The Big Comb Over

J.P. Rieger

Published by Pearls Before Press Publishing, 2024.

THE BIG COMB OVER

First edition. April 25, 2024.

ISBN: 979-8989564101

Written by J.P. Rieger.

To my Kristin - my Everything!

November 2050

Robbie took his first sip of coffee and opened his media port. He saw the subject line of the message, "23 HistoryHouse." He felt a flutter of excitement and nodded the link open. *No. Not again. Another botched test?* It couldn't be. He had scrupulously followed the instructions. He had filled both vials with saliva to the marker. He had been careful to not eat, drink, or even brush his teeth for the prior half hour. And he had done all that for the first test. 23 HistoryHouse used the word "inconclusive" for its tests. The other company, GeneTree, had used the word "incomplete."

He groaned to himself. As before, he would log onto the account and receive the message that a new kit would be delivered at no charge. He glanced over at the unopened box on top of his dresser—an unused third test with GeneTree. He hadn't bothered with it. He had elected to shell out yet more of his hard-earned money and try a DNA competitor. And for naught. But this time he would contact the company and try to talk to a live person. Somebody needed to explain to him exactly what the heck was meant by "inconclusive."

It was embarrassing. All of his friends in the Hundred A Year book circle had been sharing stories about their DNA results, some surprising and many hilarious. Ancestry research through DNA had made a comeback. You could now complete an accurate family tree based solely on DNA. Genealogical research was no longer needed. People were finding out that they were related to one another in unpredictable and sometimes hilarious ways. He wanted in on the fun.

His therapist supported the book circle idea. Thanks to therapy and his longstanding drug regimen, he had been able to tamp down most of his feelings of uncertainty and loneliness. Taking the plunge by joining the book group was good for him. A friendly bunch of readers sharing information about the books they were enjoying—or not. And now DNA was the rage. He wanted a turn!

He didn't think his family tree would be all that interesting. His parents, Will and Megan, were boring but successful. An aging attorney dad who refused to retire and a retired neurosurgeon mom. His big brother, Doyle, was a club lacrosse jock and a bigshot in sports marketing. And Doyle and Peg managed to have a couple of great kids, too—D.J. and then Mack. He hadn't seen Doyle or the kids in a long time. The kids would be teenagers now. Or maybe D.J. was in his twenties? Maybe even Mack by now?

He nodded the reader to "standby" and wandered over to the bathroom. He glanced at the mirror. He grimaced at the face of the pudgy, bald man staring back at him. How the hell had he wound up looking like this? The adaptive lighting of the bath décor was doing him no favors. He moved his head around a little before the mirror, moving closer and farther away to get the lighting to settle down. He stared again and blinked. He looked more like his crazy uncle tim tim than himself. He sighed. He hadn't thought about his uncle for a long time, probably since the funeral. And that was a good thing. Purging tim tim from his memory was something he had worked on for decades. He had all but forgotten tim tim. He peered down at the drain in the sink. He glanced back up at the mirror and shook his head. *If the young me could have seen the old me, he would have been shocked.*

And then it hit him like a lightning strike. He gulped and stared at himself again in the mirror. His hands began to tremble. It all came rushing back to him. That morning on the beach. The guy he had seen out of the corner of his eye, just for a second. That guy was staring back at him, now!

. . .

THE BIG COMB OVER

Spring 2023

tim tim

"You need to get your nose out of your game and look around." Megan raised her arms upward, as though to display the Spring Festival scene to Robbie.

Will nodded, "Your mom's right, Robbie."

Robbie looked up from the picnic blanket. Not much to see.

"After three years, we might actually be free of the pandemic. Everything is almost back to normal. It's a beautiful spring day! Life is surrounding you, Robbie. Not Pokémon."

"It's not Pokémon, Mom. Pokémon is for babies."

"Well, whatever it is, try putting it aside to enjoy the music. Look, your brother is over there with the Purdees. Why don't you join him at their picnic blanket?" She thought that the one Purdee daughter would also be a sophomore like Robbie. Robbie would need dates at some of his dances next year.

Robbie ignored the suggestion. The Purdee sisters had always been mean to him. They tolerated Doyle, because he was a lacrosse jock.

Megan looked toward the stage and nudged Will. "Oh, good Lord, is that your brother up there?" She pointed toward the pale bulgy creature in the orange Orioles tee shirt and green manpris cargos. A rumpled luminescent orange Orioles bucket hat completed the ensemble.

Will looked up from his phone. The man was dancing by himself in front of the bandstand. The oldies group was blasting its way through "River Deep – Mountain High." The dancing man was scrunching his frame downward toward the pavement for "river deep" and then stretching himself upward, dramatically, for "mountain high." Each time. The audience loved it. They were cheering.

"Yeah, that would be Tim."

Megan sighed and shook her head. She was damned glad she had wrested Robbie away from the clutches of Will's whacko brother. She was not going to pick up the phone one day to find her youngest in the hospital with his jaw wired shut too. She was not having it.

Robbie looked up from his handheld toward the stage.

"You see what's happened to Uncle Tim? This is why you stay away from him. A lonely old guy who's stuck dancing by himself."

"Okay, Mom." Robbie was back to his handheld.

The band had moved on to "Whoomp! (There It Is)." Will wished that some other people would get up to dance so that Tim wouldn't look so foolish. His wish did not come true. Tim tim was now mouthing the lyrics to "Whoomp!" pantomiming a highly personalized interpretation.

Robbie looked up from his game to the stage again. "Wow. Look at tim tim! He knows all the words! And he's working in his karate moves!" Tim tim moved about the impromptu concrete dance floor, flinging air karate chops and frighteningly unsteady high kicks.

Megan shook her head, scornfully. Will gently took hold of Megan's hand. "Look, Tim is Tim. I'm glad to see him having some fun!" Will was secretly wishing that Tim would sit one out. *Just one. Please.* It was getting kind of embarrassing.

Robbie understood his parents' concerns. Tim tim said and did a lot of weird things. But he was also a nice guy. He had really missed hanging out with tim tim. It had been almost four years now.

. . .

Late Spring 2019

"Why are you stopping here?"

"Look at that, Robbie! Look at his moves!"

Tim tim had stopped the Corolla on York Road in front of the car dealership. He was staring up at a gigantic, sinewy tube man, spellbound.

"Just look at that thing! Wild!"

Tim tim began to imitate the tube man's undulations, while seated in the driver's side of the car.

"You shouldn't just stop here in the middle of the road like this tim tim! There's traffic!"

Tim tim glanced in the rear view. "Sure, sure. I'll put the hazards on." He kept on moving his torso and arms, trying to sync up with the tube man.

Within a few moments, the traffic froze to a stop. Horns blared angrily. An outraged motorist roared past tim tim, gunning the engine in dissatisfaction. Robbie noticed the single digit wave from the driver.

"Geezy peezy, everybody is in such a rush these days. They need to pull over once in a while and smell the roses. Or the vinyl, in this case." Tim tim was still gazing upward, spellbound by the dancing giant. More car horns bleated hostilely.

"Tim tim, I think you need to move, now. You know, you can't just park in the middle of York Road?"

Tim tim sighed and turned his attention back to the road. "Yes, yes. I'm moving. But what a feat of science! Seriously!"

They eventually pulled into the parking lot of the shopping center a quarter mile away. Robbie couldn't believe their good luck. A guy was pulling out of a perfect spot right in front of the comic book store. Tim tim duly clicked his turn signal on and waited patiently for the car to leave the space.

But a new suitor had arrived from the opposite direction. The SUV saw the same space. In an instant, the SUV bullied its way into the spot, barely avoiding contact with the exiting car. Robbie was dumbfounded. He reached over to blast the horn at the SUV. Tim tim brushed him back.

"Hey, hey, Robbie! It's okay, there are plenty of other parking spots. Let me back up and get us one."

"Aren't you mad?" Robbie was seething.

"What?"

"That guy in the SUV stole our spot. That's not right!"

"No, it's okay, Robbie. We always let the other person go first. It's in line with the mission."

"What? 'Let the other person go first?' Why should everybody else go first? That's not fair."

Tim tim had backed up. There was not a single other open space in the lot. He pulled the Corolla out of the lot to seek a space on the street. Robbie was infuriated. Somehow, they always wound up parking on the street, a ten minute walk from the store.

"Well, maybe when you're just a little older I can tell you more about the mission. But for now, I can say that, basically, letting others go first is in sync with the mission."

Robbie was fuming. He did not want to take that ten-minute hike in the heat. "I'm ten now, tim tim. That technically makes me a teenager. And being a teenager means I'm pretty much an adult."

He was hoping to get tim tim to divulge the big secret, knowing from experience that the revelation was going to be extremely disappointing.

"Okay. Yeah. It's probably time to give you the basics of the mission."

They parked and began walking to the comic store. Tim tim was sweating profusely. His naturally distressed tee shirt was getting soaked. The hardened yellow underarm rings were beginning to soften.

"So, I know you like those superhero comic books. What if I were to tell you that we had superpowers too, and were expected to use them? What would you think about that?"

Robbie was glad that they were almost to the store. He couldn't wait to feel the air conditioning. "Sure. I'm in. I'll be the Flash."

Tim tim chuckled. "I love the Flash! The Flash and Green Lantern were my favorites. Do you remember the Justice Society?

I used to have a comic book where they went up against Solomon Grundy. I think your grandma threw that one out when I joined the Army."

They had finally arrived at the comic book store. Tim tim browsed through the "classics" bin. The prices were outrageous. As usual, Robbie, methodically, began at the first aisle by the cashier and slowly worked his way through the entire store. Forty-five minutes passed. Tim tim had taken a seat on the floor, cross-legged, in the very rear of the store. The foot traffic there was minimal. He had done this with every visit.

Robbie finally waved for tim tim. Time for tim tim to pull out his super wallet.

. . .

They arrived back at tim tim's rowhouse on 25th Street. The AC in the Corolla had ceased functioning years ago. They were both drenched in sweat. Tim tim plugged in the sole window AC unit located in the dining room. The lights in the kitchen dimmed and flickered in rhythm to the straining AC unit.

"Phew! It's a hot one! And it's not even summer yet! Let's get some ice cream to cool down. Do you want a float? Pepsi?"

"Yes, please!" Robbie knew that the lack of AC would always be rewarded. He began rifling through his selections, drawing them out of the plastic bag, laying each one out on the kitchen table, side by side.

Tim tim looked on. "That one looks good. 'Superman vs. the Flash, the Greatest Race of All Time.' I had a comic once where they both raced. They raced a few times."

"Well, this is actually a graphic novel."

"A novel? Really? Looks like a comic book."

Robbie sighed to himself. "Well, they call the longer type of comic books with more complicated plots, graphic novels."

Tim tim picked up the "novel." "Huh—could've fooled me."

. . .

Tim tim washed up the ice cream glasses and spoons while Robbie read.

"So, do you want to hear about the mission?"

Robbie looked up. "Uh, sure, tim tim." He went back to reading.

"Okay. So, basically, our side of the family, you know, your Dad's, has been around for a long time. Like a long family tree. Anyway, early on, we evolved here on Earth to help other people. That's the mission. It's our job to always assist people where and however we can. So it's my job as your uncle to kind of instruct you on that. You know, help you understand your role. Your mission is to do good. To always help people. Like a superhero would."

"Okay, tim tim. Sounds good." He was still reading his comic book.

Tim tim dried his hands and joined Robbie at the table. "So, does that make sense to you?"

His parents had warned him. "Do not get into a religious discussion with Uncle Tim. You will be trapped for hours." "Sure, tim tim."

"Okay, Robbie. Now, look, I know your dad is an atheist. You know what that means, right?"

"Sure." He kind of knew. He knew his mom was, too.

"Okay, the fact that your dad's an atheist is perfectly cool. But we believe in God, right? I mean, we've been handed the mission by God. So, that kind of proves there is a God. Very definitely. Do you see that?"

"Sure, tim tim."

"Phew! Okay, good! I was a little worried. Now, there are really two kinds of atheists. The ones that are more adamant, you know, more vocal about it, like your dad. And the regular ones. Each type is okay and cool with us. The adamant ones are cool because they are obviously secret believers. They don't want to, but can't help it, and so they're more vocal in their views. They're more mad at themselves than mad at us. The quieter ones are fine, too, because they're not mad and may come around at some point. All good."

"That's good, tim tim." Robbie was reading his comic.

"Oh. But I don't want to give you the wrong impression. Atheists don't have to worry. God loves atheists just as much as everybody else, and he won't let them down. I just thought it'd be easier for me to explain stuff if you already believed in God."

"Sure, tim tim."

Tim tim looked at the graphic novel again. The Flash and Superman were racing stride for stride on the cover.

Robbie looked up. "I like the Flash a lot because he can time travel."

"Yes! I remember he had that cosmic treadmill and could run himself all over the place!" Tim tim then got serious again. "You know, there's no such thing as time travel?"

"Sure, tim tim."

"It's because there's actually no such thing as a past or a future. People invented those because they seemed to feel right. But actually, there's only a present. The past is just our memories. The future is our imagination. That's why there's no time travel. Because there's only now. There's no place to travel to."

"Okay, tim tim."

"You see, God lives in the present. Basically, he's inventing the present every second we live. It's a continual process. Does that make sense to you?" Tim tim figured that it was probably too early to explain about the significance of the name. He'd fill Robbie in on that once they got to the Bible.

Robbie was getting annoyed. He thought, *If there's no past or future, then why do you have that calendar on your bulletin board and clock on the wall?* But he kept it to himself.

"Sure, tim tim."

. . .

Tim tim dropped Robbie back at Will and Megan's in Catonsville. He decided to stop over at the American Legion Post to take advantage of the hospitality and free air conditioning. Sometimes they had pretzels. And he liked shooting the breeze with fellow servicemen.

He found his way over to the bar counter in the rec hall and ordered a Pepsi. A man in a yellow golf shirt took a seat on the adjacent barstool.

"Don't believe we've met? I'm Howard Ratliff."

Tim tim turned and shook hands heartily. "Hey, Howard. Tim Elders, but my friends call me tim tim."

"Pleased to meet you . . . tim tim." Howard was a little uncertain about calling the guy "tim tim," but figured, *What the heck, if that's what the guy wants . . .*

"So, tim tim, what branch?"

"Olive. Strictly peacemaking."

Howard chuckled, "Ah. Got ya. Good old OD Olive Drab. Best color going. Army?"

"Yes! How about you, Howard?"

"Same. US Army. Where did you serve?"

"Well, I was a CO—actually 'the' CO—at the Edgewood Area at APG. You know, the old Edgewood Arsenal here in Maryland? Back in the late '90s."

"Of course. Edgewood, sure." Howard knew of the Aberdeen Proving Grounds and Edgewood but wasn't entirely sure what sort of munitions were tested there. He was impressed that tim tim had a post as Commanding Officer.

"That must have been quite a responsibility?"

"Well, yes. Like I said, I was 'it' back there. And there was plenty for a CO to do."

Tim tim's mind wandered back to his early days at Edgewood. As far as he knew, he was the only Conscientious Objector ever allowed to join the Army voluntarily.

Howard took a sip of his beer. "Did you serve overseas?"

Tim tim awoke from his reverie. "Oh, no. Back then I was grateful just to be stationed here in Maryland. They wouldn't have shipped me out, based on my status."

"Ah. Of course. Understood."

Howard figured that tim tim must have been commissioned, probably a DCO. Obviously, if tim tim was not sent overseas, it was because he was a hotshot officer of some sort. But he didn't want to compare rank or duty. That conversation could be a little touchy among vets.

"So, tim tim, if it isn't classified, what sort of materials were you working with at Edgewood?"

"Oh, it's all declassified, now. I was involved with remote viewing for intelligence-gathering. We used printed materials. Basically, what could we make out of the printed page?" Tim tim thought back to the crazy instructor, Sean, and his insistence that the tests would be much more successful if the text was initially produced at minimum size of 32 points on white paper and viewed in a well-lit room. It would be easier for the viewer to read the text that way. You'd start that way and then, with time and practice, improve the accuracy of your views.

"Ah recon work. That's interesting. And printing? So you guys were using 3-D even back then? That's quite advanced." Howard hadn't realized that 3-D printers were used in the '90s. Those things could definitely produce weapons, now.

"Yes, probably more accurately 5-D, based on our protocols." He recalled how Sean felt that remote viewing was enhanced through the other two dimensions, not the traditional three. *Whacko.*

"5-D? Really? What kind of stuff did you do? Inerts?" Howard had never heard of a 5-D printer. He was wondering what sort of ordinance could be produced that way and figured it would be dummy items for training.

"Inerts? Yes. Very definitely. But some of the real stuff we did was quite dangerous." Tim tim thought back to the inert compounds prescribed by the Army docs. It was always pretty obvious you'd received a placebo once you'd taken one of the actual mescaline derivatives. *Night and day.*

"Understood! I don't think I'd have the stomach for surrounding myself with dangerous materials. Hat's off to you, tim tim!" Howard reached his beer cup over and tapped tim tim's soda glass for a toast.

"Well thanks, Howard! Did you wind up overseas?"

Howard smirked to himself. "Yeah. I was a lowly supply grunt. It was 'Nam, '69, and we were allegedly well behind enemy lines. But that didn't stop a couple of local kids on bikes riding by and chucking a couple of grenades into our quarters. This happened, and I got mustered out on medical."

He held up his left hand to show where his little finger and ring finger had been amputated. He laughed. "I got a Purple Heart for this."

"Wow! So sorry to see that, Howard. Thank God you made it back!"

Howard was beginning to tear up. "Thanks, tim tim! The Lord's been good to me! I came back, found a job, and got myself married to a wonderful woman. Six grandchildren so far and a great grandchild on the way!"

"Wow! That's excellent, Howard! Congratulations!" Tim tim was tearing up a little too.

"So how about you, tim tim? Did you tie the knot, have some kids?"

THE BIG COMB OVER

Tim tim looked sternly at his glass of Pepsi. "No. I realized that marriage wasn't going to work for me, mainly because I learned I wasn't going to be able to have kids. But it's okay. Sometimes you need to just suck it up and stay on mission. The rest sorts itself out."

Howard felt true sorrow for tim tim. And he felt bad about even mentioning kids. Why was he such a jackass? "Oh, hey, tim tim. Sorry about that! I need to stop being so damned nosy."

"No, no, it's perfectly okay, Howard! I'm very comfortable with my life now. In fact, I've got a ten-year-old nephew who loves to pal around with me, so it's almost like having a kid. Especially now that it's time to fill him in on the mission."

Howard wasn't entirely sure what tim tim meant by the "mission," but figured he had pushed enough.

. . .

Roy

"Boys, no ass-sittin' in the creek. There's been all sorts 'a mite bugs and pfisterianias and such pollutin' the water. If you boys want to go in, it's okay. Just put on your creek shoes and keep movin' 'round so nothin' gets on ya."

He had pronounced "creek" as "crick" and "water" as "wood-er." He scratched at his stubby beard.

"And 'member to keep way clear of Uncle Roy's two lines over there. You don't wanna scare off any of my crustaceans." His weathered finger pointed to the side of the ramshackle, partly sunken wooden pier.

Roy shook his head. It was tough being a mostly retired waterman these days. In the old days he could roll out the skiff by around 4:30 a.m. and practically be guaranteed a bushel by 6:00, maybe 6:30 a.m. Nowadays, it didn't pay to get up early. He'd be better off dropping his lines in the afternoon and taking whatever came along before sundown. Between his pots and his line work during the day, there was usually enough dinner for him and Sonny—when the crabs were running, of course.

"See, those two're legal pots down there. That's what them plastic ID stickers are sayin.'" He pointed to the spot on the pier where the pot lines had been dropped. "I got an o-fficial license." He also had an unofficial license that allowed him to slip a few other unlicensed pots below the pier after sundown, when DNR patrols had ceased.

Doyle let Robbie do the talking. "Okay, Uncle Roy."

"Them crabs been runnin' good—like cocktail dresses at a Dundalk funeral. Plenty of 'em!"

"That's good, Uncle Roy."

"So do eithers of yous have any interest in bein' a speaker like my Sonny? That's where he's off to this week. One of them special speakin' courses or camps where you learn to argue or give lectures, perfessionally. A bunch of them boys from his school are goin.' I think they all hang 'round and learn to talk proper and logically and so forth. That was his class he liked in school. Forensicals. He was in the Forensical club there, too. They called it the Forensical Society."

Robbie spoke up again, "Not really, Uncle Roy. I like reading, and Doyle likes lacrosse."

"Well, that's okay! Two good things ya can use. I daresay my Sonny is going to be a smartie when he gradji-ates from high school next month. You know he got himself into college next year as a scholar. Won himself a scholarship. Smart boy, like his mom."

Roy thought about Mardi for a couple seconds but didn't want to dwell on her and get the boys all sad. It had been three years now.

Doyle finally spoke. "That's cool, Uncle Roy. Good for Desales." He was thinking it was cool for them too, not having that pain in the butt around for the week. Every year, his mom handed them off to Uncle Roy, ostensibly to give the boys a chance to get out in the "fresh air" of Essex and experience nature. Of course, Doyle understood that their parents were really just glad to get rid of them for a week every summer. With Desales around, it was usually an absolute misery. Finally, they had a week to just hang out with Uncle Roy. *All good.*

. . .

Stefan

She looked at the ring on her left hand and smiled.

He glanced down, proudly, at the modest engagement ring. He kissed her and held her closely on the concrete bench. She had said, "yes," just two days ago. He had been sweating bullets. They unfolded and went back to eating their sandwiches.

He sighed, "You know, I think a simple wedding, maybe just close family members and friends, would be best. It will be summer, so it could be outdoors? We could convert this quad to our venue. Maybe spruce it up with a string quartet?" Stefan pointed to the area in front of the park bench. "Maybe twenty or even thirty people?" He would have preferred five or six guests. He was hoping Flo would settle on twenty.

Flo smiled and thought, *Poor Stef. Time for his reality check.*

"Well Stef, brilliant. Truly brilliant. But there is the one little, tiny problem."

"A problem?"

"Well, nothing bad. But you keep forgetting. I am a 'royal.' It is not possible for me to have a small wedding. It will be all posh and plummy with appropriate swagger. You know, Pomp and Circumstance."

Stefan did not like the sound of this. He was an introvert. Yes, certainly the most extraverted introvert going, but an introvert nonetheless. "What does that mean, exactly, babe? What do you have in mind?"

"Well, it's not what your 'babe' Flo has in mind. It's what our keepers at Bucky P. have planned for Lady Florence Stour."

"What would that be? A larger reception somewhere in a hall?"

"A hall?"

"That's what we call those places back home in Baltimore. You know, you rent the local American Legion hall and hire a DJ and so forth. You know, a reception hall. Were you expecting dancing?"

Flo sighed. This was not going to be easy. "Okay, Stef. Now, this will seem crazy, but think about it. Technically, I am in line to be the Queen of England. Yes, some bizarre tragedy would have to befall roughly twenty-eight of my lovely cousins before my coronation date is penciled in, but the end result of this nonsense is that we will be married in an Anglican Church presided by a Bishop of the Church of England. And the reception will be in one of our ancestral homes or in one of the more posh hotels in London. I opt for posh and London. We can get St. Paul's for the actual wedding. I suspect we'll be inviting roughly two fifty to three hundred guests. And that is the 'small' version for us most distant twigs on the family tree. You know, Charles and Di had over ten times that."

"Good Lord!" Stefan was having a sinking spell. Anxiety had taken over. He'd have to clean and dust the flat again for relief.

Flo didn't want to tell Stef that the wedding site would actually be in the crypt, the Chapel of the Order of the British Empire, not above ground in the main church. She knew he'd freak out if she mentioned the "crypt."

"So, my lovely Stef. Have you ever worn formal evening attire?"

. . .

Will heard the chime and checked his phone. Megan. *Probably another butt dial.* Ever since she got that new phone, she'd been on a mad butt dial spree, usually one or two a day. But he was between appointments, so he took the call.

"Megan, are you there?" Usually, he would only hear Megan's voice, off in the distance, distorted, speaking with others, usually medical people. It was extraordinarily frightening at first. He thought she had been in an accident.

"Yes, Will. Bad time?"

"Oh, no, this is a good time. I have about ten minutes until my next meet."

"Good. Now, you won't believe this. My brother—Stefan—he's engaged!"

Will was thinking it was actually believable. Stefan was the most normal brother Megan had. Roy and Roland were batshit. "That's great! Let me guess. The lucky bride is a Brit? Somebody he met at Oxford?"

"Yes, but it's better than that. Here's the unbelievable part. Not just a Brit from Oxford. An actual member of the British royal family."

Will thought the phone had cut out or distorted, because the garbled words sounded almost like "royal family." "What, Megan?"

"I said 'royal family.' You know, the Queen of England?"

"What? He's marrying the Queen?"

"Ha! No. But his fiancé, Flo, is a relative of the Queen. Technically, Flo is in line to be Queen, if unbelievable circumstances occurred. Stefan tried to explain the lineage, but it was a big blur to me."

"Wow. That is unbelievable. Incredible!" He felt the other shoe was about to drop. He smirked to himself. "So, are they having the wedding back here in Catonsville?"

"Ha! Nice try. That's why I'm calling. It's set for Friday, August fourth. And in London, of course. St. Paul's if you can believe it."

Will was glad he was booked for his biggest trial of the summer. A jury trial with a three-week schedule. *Saved!* "Gee. That's during my big trial. Remember?"

"Shit. The con man case?" He had been talking about that damn case for months.

"Con man? No. We tried that case like six months ago and won. It's the human trafficking case. Remember? The dead migrants found in the freighter that made port here in Baltimore? It's going to be 24-7 those three weeks."

"Can't you hand it off to someone else?"

18

"Uh. No. I'm the only one completely up to speed. There's no one in the office that could take my slot."

"What about the boss guy, Dave?"

"Well no. Dave's running dozens of cases. I think you're going to have to go this one solo."

There was a stony silence.

Will spoke, fearfully. "They didn't invite the boys, too, did they?"

Megan sighed, "Yes, of course, Will. He's my brother, so yes, of course the kids are invited."

Will was picturing Megan dragging the two boys around England. This was not going to be fun for her.

Megan spoke. "You seem to be forgetting something."

"What?"

"My commitment to Médecins Sans Frontières. It's the same damn time! And I cannot pull out of it. Backing out on that commitment is not an option."

There was more uncomfortable silence.

"There's absolutely no one in that entire office that can run that fucking case? Seriously?"

Will gulped. "No. It's on me." He paused. "What about your brother, Roy? He'll be going, right? And he's got Desales?" Will was thinking that Desales was clearly the adult in that family.

"Sure. We could ask Roy to take the kids. But they might have more fun with Roland, right? He'll be going and he's . . . well . . . lively and . . . urbane." She was choosing her words carefully. Roland was a lovable teddy bear. Roy was still getting over the loss of Mardi. Roy had been distracted and a lot grumpier the last few years. Maybe not as reliable. And the kids did not like Desales at all, for some reason.

Will thought Roland was okay, except, perhaps, for the CBD gummies he seemed to constantly chew. He was a little curious about precisely what was in those gummies. He had happened upon Roland sneaking away before Thanksgiving dinner to devour a large bag of corn curls on the porch outside the kitchen. The gummy thing could be a problem. Roy with Desales would be the better plan. The kid was smart as hell and a total winner. Completely cool under pressure. He thought back to the time he had given Desales a tour of his office in the Federal Building and let him sit in on one of his court hearings. He encouraged Desales to get on the mock trial team at his high school. He did, and had been winning awards ever since.

"Look, I love Roland, but Roy's a parent. And Desales will look out for the boys. And there'll be plenty of chances for all of them to hang out together once in London, anyway, right?"

Megan sighed. "Yeah. Okay, Will. Sure. I'll phone Roy."

"And please, just make sure Desales is going."

. . .

Roy hung up the yellow princess style rotary wall phone in the kitchen. Deep coal-like smudges emblazoned the sides of the handset. The earcup was encrusted with a rippling orange waxy substance. The yellow coiled phone line was stretched beyond all believable proportions. It had looped itself around the ancient spinet piano, freshly painted canary yellow a mere thirty years earlier.

"Well, go to war, Miss Agnes!"

He took a seat at the Formica top kitchen table with Robbie and Doyle.

"Boys, that was yer momma. She was in between patients, so she didn't have a chance ta talk to yous right now. She said she'd call agin tonight, like usual. But the reason she was phonin' us, now, was ta tell us some good news! Your Uncle Stefan's gettin' married! Some nice English girl. And we get to go ta England for the wedding! Can you b'lieve that? Yer mom and dad can't go cuz of their schedules, but Uncle Roy's ready, willin' 'n able. I'll be like yer chaperowner—you know, somebody makes sure you got company and are taken care of and fed. And Sonny will be there with us too. Your mom said Stefan is gettin' us real good tickets for businesspeople on the plane and that they'd be puttin' us up at a fancy hotel there in London. I ain't never been on a plane ride before. Did take a train, oncet. Should be excitin'!"

"Did you say we're going with you, but Desales is coming, too?" Robbie looked glum.

"Yessir. Sonny's been on a few plane rides before, so he'll know the ropes. You boys ever ride a plane before?"

"No."

"Okay, me neither, but we'll all be together. It'll be just fine."

. . .

Roland

Roland wheeled his ridiculously overfilled mini shopping cart to the checkout. He had entered the supermarket with a small list, but other things seemed to jump into the cart somehow. He also grabbed a *People Magazine* from the rack alongside the checkout belt. And then he quickly grabbed an *Enquirer*, although more guiltily. He tried to place the *Enquirer* face down, but the page-sized ad on the back for a hair follicle helmet was even worse than the front, so he quickly turned it back over. And dammit, he wanted that helmet.

A middle-aged woman took her place behind Roland. Her orange tee shirt said, "God First, Family Second, Then Orioles Baseball." She quietly watched the unloading process. The process was endless. Items were being removed from every square inch of the tiny cart. The crannies had crannies.

Roland paid the freight and wheeled the tottering cart, now overflowing with bagged groceries, into the parking lot. The middle-aged woman followed behind with her own. He popped open the trunk and began removing his bags from the cart.

"Excuse me, sir. You know, you could have used a larger cart. That smaller cart isn't really holding everything properly. You should have used the bigger-sized cart."

Startled, Roland looked behind to see the woman standing there with her cart. He gritted his teeth. "Oh. Well gosh, Karen! I appreciate the advice, but doing it this way is cheaper for me." He smirked to himself.

"Cheaper? How so? And, by the way, my name isn't Karen, it's Brenda. Why did you think my name was Karen?"

"Oh, I'm so sorry, dear. I thought for sure you were a Karen. So nice to meet you, Brenda." He was having a hard time keeping a straight face. "Well, shopping with a smaller cart is always statistically cheaper than shopping with a larger cart. Makes sense, right? Typically, your larger cart, filled to the brim, will be more expensive at the checkout than my smaller cart filled to the brim. And that's what a savvy shopper should be concerned with. Statistics. You know, over the course of the year, you'll want to keep costs down on a statistical basis. So, by using the smaller cart, I've greatly increased my chances of paying less at the cashier. Because, over the course of a year or so, ultimately the statistics will win out. I will have saved money. Does that make sense to you, dear?" He was trying not to laugh.

Brenda scowled. "Well, I can see what you mean, but I was just trying to help you so you'd have an easier time shopping. Fitting all that stuff in that little, tiny cart seems like it would make shopping more difficult. But, if it's cheaper like you said, it sounds like it's worth trying. Maybe I'll try that?"

"Thank you, dear. I hope you do! Have a pleasant day! And happy shopping, in the future!"

"You too, sir!"

He left the supermarket lot. Almost as soon as he turned his Corolla into Caswell Street, he heard some idiot honking the horn at him from a black SUV. He ignored it. He wasn't doing anything wrong. *People.*

. . .

Roland pulled his Toyota Corolla into the parking lot in the rear of his apartment building. He parked as close to the building as he could get away with. The fewer steps the better. He had a lot of bags. Yes, it was technically a handicap spot, but he was dealing with several serious handicaps. He was tired, weak, overweight and depressed, and wanted to get his bags in as quickly as possible before any nosy neighbors or the apartment manager chatted him up just to peek inside his bags. His hair and diet products were none of their business. He had been trying absolutely anything and everything to get his hair to grow out thicker. Anything to fight the damned infringing baldness. He would only be in the spot for a minute, just to get the groceries into the rear hallway.

Mrs. Barnwhistle appeared in the rear entrance doorway. "You can't park there, Mr. Biv. That's reserved. It's a handicap space. I've told you that before."

Roland gritted his teeth. "Does severe depression combined with alopecia and morbid obesity qualify as handicaps? I believe so. Have you ever heard of the Americans with Disabilities Act?"

Mrs. Barnwhistle clutched the neck of her house dress defensively. "Well of course. I'm management here as well as a tenant, and they make us learn all of that stuff. And, no, those are not legitimate disabilities, and even if they were, you are still missing the required handicap hanger for your car mirror."

"Okay, dear. You win. I'm going to repark, now."

"Good. But don't be a silly goose. At least bring in those two bags you have in your hands awhile before you repark." She wanted to take a look inside the bags while Roland reparked.

Roland sighed. "Okay, let me know if you see anything you like."

He wound up parking in the last spot in the lot, about as far away from the rear door as imaginable. He cursed to himself, but spoke out loud, "Life's not fair." He struggled carrying the first set of plastic bags across the lot. The bags seemed heavy as hell, and the handles were cutting into the sinews between his thumb and forefinger. "Gravity's a bitch!" And that was just round one. There were seven more bags in the trunk. And he had to put the trunk lid down each time to lock the groceries in because the neighborhood was just lovely and someone could stop by and grab his bags. Or, Mrs. Barnwhistle would pop over to inspect them. Double whammy.

He dragged the last of the bags into the hallway by the elevator. He no longer noticed the perpetually lingering smell of floor wax and pesticide. Mrs. Barnwhistle was holding the door of the elevator for him with one hand, while continuing her grasp of her house dress with the other. The door kept trying to close. She kept pushing it back open, creating a noisy, impromptu metronome. "All aboard, Mr. Biv."

. . .

He had dragged all the plastic bags into his apartment after struggling to hold the building's lone elevator. He heard his landline ring. *Megan.* None of his friends ever called him on his landline. Cell only. He knew it had to be Sissy and was tempted to ignore the call, but figured it could be important, Megan being a surgeon and all.

"Yes, dear."

"Hey, Rolie Polie. How have you been? Warm enough for you?"

"Oh, Sissy. What a surprise! Yes. Hot as hell, and it's not even summer yet."

"I know! Right? So, asshole, you didn't notice me today. I was just across from you in traffic. I waved like a hundred times. And then I honked to get your attention. And you still didn't see me."

"You know, don't take this the wrong way, but I don't really look into each car as it approaches to see if I know the occupants, right? So that I can give them a friendly wave? That's like a full-time job. Nothing personal, dear."

"Jesus, idiot! I wound up giving you the finger just to see if that would get your attention! It didn't. You don't know your own sister?"

"Well, not when she's driving around in a generic black SUV with her windows tinted. Like you're from the hood or something. Why don't you paint it pink? Or slap on that rainbow bumper sticker I gave you a while back. That would make your vehicle stand out more."

"Idiot. Okay. Look, here's why I've called. You're not going to believe this. Stef's getting married!"

"Wow! Our little Gremlin. Really? Who's the unlucky bitch?"

"Don't be mean! He's marrying a girl he met at school. At an animal rights rally, of all things."

"Shocking."

"Let me finish, goof. Here's the unbelievable part. His fiancé is a member of the British royal family. Lady Florence Stour."

"'Stour?' Lovely name. Sounds almost German, like sauerkraut. Did you say 'royal family'? Like the Royal Farms store? She's the Fried Chicken and Sauerkraut Heiress?"

"No, tiny dick. Listen. The British royal family. You know, the Queen of England? Heard of her?"

"I'm not on speaking terms with that particular queen, no."

"Silly ass. Be serious. I need your help."

"Okay. What?"

"So, the wedding is happening this August. And Will and I can't make it."

"What? You can't make it? Why? There's a better gig? A crab feast in Parkville?"

"Idiot. No."

"Okay. Where is it being held? Bavaria? Land of stourkraut?"

"No, dumbass. In London, England."

Roland heard magic words. "London, England."

"So, Sissy, how can Sir Roland assist?" He was beginning to salivate.

. . .

"Boys, that was yer momma on the phone." Roy walked the yellow handset and elongated cord back to the wall phone. The movement of the cord excited several dust bunnies, which skittered away—tumbleweeds on a linoleum desert. "She says we should all go ta the store ta buy some fancy clothes, like suits 'n ties 'n such ta wear to the weddin'. Says you boys will need proper a-ttire. Yer momma's goin' ta re-numerate Uncle Roy, later." He nodded, solemnly, evidencing his consent to the deal. "Sonny's already got plenty 'a suits and such, but yer ole Unca Roy needs a proper suit and tie. And you fellers, too." He nodded again to the nonplussed faces of Doyle and

THE BIG COMB OVER

Robbie. They wanted to continue exploring the woods that morning. Doyle had caught six salamanders the day before.

Robbie responded. "Okay, Uncle Roy. Are you taking us in the Mustang?"

"Naw, that's Sonny's, so I think we'll all hafta scrunch ourselves up in the truck. But it ain't that long a ride."

The three trudged over the gravel and crabgrass "lawn" of the front yard. The yard held a partially rebuilt engine on a rotting wood pallet and a discarded beige computer monitor. Roy had meant to take the old monitor to the dump. It was now an unnoticed part of the permanent landscape.

Roy saw that the passenger side of the 1980s-era rust bucket was heavily guarded by a wild bayberry bush. He had meant to cut it back. "Hang on, boys, let me pull some 'a this daggone bush outa the way." He held back the bush with one arm while opening the passenger side of the truck with the other. Doyle let Robbie go first. His leg could barely reach the floorboard, so Doyle gave him a boost upward. Doyle followed behind. Once seated, Roy gave the door a slam, which pushed Doyle over snuggly next to Robbie.

"Stop pushing me, Doyle!"

"I'm not! It's just cramped!"

They sat fuming while Roy worked his way over to the driver's side. Robbie noticed the palm-sized plastic yellow Holy Family statuette fixed to the top of the dashboard with duct tape. The ends of the tape had become dry and now curled upward in an inadvertent display of piety.

Roy hopped up into the driver's seat and gave the ignition key a turn. There was no sound.

"Crapsake! Geezy Christmas. I fergot ta pull off that dang battery cable again! She's dead as a doorstop, boys."

He had been removing one of the lead cables from the battery after each use to prevent it from being run down by the juice-stealing

'80s electronics. He contemplated giving the truck a jump, but revised the plan. "Okay, boys, we'll take Sonny's car this time. He ain't around ta use it and won't mind his ole dad borrowin' it."

The faces of Doyle and Robbie lit up in ecstasy. The perfectly restored white 1966 Mustang convertible!

. . .

With the top down, it was a little hard to hear what Uncle Roy was saying. But they didn't care. This was a thrill ride. Roy looked back over his right shoulder to speak. He had to yell over the sound of the fierce wind.

"Ya know, me 'n my Sonny built this Mustang together!"

They knew and had heard the story a dozen times.

Roy looked back again. "So, one day Sonny tells me, 'Roy, they gotta new heap over ta scrap yard on Pu-laski Highway!' So I says, 'Okay, Sonny, let's get over there in the truck and check 'er out!' And sure 'nuff, there she was. But the frame was all rusted out. Body was okay, though. An, no engine. But we'd already got a good engine. So we put it all back together again in that ga-rage we used downa road on Philadelphia Road. We was rentin' it back then."

The boys didn't bother to answer. They were enjoying the windstorm. And the speed. *Go Roy!*

"Now, yer momma said ta go ta the Macy's store in White Marsh, but them stores 'er all too fancy 'n that's kind of a drive, so I had a good idear to go to tha ole Sears discount store. It ain't technically run by Sears anymore. They closed it a few years back and some nice folk bought it up an still sell the same kindsa stuff including clothes. An it's a lot closer, just downa ways on Pu-laski."

As he drove the Mustang, he remembered the happy afternoons spent with Sonny working on the car. It was a good move. Mardi had passed away, and Sonny needed more love and attention than ever. He was a good boy. And he was so proud of him.

He thought back to the first time he met Mardi. He was young and had taken over his dad's business. His younger siblings weren't interested. Megan had plans for medical school. Roland would be an actor. By the time Stefan had come along, the family had moved from Baltimore to Parkville. Roy bought out the others. He turned their old summer shack on Brown's Creek in Essex into a home.

He joined a duckpin bowling league operating out of Dundalk, which he found a little distasteful and embarrassing. He obviously would have preferred to bowl out of Essex, but there were no leagues open then. Some of the guys in his duckpin league had encouraged him to sign up for the "show and tell" pet day at the local nursing home. The residents loved seeing and playing with the pets. Roy didn't own a dog or cat because they'd scare his crabs away. So he brought along three undersized blue crabs in a gallon jar serving as a makeshift aquarium.

That's when he first saw that beautiful nurse. Her smile gave him pure happiness. Her ID tag said, "Mardi Gras Luison." She laughed at his makeshift aquarium and crabs. Certainly the oddest "pets" she had ever seen in her life. They started going out. Before long, they were wed.

When Sonny came along, Mardi was hell-bent to raise their boy without any discernible accent—neither her Creole nor Roy's "Balmerese." At first, Roy was a little surprised and offended. He told Mardi, "I don't have a accent. I sound just like everbody else 'roun here." Mardi won that battle. They both worked hard to afford the private elementary school and accent modification tutors. They had succeeded in beating most of the Bawlmer out of Sonny's speech. Maybe a bit tougher losing all the Creole. Roy didn't mind because it reminded him of Mardi.

. . .

Will and Megan tried not to laugh, but it was tough. The two boys had emerged from their rooms wearing matching robin's-egg blue seersucker suits, complete with matching blue- and red-striped clip-on neckties. Will was wondering if there were straw hats, too.

Doyle spoke first, "I'm not wearing this, Mom. It is totally lame! Forget it!"

Megan choked back an involuntary guffaw. "Those suits are fine, Doyle." She had to turn her face so that the boys would not see her holding back laughter.

"No way, Mom. I'll just stay home."

Seeing Megan's inability to respond, Will jumped in. "Listen, think of it like this. No one over there is going to know you. They won't care what you're wearing. Your friends won't be there. They'll never see you in those suits. And—here's our promise—when you get back home, we will send both of those suits off to the Goodwill. You'll never see those suits again."

Will was conscious of his tiny fib. There would be wedding photos. *Oh well.* But kids never looked at those anyway.

Robbie spoke up, "Can I keep the tie?"

Will tried on an earnest expression. "Yes, of course, Robbie. You may."

Megan had composed herself. "So, Doyle, tell Dad what kind of suit Uncle Roy bought?"

Doyle shook his head in disgust. "The same. And the same tie, too."

Picturing the three of them in matching seersucker suits and ties was too much for Will. He burst into laughter.

Doyle looked pleadingly to Megan. "Mom, c'mon man. Don't make us wear these! Even Dad is laughing!"

Will caught his breath. "Look, Doyle. You have to wear it. Think of Uncle Roy. You'd break his heart if he showed up for the trip, the only one wearing the seersucker. He'd have his feelings hurt." Will figured that crusty old Roy probably had no feelings to hurt, but kept that part to himself.

Megan agreed. "Look, Doyle. Suck it up. Shake it off, buddy. You're wearing the suit. End of story. And when you're back—tell you what—we'll let you guys burn those suits in the backyard pit!"

Robbie's eyes lit up. "Really?"

Doyle looked on sulkily. He hesitated and then spoke, "Okay, Mom. You win. But I really do want to burn the suit. So you have to keep your promise! Do you promise? We'll actually burn the suits in the pit?"

She sighed. "Yes. When you guys are back, we'll burn the suits."

Doyle pumped his fist into the air. "Yes!"

"Don't forget, I want the tie."

"Okay, Robbie."

. . .

"So, I had this great dream that I'm going to work into my musical."

Roland looked on, puzzled. "The musical about the scientists?"

"Good Lord. The scientists with the thought experiments? *Fridays*? No, not that one. I put that aside like twenty years ago."

He had almost forgotten that one. He had put it aside because, although it was easy finding scientific words that rhymed, not everyone in the audience would know what the lyrics meant—what the actor was singing about. He hummed the one part to himself: *Cytology, spectrometry, do you see a difference? Histology, optometry, no I do not see!* Very difficult.

"Oh, the one with the haikus and limericks?"

He thought back to the unfortunate haiku venture. Limericks would be sung for the "funny" parts and haikus for the "dramatic dialog." But it was doomed from the start by naming the principal characters Venus and Chuck. *A mistake.*

"No. Remember? The one about the big, fancy hotel and all the crazy staff and waiters? There's a lot of oddball characters, etc." He knew there was a perfect part for Roland, due to his commanding physical presence.

"Oh, okay." Roland was thinking, *Yeah, it's called Grand Hotel, Chris. Next . . .*

"Okay, so I dreamt this scene from, like, a breakfast room at a hotel. Like a big dining room with a lot of big round tables. Nice white table cloths and silverware. It's like a buffet where you bring a plateful of food back to the table. But it was apparently possible to also reserve a table in advance for a large party."

Roland had never heard of that, but let it pass.

"So, there's a lady and man sitting at the table with their plates. Like a husband and wife. Every time a guest brings a plate over and takes a seat, she tells them, 'This is a reserved table. We have a party of four joining us, so we have to make sure we have room for them.' And then she makes sure the other party won't be too large, etc. She tells them, 'I've got an appointment this morning with Mr. Lawrence. He's head of hospitality here. It's a job interview. I thought it would help to stay here and have breakfast. I'll be able to talk about the food and service, firsthand.' And, naturally, the guests that come by either say, 'Okay, thanks,' or 'Oh, our party won't fit, so we'll sit somewhere else.'"

"Got it."

"So, guests come and go, and her other party still hasn't shown up, but she keeps repeating the same story to everyone that comes by about the reserved table and job interview and Mr. Lawrence. The husband just looks on silently. Some stay, some leave. Eventually, the husband gets up to get some more food from the buffet. Then, a big guy—kind of a mess—overweight, slovenly, and with bed hair, no shave or shower, etc.—you get the picture—comes by and sits right next to her, where the husband had been sitting. She tells him, 'You can't sit there, that's my husband's seat. And by the way, this is a reserved table, and we need the seating for some other people, so you can't sit at this table.' But he absolutely ignores her. Stays seated. Munches through his food. Says nothing to anyone. The lady says, 'Excuse me. Didn't you hear what I just said?' and then repeats the whole thing all over again. She says, 'I think it will be a good idea if you find another table.' And she's ignored again. The other guests at the table are getting a little creeped out over the discomfort of the situation."

"Okay."

"So, the husband comes back with his new plate of food and sees his spot is taken, but just takes a seat next to the big guy. Doesn't say anything. Doesn't seem to care."

"Mm-hmm."

"And a few of the guests kind of finish up fast so they can move away. But a few other guests fill in the few open spots. And she runs through the whole thing again, every time, but now she adds, 'And this incredibly rude man here'—she points to the big guy—'not only has ignored me but took my husband's seat.' Again, this freaks out some people. The guy just ignores it all. He's now buttering and jellying his toast.

"One of the new arrivals sits and looks around and says, 'Oh darn. I don't think I have any silverware.' So the lady grabs the knife of the big guy—it's got butter and jelly on it—and slides it across the table to the guest, saying, 'This man took your place setting. So this is actually yours.' The guest looks on, bewildered. The big guy doesn't say anything."

"Mm-hmm."

"Eventually, the big guy gets up and moves on. She says, 'Finally! That rude lummox took my husband's seat and refused to move!' Then a new guest comes by and sits, and she runs through the whole litany again. The guest says, 'Did you say Mr. Lawrence? I just saw him leave your table and head back to his office.'"

Silence.

"So, do you get it? The big guy was Mr. Lawrence."

"Oh, yes, Waxley. That was a good one." Roland looked at his watch. All the talk of food made him hungry and he was hours away from lunch. *Dammit.*

"So, Christopher. You won't have old Roland around here to flog about this coming August."

"Really? You landed a part somewhere?"

"Well, yes, I'll be playing the part of an incredibly good-looking, dutiful brother in a humongous show in London. It will make the news. Look for me. I'll be in St. Paul's Cathedral, participating in a royal wedding! Presuming lightning doesn't strike me dead. You know, desecrating a holy place? Can you believe it?"

"Wow—so it's actually a show in London? What's the show called? And it's a musical?" Waxley figured it would have to be a musical. Roland loved to sing and sang almost as well as he. *Almost.*

"It's called 'reality.' Seriously. No. It isn't a show, silly. I'm actually the best man at my brother Stefan's wedding. The little bastard has got himself hitched. And no bullshit, it is a royal wedding."

"What? How?"

"Well, Stefan's betrothed is actually related to the Queen and is something like tenth in line to become Queen should the old gal and a bunch of her old crows cash in their chips. Her name is Lady Florence Stour. Stefan calls her 'Flo.' 'Stour' is, like, a river around their ancient old mansion out in the country somewhere. Lucky her. Named after a river. Look at me. Named after a 'biv.' I don't even know what a 'biv' is."

"Wow! Truly unbelievable! Woo hoo! I'll have to get up early and watch the coverage!"

"Well, the wedding is I think like six p.m. there, so unless you really sleep in, you won't need to worry about getting up early."

"Okay. So, did you say you're going for the whole month of August? You're not going to miss the Ravens thing, are you?"

"Oh, no, no. Just a long weekend, like three, maybe max four days in the beginning of August. The Ravens night is not until like the second or third week in August. All good!"

"Excellent! Do you need any help booking your flight or getting a place to stay? I still have that travel agency going on. It's for specialty travel, you know, niche stuff. But I'd be happy to help you? I can book all the normal stuff, too."

"Well, gosh, Chris. That's very kind, but Stefan and his fiancé have already worked that out for us. British Air, Business Class. But I have to fly out of Dulles, which is a bitch because of the drive." He was glad he had orchestrated the Dulles thing because he sure as hell was not going to fly seven hours with his loony brother Roy and those damn kids. Especially Sonny, who was a gargantuan pain in the tush.

"Ah, got it. Let me know if you need a ride to Dulles or anything."

"Thanks, bud! So, how has your travel thing worked out? You had said you were doing, like, covered bridge destinations?"

"Well, yes. I started with that because, you know, a lot of people really connect with covered bridges. There's a peacefulness. A return to simpler times and virtues. A lot of people like that."

"Sounds nice."

"But I'm not the only agent with that idea. There are actually a lot of travel consultants doing covered bridges. Old railroad lines are also big these days. Anyway, I upped the ante. I'm now working in acoustic sound barriers."

Chris saw Roland's puzzled look.

"Okay. So, it's interesting. You know you drive along the Beltway or other highways and see they've put up all those sound barrier walls, right? That way it's not so noisy for the people in their houses. The walls are all prefabricated and look about the same. But I noticed, every now and then, they stick a door in one. I always wondered why. I learned that it's so that the highway people can get access for maintenance or to get to fire hydrants or what have you."

"Yes?"

"So, I had been curious about that and thought, 'You know, if I'm curious about that, other people will be too.'"

"Okay."

"So, I surveilled various sound walls throughout the state—mostly around Baltimore—and made a list of the most interesting ones with doors. Some of them have been around like twenty years, so they have, like, a highway patina. A lot of them have plants and vines growing around them, randomly, but sometimes in very beautiful ways. So I reached out to some of the folks whose homes are affected to get a tour, as it were. The coolest thing is the 'before and after.' You know, you listen first with the door open. At peak times the noise is unbelievable. But once you close that door, there is an immediate calm. Much more peaceful. Very Zen. And like I said, the naturally occurring flora and fauna are quite amazing. Besides the plants, there were things like rodents and birds nesting near the doors. Some right on the walls above the doors. You could tell because of all the droppings."

Roland blinked twice.

"So, I worked a few deals with about a half dozen homeowners with the doors to bring travel groups in. I even lined up a retired State Highway employee to give lectures about the barrier walls and so forth. The guy really knows his stuff. It's pretty cool."

"Unbelievable."

"Yeah, it's kind of 'nascent' though. It's just starting. I need to get more buzz, so that's why the Facebook page. There haven't been that many takers yet. Although I do have one repeat couple. Older folks who have done the tour several times. Retirees. I like them."

"Wow."

"I also offer a box lunch. That way, people can kick back and make an afternoon of it. Usually lean roast beef and Swiss cheese on whole wheat. It's eight bucks, but I include a small bag of chips and a bottle of water. I also have those little plastic packets with mayo and mustard, too."

"Makes sense."

"It's weird. The brochure mentions the box lunch, but nobody wants to book the box lunch at point of purchase. So, what I do is, I bring along enough box lunches for everyone. My guy does the lecture, which is way cool because it's outside. He uses one of those Mr. Microphones they used to make. Works, too. Anyway, when he begins the lecture, I just start eating from one of the box lunches and 'voila' they all want the box lunch too. So I wind up selling a lot of lunches that way."

"Cool. So, presumably you jack the price of the lunches up a little, then, because the people didn't order in advance? What, like ten or twelve bucks instead of eight?"

Chris looked puzzled. "No. Why would I do that? The brochure says eight, so I charge them eight. And none of the sandwiches go to waste. I just eat a lot of them during the week if there are leftovers." He was thinking that he had gotten a little tired of roast beef, though.

"That's great, Waxley. Have you ever heard of a thing called Chapter 7?"

"What? Not really. But look, maybe, when you get back, I'll do you a solid. A free pass to the next tour? Box lunch included!"

. . .

Late Spring 2019

Robbie waited for his ice cream float and removed his comic books from the bag.

"So, rob rob? What's up? You seem a little quiet today?"

"Not really." He began checking out the "classic" Silver Surfer comic that tim tim picked out and bought for him along with the others. He didn't really want it. It was in fair condition, which meant beat to hell. Not really worth anything. Old.

"You're going to like that one! That comic was a game-changer for a lot of people."

"Did it come out when you were a kid?"

"No! It was already a classic when I started reading comic books in the '80s. Look—the price was just twenty-five cents in the '60s! Can you believe it?"

"No."

There was more silence.

"Did I do something to bother you, Robbie? Are you angry with me?"

He continued staring at the page, but was not really reading it. He sighed. "Well, no. But it's when you drive and stuff. You never get mad at the people who cut you off or take your space or butt ahead of us in line. And when I get mad, you give me a lecture. I can't help being mad when people do that stuff because it's not right. It's not fair. And then you keep telling me I have to ignore it. I can't, and I don't know why I should?"

"Ah . . . okay. I'm sorry, Robbie. I keep forgetting that you're still a young guy. Some of the stuff I say is not going to make any sense now. The reason I say stuff like that is because my uncle waited way too long before getting me up to speed on the mission. It would have seriously helped me understand what was going on inside me, if he hadn't been so darn careful and waited so long. I was pretty big for

39

my age and was ready for the instruction. He didn't know and just never was around much then. His uncle hadn't filled him in until he was like twenty, which is way, way too late. I was like nineteen when baz baz finally started."

"Baz baz?"

"Yeah, his name was Basil, so we called him baz baz. He would be your grand uncle. He once sat in that very chair. But he passed away a good while back."

"Okay?"

"Listen. I want you to know that as you get older, your body and mind will go through changes. All of it is okay and natural. Good training will help you understand what's going on."

"You mean like sex ed?"

"Sex ed? Ha! No. That's up to your dad and mom. I mean training for the mission. Totally different."

"Seriously? You know, here's the thing. Maybe I don't want the mission?"

"Yes! I get it. I know. I had a really tough time with it. Your dad probably told you that I had some bad experiences with drugs when I was younger. Why did I choose to take drugs? Because I wanted to do good for people, to help our country. And I also thought the drugs might help me find myself. You know, gain an understanding of what was going on with me. Who I was and what I was supposed to do with my life. But the drugs just messed me up for a while. They didn't explain the mission. Finally, baz baz started hanging out with me, and it all began to make sense."

"Were you like, arrested? For drugs?"

"Oh! No. Never. I was a volunteer. It was all legal and carefully done. But it was a waste, ultimately. I doubt any good came out of it."

Robbie looked on, puzzled. Tim tim stuck the spoon into the ice cream container.

"It's thawed enough now. Let me get the floats going."

. . .

Tim tim washed up the ice cream dishes in the sink. He glanced at the enormous rust spot. The spigot dripped. He spoke over his shoulder.

"So Robbie, I want to tell you about our family tree. Our lineage."

"Okay."

"We go back a really long way. All the way back. We're even mentioned in the Bible. In Genesis, if you can believe it. That's the earliest book!"

"What? Like Adam and Eve?"

"Ha. No. We were here before those guys. By the time they rolled in, we had already made our mark. To them we were 'the heroes of old, the men of renown.' I'm kind of proud of that. And you should be too!"

"Really? I thought Adam and Eve were supposed to be the first people." He went back to glancing through the Silver Surfer. It was more believable than tim tim.

"Well, they were the first round of human beings for sure. But we were some of the earlier people. We evolved here specifically to help all the other people in the world. Particularly human beings, who came along a bit later."

Robbie put the comic book aside. He looked up and blinked. The strangeness of the discussion had sunk in. "Are you saying we're not human?" He was trying not to laugh.

"Ah. No, you and I are definitely human, in part. That's because, way back when, we ran out of our own people to marry and have families with. We weren't able to sustain ourselves without becoming part of the human race, at least partially. You know, it was the same thing for the people we now call Neanderthals. And there were a few other groups in the same boat back then. But it was the right thing for us because God said so and instructed us to keep helping other people. That's the mission. And pretty much the only people left here are humans. And we're included because we are each part human, anyway. But you and I are slightly different because of our lineage and the mission and the whole nephew and uncle thing."

. . .

Will was not looking forward to it. Robbie almost never sought him out to discuss "things." He was apprehensive, hoping to avoid a "facts of life" discussion. He recounted his dismal efforts with Doyle. Really embarrassing for both of them. Doyle already knew everything. Will had secretly hoped that Robbie would get his information from Doyle.

"So, Robbie, what's up?"

Robbie closed the door of Will's home office behind him. He sat down in the lounge chair next to the desk. "Well, mostly it's about Uncle tim tim."

"Okay."

"So, you never told me he was doing drugs when he was younger? Is that why he's so weird?"

Will sighed in relief. *Hooray! Not a sex talk.* "Well. That's a little . . . touchy." He sighed. "Listen, whatever we talk about here has to be considered a secret, between us. Confidential. Do you understand that?"

"Sure, Dad."

"Okay. And I mean, don't even mention this to Mom or Doyle."

"Okay. Sure?" Robbie was a little surprised.

"All right. So, for most of his life, Tim has been a little . . . weird. I began to notice it as we became teenagers. You know, around puberty. You know what that means, right?"

"Sure, Dad. Of course." Robbie was pretty sure at least.

"Okay. Tim just started acting in an odd way. For example, he made the school's junior varsity wrestling team, which surprised all of us because Tim was not particularly good at sports. He had challenged one of the best wrestlers on the team to a match for some reason, even though he had never wrestled in his life. I think he was mad at the guy about something and wanted to whip him. I can't remember exactly what. So, they go to the gym. A bunch of guys tagged along for the show. But, apparently, the wrestling coach—who was also a teacher—caught wind and watched from a distance in case he had to jump in and break things up."

"Okay."

"And Tim somehow beats the guy. Made it look easy. So, the coach rolls in at the end, pretending to be pissed off and threatens both Tim and the other guy with detention. And then he basically ordered Tim to join the team, which he did."

"Wow. Okay."

"But, afterwards, Tim was a horrible wrestler. He showed nothing. He was losing all of his matches, so the coach kind of . . . well, he let Tim stay on the team, officially, but just as a sub. He was never given any more actual matches. And that was good because he really sucked at it. The weird thing was that he definitely beat that other guy who was a good wrestler. But he was never able to do it again in real matches. Just really odd."

Robbie had a blank look on his face. "Is that when he started doing drugs?"

"No. Not really. I was just telling you that because that was kind of like the beginning of the weirdness. He started to get reclusive. You know, wanting to be by himself more. He still had a few friends at school and his teammates, but he spent more time reading. Especially reading the Bible. Which was odd, because we were not really a religious type family. We were Catholic, but only went to church like once a year at Christmas. But that was because they, you know my parents, Grandpa and Grandma, liked the decorations and choir and Christmas carols. Not because they were all that into religion."

"Okay."

"But Tim somehow got into a religious thing and would talk about stuff from the Bible. He graduated from high school, but didn't want to go to college. Your grandpa was really pissed about that. And Tim was having trouble getting along with the rest of the family. That's when he started talking about being, like, a missionary. He was looking for some religious group to join and travel with. He would stay in his room and read the Bible all day and then go out at night and weekends looking for church services to go to. Religious groups he could join. But he never really found anything."

"Wow."

"So, Mom and Dad were really worried and took him to several counselors and a psychologist. He didn't like it, but ultimately, he went along with meeting those people. But he never stuck with any therapies or anything. And the next thing you know, he was trying to join the Army. But—and this is really weird—he was very anti-war. Totally. But he wanted to join the Army. And, somehow, he did. More or less."

THE BIG COMB OVER

. . .

June 1998

Staff Sergeant Breton didn't mind the thinness of the walls. It gave him the chance to listen in on the efforts of the particular recruiter rotated to his command. Sergeant Stephanie Pinder was one of the best. Male recruits loved her, and women felt at home with her. She had a hell of a smile and delivery. She could read the room and connect with virtually any personality. And there were an awful lot of those. And this was a particularly odd one.

"Mr. Elders, yes. Like I said, we have many conscientious objectors in our Army. We take great pride in respecting the moral, ethical, and religious needs of our troops. We take that as seriously as any other aspect of military service. But we can't sign up a person who has deeply held convictions against bearing arms and potentially taking a human life. If the person already holds those convictions at the recruitment phase, they'd be disqualified."

"But I don't see the difference? You're saying that a recruit can join and then later develop feelings against killing. And the Army would accommodate them. And they could do all kinds of really positive and useful things for their country? But a guy who just wants to do helpful things can't do them for the Army if he has objections to killing, earlier, before signing up?"

"Yes, Mr. Elders. I feel where you're coming from. I get it. I really do. But think of it from the Army's point of view. We need dedicated soldiers willing to take a life, if necessary, in service to their country. That's big. We may not be at war, now, but we must always be prepared to defend our home. Wars can happen very quickly and unpredictably. To be blunt, a conscientious objector places an extra burden on the Army. The law requires that we accommodate soldiers who legitimately develop those beliefs while in service. Accommodating those folks is something we do. And we do it well. But personnel and duties must then be shifted and reorganized. A review panel must be maintained. There's a built-in cost factor. Do you see?"

Tim tim sighed. "Yes. I guess I can see that. I just really wanted to serve our country. To be part of a team. A mission to do good and serve people. I figured the Army would have a place for me."

Sergeant Pinder sighed. "I hear you. I can tell you're a good guy, Mr. Elders. But there's just nothing we can do for you in this case."

Tim tim looked down at his folded hands. "Well, thanks, ma'am. I'll figure something out. And I appreciate your kindness." He stood to leave.

Pinder heard tapping at her door. She was seldom interrupted during a pitch. The door opened. She stood at attention and saluted.

"At ease, Sergeant." Breton reached forward to shake hands with tim tim. "Nice to meet you, Mr. . . . . Elders?" Tim tim shook Breton's outstretched hand, blankly.

"Yes, sir. It's Elders."

"Good, good! So, I'm sorry for listening in. That's my office, there." He smiled, sheepishly, and made a hitchhiking motion toward the wall. "Look, everything Sergeant Pinder told you regarding conscientious objector status is absolutely correct. And she's done an excellent job in explaining Army policy in that regard. Truly accurate. But I wanted to inform you of a potential opportunity. It would be something like a hybrid position connected with the Army. But not the same as being in the Army as a regular recruit."

Sergeant Pinder looked surprised. She had never been informed that any such thing existed.

"Okay? What is it exactly?"

"Well, it's a nonofficial position where we work with . . . materials . . . to do things that help our country's peacekeeping missions. And it's right here in Maryland. It's a fascinating opportunity for the right recruit. Would you like to learn more? We could grab a coffee together?"

...

July 1998

Corporal Markham entered the room and watched the four recruits come to attention. The old guy in fatigues on the end had the best form and had appropriately saluted. The others in civilian attire were a mess. He glanced over his shoulder to the lone conference table, making sure the can was there. It was.

"At ease, men."

He noticed that three of the four had already gone at ease because their version of standing at attention was being at ease. And he saw that the old guy in fatigues had not gone at ease. He still stood square-backed and stiff-necked. But at least he had dropped the salute, albeit quite vigorously. Markham sighed to himself, *Not my problem.*

He looked ahead toward the back of the room to make sure Sean was there. He was. As per usual, Sean was seated in the stark wooden chair, head bowed and eyes closed in apparent meditation. He wore his usual black turtleneck sweater, khakis, and huarache sandals. The flecks of gray in his black beard stood out against his sweater. His hair was pulled back in a ponytail.

"Men, today you embark upon an incredible mission. Needless to say, your country salutes you for your service." Markham stiffly saluted the men, which he saw triggered a dramatic and zealously robotic salute from the weird old guy on the end. He shook his head. *Okay.*

"Men, today the US is under attack from enemies of every stripe and from every corner. They are spread out upon this earth, and yet, we cannot see them. They hide under every rock and stone, afraid of being brought into the light. But pick up their stone, and watch the slimy vermin run away in cowardice. Their organizations are poisonous limbs reaching everywhere—thorny brambles and scrubs with shoots extending to the four corners of the globe. But, break off a twig, and you'll find the rot, the maggots just waiting to infest your home. Just waiting to eat away at everything you've worked for as an American. To make you and your loved ones miserable."

He saw the short guy on the other end wince and then shudder. The old guy stood stiffly at attention.

"Do we know these enemies? Yes, we do. We know them well. Do we know where they are located? Yes. These United States have the most thorough and incisive intelligence-gathering agencies in the world. None are greater than our own. But even when we find our enemies, do we always know the vital details of their plans, their fiendish plots against our freedom and safety? Sometimes, we do not. If we could just see those specific plans, maps, strategies, operations . . . you get the picture. When we have proper, detailed intel, we can beat back any enemy. And that's where you men come in."

Markham took a breath. He could tell that his muster was working on them, at least the three. He sensed their enthusiasm. Especially the bulgy balding guy next to the old guy. The old guy was still stiffly expressionless.

"Now, at this juncture, I will introduce you to your mission commander." Markham waved toward the back of the room. "Sir?"

Slowly, the bearded man unfurled from his meditative position in the worn chair. He rubbed his face with both hands and then stroked his beard. He stood and gently padded across the floor, taking his place next to Markham. His footfall made almost no sound.

"Men, this is Sean. He's an artist. He will lead and guide you in this mission."

He sensed that the men were confused about the lack of rank. Tim tim also noticed that Sean looked a heckuva lot like the '70s comedian George Carlin.

"Sir, do you have a preference? Do you want to be addressed as Commander Sean or Mr. Sean?" Markham always made sure to ask this each time. You just wouldn't know with Sean.

Sean looked on at the assemblage and paused. He looked down to his sandals and took several meditative breaths. And then he looked up and spoke. "Just Sean is fine, Corporal. Sean is my connective name. No need for extra baggage."

"Yes, sir, Sean."

"Would you call roll, Corporal?"

"Yes, sir. Now, men, when I call your name, please respond, 'here.' Adkins?"

The short man on the end raised his hand. "Here."

"Elders?"

"Here, but you can all call me tim tim." Tim tim smiled enthusiastically.

Sean looked up quizzically. "Still two syllables, Elders. I'll stick with Elders." Tim tim felt confused and a little deflated.

"Okay, Sean."

Markham continued. "Florin?"

No response.

"Florin, Myron? Are you present?"

The old guy on the end unstiffened and responded, "Here, sir." He saluted again.

Sean looked up from his sandals at the man. He held up his hand, gently, to pause the roll call. He looked directly at Florin. "How old are you?"

Florin stiffened again. "Ageless." He had been adopted and didn't actually know.

Sean gently nodded and looked back down at his sandals. He breathed twice and slowly raised his head.

"Efficient. I applaud that, Florin."

Sean saw the three puzzled faces.

"Ah, you're wondering what I mean—why would I say that?"

Two of the men nodded.

"Florin could have responded with his age, in terms of numbers—the years on the calendar—the strokes marked off on the wall of his mental cell. But that would not have been as efficient. For example, Florin could have said, 'seventy-five,' his likely chronological age. But that would have taken four syllables. 'Ageless' takes only two syllables and tells us much, much more about the man, Myron Florin. Bravo, Florin."

Florin had not flinched and did not acknowledge the praise. He continued to stand at attention.

"Continue, please, Corporal."

Markham was unfazed. He had seen it all before. "Sadtler?"

"Here."

Then silence.

Markham waited patiently. Sean was looking down at his sandals again. An eternity passed. Finally, Sean raised his head and pointed to the conference table just a few feet behind. "Do you see that? What do you see?"

The three looked at each other quizzically. Sadtler eventually raised his hand. Sean nodded.

"Sir, I see a table and a soup can. And five chairs."

Sean nodded. "Correct, Sadtler. What is the can communicating to you?"

Sadtler felt confused. He looked over to the other recruits for help. Tim tim and Adkins quickly looked away.

Sadtler rallied. "Well, I guess it's telling me it's a can of chicken noodle soup. I can see it's chicken noodle."

Sean looked away disappointedly. "Anyone else? Elders?"

Tim tim looked puzzled. "Me? Well, I'd have to agree with Mr. Sadtler. That's definitely Campbell's Chicken Noodle soup. My brother and I eat that for lunch a lot." He shook his head affirmatively.

Sean scoffed. "Nice."

"Adkins?"

"I agree about the soup, sir. That's a can of soup. Unless it's been eaten already and the can's empty. Can't tell from here." He squinted. "But, I'd guess it's a full can, sir."

Sean shook his head, gently, and looked back down toward his feet. Moments passed. "Nice. But, you've all focused on the micro, not the macro. You have to look beyond the object to see the thing the object represents."

Three of the four looked hopelessly bewildered. Florin remained at attention.

Sean stepped back to the table and picked up the can. He held it up before the men.

"This can teaches us relativity. Not in the Einsteinian sense. More literal. Perhaps perspective is a better word. I'll make it simple: This object existed before you were born in precisely the same form and size. In fact, probably before your fathers were born. It looked the same and tasted the same. The packaging was the same. And it will be here long after you are all gone, probably long after all of your sons and grandsons are gone. It was begotten long before you and will continue to be, long after you. And it will look the same and taste the same."

The three looked utterly confused. Sean looked back down at the floor, holding the can close to his breast. Another eternity passed. He looked back up, still cradling the can.

"What have you learned?"

No one dared answer.

"Adkins?"

Adkins glanced around at the others. "Well, I was thinking that Campbell's Chicken Noodle is a very popular soup. Probably more popular than, like, Vegetable, or any of the others. That's probably why it's been around so long." He nodded his head several times toward the others, hoping for affirmation. No one moved.

Sean winced, visibly. "Elders?"

Tim tim gulped. "Well, I was thinking that that particular can probably isn't all that important. Because there have been so many others exactly like it. And then I remembered that a lot of folks would have that guy Andy Warhol—you know, the artist—autograph their chicken soup cans, because he painted a really accurate picture of a Campbell's Chicken Noodle soup can once that became famous. Those autographed cans should be worth something now."

Sean stepped back and placed the soup can back on the table. "Interesting, Elders. Capitalistic."

Tim tim wasn't sure if it was praise or insult. But he answered, "Thanks, Sean!"

Sean scowled. "Sadtler?"

Sadtler gulped. "I think you're trying to say that the soup can tells us our lives are actually insignificant, even though we may feel otherwise."

Sean looked back toward the can glumly. He paused and then responded. "I asked you what the can communicated to you. Not what you felt I was communicating." He had provided air quotes with the phrase "I was communicating." He looked back down at his feet. Sadtler was crestfallen.

The three eventually looked over toward Florin. No movement.

Finally, Sean lifted his head. "Were you waiting for a response from Florin? Recall that he's already responded. He told us previously, 'Ageless.' Florin effectively handled several questions, including a future question, by responding to one earlier question. Efficiency." He nodded over to Florin, approvingly, and then looked back down to the floor.

. . .

Early Summer 2019

"So Dad said you wrestled in high school. Did you like it?" Robbie had finished his last spoonful of ice cream.

"Well, kind of! I laughed a lot!"

"What do you mean?"

"Well. It's kind of ridiculous. I was ticklish. It tickled! Wrestling, I mean!"

"What? Guys would tickle you?"

"No. Not on purpose. But the physical contact with the opponent. It tickled! I would start laughing and lose the match. It was awful. My guys nicknamed me 'the fish' because I would always roll over and wind up losing. I couldn't stand the tickling!"

"But Dad said you were good once?"

"Well. There was that one time. This guy Mike was, like, a hotshot on the team, and he would always bully my friend Travis. You know. Belittle him because he was a skinny, weak kid with thick glasses. He'd slap him really hard on his back, like he was a friend, but way too hard. It would hurt. And then he'd coax or basically extort money from Travis. He got bolder and bolder when he saw that no one was going to stop him. He started smacking Travis on his head, which really hurt him. And he was picking on more and more kids, too. So one day I saw him really smack Travis, and I felt something. Like adrenaline almost. You'll see. But not just adrenaline. And I glanced over, and out of the corner of my eye I saw the thumbs up and knew it was time. Right then and there I challenged Mike to a wrestling match because I knew he would not be able to resist beating me at his best sport."

"Wow?"

"So we went to the gym. He first tried to coax me—to bully me—into backing down. Tried to convince me I would lose. Because bullies don't want any chance of being embarrassed. But I said I was quite ready to wrestle him right there and now and that if I won, he'd have to let Travis and all the other kids be."

"So you wrestled and won?"

"Yes. And he stopped bothering Travis and everybody. And that's how I got on the team. Can you believe it? I got a letter in wrestling!"

"How were you able to wrestle the guy if you had never wrestled before?"

"Oh, I had watched a couple matches before and saw what was done. I just copied what I had seen."

"Did they throw the guy off the team?"

"Mike? Oh no. He was the star. And Mike and I became good friends. He had a lot of life issues then. Weird parents. Big family. He didn't get much attention. He was a good guy at heart. He had just been taking his insecurities out on others. He cooled out. He was okay. That's how life works, sometimes."

"I don't think I'd ever be able to be friends with a guy like Mike."

"I know. I wouldn't have thought so either. But the mission sets into motion a lot of adjustments. They often happen naturally."

. . .

Will was becoming more accustomed to his discussions with Robbie. Almost always about Tim. He was getting worried about Tim's influence. But with his trial schedule, having Robbie pal around with Tim was really helpful. It was just all the damned religious and weird stuff that went along with it. He would at least try to get Robbie to see things scientifically, to counter the crazy religious stuff.

"So, what's new with you and Tim? Did you guys find any rare comics? Or does Tim just treat you to the newer ones?"

"A little of both, Dad. But mostly I pick out graphic novels, and tim tim sometimes finds a classic he thinks I would like. They're kind of old fashioned, though. But I read them."

"Cool, cool!"

The conversation paused.

"So what's on your mind? Is it Tim?"

"Well, yes."

There was another uncomfortable pause.

"Is it about his religious stuff and the Bible?"

Robbie sighed. "Yeah. So, tim tim says that just because we can't see God, doesn't mean he doesn't exist. But I know you and Mom don't believe in God, right?"

Will scowled to himself. "That's right. Your Mom and I don't believe that a god exists. We believe in things that we can see and observe. Not invisible beings and things we can't observe. We believe in the scientific method. Ghosts and gods and magic and other superstitious stuff just distract people away from living their lives freely and rationally. Santa and the Easter Bunny are fine for kids, but at some point we have to grow out of irrational beliefs."

"Tim tim says we can't see germs either, but they exist. And he says that scientists don't really understand what electricity is, either, and it's invisible. But it exists."

Will sighed, heavily. "Well, what we can't see with the naked eye, we can observe using scientific instruments like microscopes and telescopes and oscilloscopes. Instruments proven trustworthy thanks to the scientific method. We know germs exist because we can see them under a microscope, which is part of the rational world that we can trust. And we know what germs can do to people thanks to modern medicine. Yes, in the old days, people didn't know about germs and viruses. You couldn't see them with the naked eye. Some doctors felt there must be something making people sick, but there was no way to find the cause. Then the microscope was developed and taught us about another whole world of things."

"Do you think they'll ever come up with an instrument that could maybe find God?"

"No, because God doesn't exist. So there can't be an instrument to find God. Do you understand?"

"Okay."

There was another pause.

"What about electricity? It exists, but no one can see it? And scientists don't really understand it?"

Will scowled. "Yes, it exists. And no, we can't see it, and scientists may not understand it fully, but we see what it does. You flick the switch, and the light goes on. Remember, science teaches us that just because we can't see a thing doesn't mean it can't exist."

"Okay, Dad. Thanks."

"You're welcome, Robbie. Put your trust in science. Science is real."

Robbie pulled himself out of the lounge chair and gently closed the door behind on Will.

Will leaned back in his office chair. He was glad that Robbie shared with him. But, somehow, he felt unsatisfied in how the discussion went. He couldn't quite put his finger on it.

. . .

Tim tim cleared and wiped down the kitchen table. He dried the surface with the dish towel. "Can I take a look at what you found?"

"Sure." Robbie pushed the comic books over to tim tim's place at the table.

"Wow! Look, you got one with Galactus! He's considered a classic character. He's gigantic."

"Yeah, and he has to devour planets to survive!"

"Yep, I remember! And later he became a 'good guy' and then a 'bad guy' back and forth."

Tim tim handed the comics back over to Robbie. "You know, Robbie, seeing Galactus reminds me of some stuff to tell you about the mission."

Robbie sighed. He really hated the mission talk because it sometimes led to Bible talk. "Okay, tim tim."

"So, I've mentioned how our ancestors were loved and held in great esteem by everyone here way back when."

"Yes."

"Okay, because of some poor translations of the Bible, we are mentioned in a few other places as being the 'bad guys.' Galactus reminded me how some people thought we were giants or warrior types."

"Okay."

"But this was simply not true. We never killed other people. We were, and are, peaceful people. And we were never giants. Maybe physically a few inches taller than others, but definitely not giants."

"So, we've always been the good guys? Never the bad guys?" Robbie figured this could shut the discussion down.

"Well, this part is tricky. Free will comes in different flavors."

Robbie looked up, puzzled.

"Well, I can explain. When people do bad things, it's because they've chosen those things. They have a mind that lets them choose between good and bad, and they choose the bad thing. Being able to choose between good and bad is free will. God gave free will to human beings as a gift. It's the thing that makes humans most like God. It's huge. Not all people have that."

"What? You mean, like, people with brain damage or something?"

Tim tim sighed. "Well, yes, some folks have brain injuries that mess up their thinking and stuff. But I'm really talking about us. Because you and I are very much human, we're born with free will. And we keep it until around puberty, when it—well—transitions to our particular flavor of free will. Our ancestral free will. You know, the free will we were given when we first came onto the scene, way back when."

Robbie looked puzzled again. "You're saying once you get older, you think differently?"

Tim tim looked out toward the kitchen wall. There was a gravelly stain along the stove's exhaust fan. "Well, I think the same way in most areas, as long as it's in line with the mission. To do good for people. To help them. But we don't kill. We've never done that. We can't choose to do that. So, even though there are a couple places in the Bible where we are mistakenly identified as warriors working for the bad guys, that never happened because it simply couldn't happen. That's not how we roll."

. . .

October 1998

Tim tim disliked the "rap" sessions. He just didn't understand the purpose. And it was physically uncomfortable. The six men sat on bath towels, cross-legged in a circle. The tile floor was always cold. The towels were no help.

Sean spoke, "I want to introduce you to one of our project facilitators, Belize II." He gestured toward the man sitting next to him. Belize II was also wearing a black turtleneck sweater and had the same basic facial hair as Sean. He, too, had a fairly lengthy ponytail. But his features and hair color were darker.

Adkins raised his hand. "Are you, like, Belize Junior, sir? Because some dads name their sons, you know, junior, but some use the Roman numeral to mean, like, the second?"

There was a lengthy pause. Sean looked down to his folded legs and gently shook his head in disdain.

Belize II finally spoke. "It's Belize II. That's my name." He had gotten used to the name. The oddness was almost a calling card, considering his profession in the field of psychical therapeutics. He never told anyone that his parents named him that because he was conceived on the second day of their weeklong vacation in Belize. Not relevant.

Sean spoke again. "Like myself, Belize II is an artist. He's Non-Representational, while I'm simply an Abstract Expressionist." Sean looked down humbly. "I am also a student, learning something new every day from Belize II. And, because of his advanced experience and training, he has been chosen as your cofacilitator for your remote viewing exercises."

"Thank you, Sean. And for the record, I would consider myself more of a Neoplasticist than a Non-Representationalist."

"Yes, of course. Mea culpa."

There was another long pause.

Belize II finally spoke. "There is a spiritual side to our endeavors, our travels. There is a multidimensional side, too. I feel these are integrated states. That may not be the case for everyone present in this circle, though. And that's okay. Your ability to free your mind and travel through space-time's dimensions in your gentle energy stream is the key to finding that real-world destination. Seek it however you may. There are many doors. There are many keys. When you find the key that fits your door, you will find your gentle stream. Now, meditate on this. Contemplate the doors and your personal keys."

He and Sean looked down serenely at their crossed legs. Tim tim was wondering what the heck Belize II was talking about. He thought of his keyring in his pants pocket. He didn't think that's what Belize II actually meant, though. Tim tim looked over to Adkins with a puzzled look on his face, telegraphing his confusion. Adkins shrugged. Sadtler noticed tim tim glancing over. He ignored him and went back to looking at his own legs. Florin had never stopped looking stiffly ahead.

Fifteen endless minutes passed. Finally, Belize II raised his head. "Men, I hope some of you have found your key or perhaps even your door. Now, I don't encourage false spirituality. Each man must find his own way. I, myself, do not believe in a traditional god. But I believe in an ethereal spirit force that guides us and inspires us. Depending on my perceptions and sense of surrounding, I may give my spirit force a name. Sometimes it's "Ocean." Sometimes, "Sunrise." It may depend on your connection and comfort with the energy source. Let's contemplate that."

Both he and Sean, again, looked down, placidly. Ten minutes passed. Finally, Belize II looked back up. "That was refreshing." Sean nodded in agreement. "So, Adkins, did you feel a connect? What name do you give that force?"

Adkins looked around, panicked. "Sir, I don't know. I've never thought about it. I didn't think you were asking us to come up with a name."

Belize II made a soothing hand motion. "It's okay, Adkins. It's okay. When you feel a name, there will be a name."

"Sadtler?" He looked up startled. "Ah, me neither, sir. But I'll think about it more."

Belize II again made a calming motion. "That's fine. Perfectly fine."

"Elders?"

"I am."

"I'm sorry, Elders. You're what?"

"No, sir. His name is 'I am.' At least, that's what he told us to call him."

"Interesting, Elders. But what does that mean to you?"

Tim tim looked down to the floor for a moment and then looked back up. "It means that he is all being, all existence, the source of all life for all of the universe, forever. He's the one who is. Something like that, I think."

Belize II looked on respectfully. "That's very beautiful, Elders. Encompassing. Very Eastern. I like that. It's just a shame that our conventional Western theologies couldn't come up with something so beautiful. Think of how different our world would be today?"

. . .

Summer 2019

"I heard Mom tell Dad you're a Jesus Freak. She said you were a born-again Christian."

"What? Really? Well, I do love Jesus. Very much. I mean, who couldn't, right? But I don't belong to any organized church or religion. I'm not a born-again Christian. I just do what I do and stay on mission."

"Well, you had said that God created the universe, but Mom said that there is no God and that the universe was created by the big bang, not God. She said the big bang happened from just a super small, tiny point, which blew up and expanded like crazy and became the entire universe. She said God played no part in it because God doesn't exist."

"Okay. Well, then who put the tiny point there?"

"I don't know. I'm just telling you what Mom said."

"Okay. Well, tell your mom she's correct about the big bang and that the tiny thing in the beginning was a mustard seed."

"What? A seed? Like an actual seed from a plant?"

"Well, no. I'm being facetious. You know what facetious means, right? Means I'm being a smartass. Look, your mom is a fantastic mom and surgeon and super well educated and way smarter than me, but I have . . . like, inside information. Don't worry about how the universe came to be. Trust me, it's here because of God. He created the universe to give us life and freedom because those are the things he enjoys the most."

"Yeah, but Mom says there isn't a God because a real God would never allow people to suffer from things like diseases and hurricanes and wildfires and stuff like that. He wouldn't allow all the bad things to happen."

"Okay."

"And Dad said that when he went to CCD class as a kid, they told him that bad things happened to people as a test from God. To make sure they were really faithful and would accept his hardships."

Tim tim sighed. "Well, I can tell you that none of that stuff is true."

"But then why do bad things happen to people if there's a God?"

"Well, I do have the answer for that. Again, it's insider knowledge, but it's probably time to share it with you. You're old enough."

"You're not going to say, 'there's no answer and we have to just accept it,' right? Because that's what Doctor Forbes said."

"Who's Doctor Forbes?"

"Well, I didn't tell you, but Mom and Dad hired him to help me understand things. He's like a guidance counselor. They said he understood kids and could help me. I'm embarrassed because I didn't want his help, and so I didn't want to tell you."

"Oh. That's okay, Robbie! My parents did the same thing for me. I wound up talking to a lot of people like that when I was young too. That's because I didn't understand the mission yet, because baz baz wasn't on the scene for me, at that point. But all is well, rob rob, because you're probably beginning to understand the mission more and more, right?"

Robbie scowled sourly. "Well, no, tim tim. Not really. I still don't understand why I'm expected to be and act differently about people and things. I think I never will."

Tim tim thought, *Yes, you will. We all do, eventually.*

"Well, that's okay, Robbie! Rome was not built in a day. A thousand-mile journey begins with the first step. I'm pleased with everything you've done so far. You will definitely get it soon. Don't worry!" He nodded supportively.

"Okay. So what's the inside information to explain why people have to suffer? It doesn't make any sense to me."

"Okay, yes. I'll explain it to you like baz baz explained it to me. Imagine for a minute that you are a different kind of creature, but just like a normal person, you feel and think for yourself."

"Okay."

"You start out straight and strong. You have a family of like three or five others just like you. You love movement and exercise and you like to glide, upward and downward, surrounded by warmth and fulfillment. Your family loves the same. Motion, warmth, purpose. Sometimes you are all moving so well and happily together that you feel a greater purpose to what you are doing, and this makes you glad. You like your environment, which is quite beautiful to you and very interesting and comfortable. So, that would be like a happy person in good health surrounded by a happy family in a safe and pleasant environment. Maybe even a person who believes in and thanks God."

"Okay."

"But there are times when your movement is slow and feels rough. You watch a family member struggle and shut down. Things don't feel right. You're not feeling any kind of higher purpose. This would be a person facing a hardship or illness."

"Okay."

"And worse yet are the times when things come to a complete stop. No movement. No feeling of warmth. Just coldness. Loneliness. Your family is no longer your support. They've shut down too. You feel that there can't be a greater purpose because a loving God would not allow this to happen. This is a person facing the worst. Sickness, death, and loneliness. Maybe an accident or disaster. A person would, naturally, begin to doubt the existence of a loving, caring God."

"Okay."

"So, here's the answer—you are actually a piston in a cylinder in an internal combustion engine inside of a car—a race car. God made the car, piece by piece. The car is his universe, and God is driving the car. And God loves to race and share his happiness with all the parts of the car—every single wire and switch and pipe and all parts of the engine. But, sometimes God has to brake and decelerate the car, naturally. And there are pit stops and maintenance when the car has to be shut down entirely. Slowing down to take curves carefully or parking the car for maintenance are things that have to happen in order for the car to drive safely and work properly. They are temporary, because God absolutely loves the race and sharing his joy during the race. The slowdowns and pit stops are just as much a part of the race as the movement and acceleration. The race will continue. But the piston doesn't see beyond his own cylinder and the cylinders of his family. He doesn't know about the car or that he's even part of a car. He only knows what feels right to him based on the world he inhabits. And that's okay. That's how it is supposed to be. He'll feel better once the race resumes, but there will always be pit stops and maintenance required. So, being people, we are not getting the complete picture. We can only see what we can see and, naturally, we judge the situation based on the knowledge we have. And that's okay. But God loves us and wants us to know that, although the pit stops and shutdowns seem to take forever, the race is on and is actually quite short. When the race is finally over, every piece of the car feels the victory and shares the trophy. Does that make sense?"

Robbie blinked a few times. "Well, why doesn't he just tell the piston about the race and the car?"

"Ah, well, he did at the beginning when he made the car. And the old original pistons were told to pass it along to the newbies whenever the old ones were replaced. And they tried, but being made of metal, sometimes there were flub-ups in the communication. But that's why I'm here. I'm an old piston, telling you about your engine."

Robbie still looked puzzled, but tim tim figured it was time to change the subject.

"So, I heard that you and Doyle are going to merry old Londontown for your Uncle Stefan's wedding later this summer? Are you stoked?"

"Not really. Because we'll be stuck with Desales. He's a big pain in the butt."

Tim tim chuckled. He had met Desales a few times at family gatherings. It was true. The kid was a pain. "Well, hopefully your Uncle Roy will keep him under control."

"Are you coming, tim tim?"

"Well, no. Stefan is your mom's brother, like Roy and Roland. I'm your father's brother. So I'm only related to Stefan by marriage. But you are a blood relation to Stefan because he's your mom's little brother. So, they can't have every possible relative go to the wedding. They have to limit the invitations. But that's okay. I'll be looking forward to hearing about your adventures!"

. . .

October 1998

Both Sean and Belize II were leading today's project. They sat on identical wooden stools while the four men sat cross-legged on their bath towels.

Sean spoke first. "Okay, you men have worked your first pre-con mission. You've received your allotted enhancers." Sean felt it better to refer to the mescaline derivatives as "enhancers"—it sounded less clinical than "doses."

Tim tim thought back to the pre-con mission, hours before. Basically, the four being driven around in two old Army vans with maps and told to direct the drivers, Sean and Belize II, to specific geographic destinations. He was stuck with Sadtler, a very "down" guy. *Then again*, he mused, *it could have been even worse with the nearly mute Florin.* But Sadtler was directionally challenged. Sadtler kept holding his map upside down, placing the obvious landmarks on the wrong side. It took him hours to direct Sean to the destination, an abandoned Nike Missile silo. His was easy. A public school playground in Havre de Grace, featuring large plastic playhouses and a metal swing set. *Cakewalk.*

Sean looked over to Belize II, who took over. "Yes, men, nice work today, but it's time for us to get into our zones and explore what we've seen. You should experience your recollections much easier thanks to the enhancers. Now, eyes closed."

Tim tim was a little distracted. He was wondering about Belize II's driving skills. Sean's were quite poor. He kept braking well before he approached a car ahead or a light. And the old van had an automatic. No excuse. The jiggling around had made him a little car sick. Maybe next time he'd get Belize II as driver?

Belize II and Sean breathed in, deeply, twice. There was a long pause. The room was still and quiet.

"Now, picture your destination. How does it look to you? How does it feel to you? See it in your mind's eye. Now, keep those eyes closed, and give your body some deep breaths. Happy, fulfilling breaths. The air is your food and drink."

Another long pause. "Now, relax and feel yourself floating downstream. Easily. Gently. Can you feel yourself move through the space-time of your recollection? Can you grasp that space, feel that destination? Now relax. Relax. Feel yourself float in your gentle energy stream to that destination."

Tim tim couldn't help but open his eyes. The medicine had made him a little nauseous. Or perhaps it was leftover car sickness. Or both? He thought it best to get to the latrine. He tried to stand, but the floor had turned into rubber. Like a trampoline. He looked toward Sean and Belize II, and their images had become blurry blobs of moving color.

"Elders? What's the matter?"

Tim tim was now on his hands and knees trying to stabilize himself against the movement of the floor. And his left leg had fallen asleep. Or worse. He felt a stabbing pain in his calf. *Crap.* A charley horse.

"Sorry, Sean! Charley horse! Gotta stand up." Sean and Belize II continued to observe from their stools.

Hearing the words "stand up" triggered Florin to do the same. He stood erectly and walked calmly to tim tim, helping him up, steadying him.

"Thanks, Myron!" Clenching Florin's shoulder, tim tim tried to work the kink out of his leg. But that made the floor move again. He said, "Bouncy house."

Sean responded. "Good, Elders. Mission accomplished. You are seeing and feeling your prescribed destination."

. . .

November 1998

Sadtler whispered to tim tim and Adkins, "Florin's AWOL. He's gone."

Adkins looked shocked. "How do you know?"

"His quarters are next to mine. I thought I heard him moving around last night after curfew. I looked in his room this morning. Just his fatigues, socks, and underpants. All folded on his cot. And he's not in the latrine or shower. I checked."

"Holy shit!" Adkins grimaced. "I wonder if Sean and Belize II know?"

"We'll find out at muster."

. . .

Sean said, "At ease, men. I'm sure you're wondering why Florin is not with us today. He's completed his mission here. He's moved on."

Tim tim raised his hand.

"Elders, you know you don't need permission to speak, right. What is it?"

"Ah. Was wondering why his clothes and underwear are all, like, folded on his cot? Basically, what's he wearing?"

"Wearing? Well, that's up to Florin. He's most likely wearing what Florin wants to wear."

"Ah, okay."

"Look, don't worry about Florin. We have a lot to accomplish today. Belize II, could you hand out the enhancers?"

Tim tim raised his hand again. Then he remembered and quickly brought it down. "Ah, Sean, I don't mean to be a wimp, but I don't know if I can handle the enhancers today. I'm still, like, sick from yesterday and before. Like, nausea. And I'm having trouble focusing because things still seem distorted. So, would it be okay to have a day without the enhancers? Or you could give me the placebo?"

Sean looked over to Belize II. Then he looked down at the ground and scowled. Belize II responded. "Elders, people out there would give their eyeteeth for this experience. True patriots, willing to take one on the chin for their Army, for their country, for their fellow Americans, too. I hope that answers your question." He began giving out the tiny paper cups of liquid.

Tim tim sighed. He drank it down as did the others.

Sean grabbed a sheet of letter-sized paper from the table. "Okay. Look at this." He held up the paper. "Can you see it? Can you read what's written?"

The paper said, "Paris in the the spring." The text size was approximately 32 point. The font was Times New Roman.

"Now, we rapped about sight, lighting, vision. The rubber hits the road with paper and text. So, this next part of the training will be challenging. But we're starting off with something basic, to ease you in. Belize II will be driving you to a destination in the van. It is a room in a small building. Watch and feel your way there. Absorb that journey. Make use of those extra two dimensions if you feel them announcing themselves. Belize II will take you to the room. In that room will be a table. He will show you how the sheet will be placed on that table. See and feel the lighting in the room, which will be bright. Absorb the room. Make it familiar. Because later today, when you are here, you will take a mental journey back to that very room. Although the door to the room will be closed, you will enter the room. The room will be illuminated just as before and there will be a sheet of paper, just like this one, with the same font and text size."

He held the paper up again.

"But the paper will have other words. A different phrase or sentence. See those words. Absorb the words. Remember the words. When you come back and are ready, you'll report to me with the text that you read. That is today's exercise. Simple, but challenging nonetheless."

Tim tim felt even more nauseous.

. . .

Summer 2019

There never seemed to be a parking space anywhere near tim tim's house. Robbie had gotten used to this simple fact of life. Tim tim, again, made another painfully slow pass along 25th Street, craning his neck from side to side. He finally found a spot. And, as usual, it was nearly two blocks away on a side street. He carefully parallel parked the Corolla.

"Okay, Robbie, not too bad of a hike this time."

Robbie put the graphic novel back in the plastic bag. "Sure, tim tim." Another walk in the heat.

As they turned the corner, they heard a muffled sound. They saw two figures struggling on the sidewalk a half block away. They began walking faster toward the scene to check it out—a woman struggling with a man wearing a ski mask.

"Uh oh! Lady's in trouble. Hurry." They began jogging toward the altercation. Robbie saw the man ripping at the woman's handbag. The woman must have looped the straps over her arm, because the guy was nearly yanking her arm off to steal the bag. She was yelling, weakly, "Help! Help me!"

The masked guy pushed her onto the ground, roughly, and continued pulling at the straps. "Let the fuck go, bitch!" He had worked the tourniquet down to her forearm. The woman was now crying out in pain.

"Ow, ow! Stop it! Stop! Please!"

He saw the two men approaching and he began yanking even harder. The loop was now down to her wrist. He was mercilessly yanking the bag upward, nearly pulling her up from the sidewalk.

"Ow! Stop! Stop!"

Tim tim and Robbie came to a halt. Tim tim spoke calmly, "Sir. You need to stop that. Right now!"

The thief glanced over at the two. "Get the fuck away! Keep out of this!" He continued pulling at the bag, nearly pulling the woman's arm out of her shoulder socket. The woman continued writhing on the ground, now moaning in pain.

Tim tim took a deep breath. "Sir, I don't want to hurt you. But you do have to stop that, now!" He had nearly pulled the bag free. He glanced over. A pudgy bald man and a kid. No threat.

"Fuck you! Fuck you!"

He saw quick movement. He watched the pudgy guy break into a cacophony of air karate chops and loud grunts. "Yeep! Hiya!" The guy's moves were ridiculous. He stopped pulling on the bag, dumbstruck by the performance. The man was drawing closer with his karate moves, including an absurdly awkward kick into the air. He wasn't sure if it was a joke. He began yanking at the bag again.

Tim tim continued his chopping motions, adding even more martial arts shouts and grunts. "Yip yip!" He moved closer and closer to the thief. He gave another flaccid air kick. He was running out of steam. Tim tim took another deep breath. "What's your favorite ice cream?" Robbie looked on, astonished. The woman continued to moan and struggle. The thief had ceased pulling at the bag.

"What the fuck you talkin' about?"

Tim tim continued his moves. "I like vanilla. But with chocolate syrup. Warm. And with whipped cream." Tim tim was now fluttering near the man's face with his hands.

The man realized he was thinking about ice cream. Strawberry ice cream. Somehow that made him think of warm strawberry pie. Iced with a glaze of white sugar. He could almost taste the sugar mixed with the sweet but slightly tart strawberries. He did taste them. And then he began to smell the warm, flaky shortening crust, fresh from the oven. He tried to put aside the distraction. He was about to give the bag one more yank, when he saw the pudgy man's hand just along the side of his face—his thumb and forefinger. He felt a sharp pain in his left earlobe. The crazy guy had just flicked his earlobe! The pain was excruciating. He dropped his grip on the bag and yelled, instinctively, "Fuck! Motherfucker! That hurts!" He grabbed at his ear and tried to rub away the pain.

The woman on the ground began to roll upright and clenched the bag to her chest like a safety vest.

"I know. I'm sorry to do that, man, but you have to go now."

The man began moving away from the scene, holding his ear. He yelled, "Fuck you!" and jogged away.

Tim tim and Robbie helped the woman to her feet. She was still clutching at her handbag.

"Are you okay, Mrs. Watts?" She was now upright, rubbing at her shoulder, wincing.

"I don't know. I think so." She paused and looked at the two. "How do you know my name?"

"I'm your neighbor. Just half a block down." Tim tim pointed to his house. "Tim Elders. We've met before!"

She looked down the street to the house. "We have?"

"Oh sure! Several times! I'm the guy that sends you Christmas cards! Tim tim!"

"Oh. Okay. I don't remember. But thank you, sir! Thank you for saving me!"

"You're welcome! And this is my nephew, Robbie."

Robbie held out his hand. She shook it tentatively. "You both live 'round here, you say?"

"Well, I do, Mrs. Watts, but Robbie lives with his folks in Catonsville." Robbie nodded in agreement.

"Oh. Okay." She continued rubbing her arm and shoulder while clasping the straps of her bag for dear life. "Well thank you, boys! And God bless you both!"

. . .

Robbie's adrenaline was still pumping. Tim tim calmly placed ice cream floats at their places on the kitchen table. He took his seat next to Robbie. "Man, all that exercise got me especially hungry for this!" He took a generous first spoonful. Robbie was already working on his second.

"So, there you go, Robbie. That's the mission. What do you think?"

Robbie was still mulling over the craziness. "That was weird. But awesome!"

Tim tim spooned another chunk of vanilla into his mouth and mumbled. "Mmm-hmm!"

"Do you know martial arts?"

Tim tim took a breath before delving back into the ice cream. "Uh oh! Ice cream headache! Gotta slow down! Martial arts? No. But I've seen it in the movies. I was just copying. Copying what you've seen always works. But I am a little out of shape. Gotta exercise more."

"I thought you might wail out on the guy, but you just ticked his ear with your finger? What made you do that?"

Tim tim's headache time-out was over. "Well, we never want to injure a person. The rare times when we have to interact, physically, we want to make it as absolutely harmless and painless as we can under the circumstances."

"Okay. Why were you talking about ice cream?"

Tim tim finished his last chunk of ice cream. "Ah, well, it's a technique I've found very useful over the years. If you think about a food or dessert that you love and begin talking about it, it's a good distraction. The other person hears it and then can't help thinking about it! And that leads them to maybe think of similar foods and flavors that they love even more. I'm not sure why it works so well, but it always seems to. I've never thought about it much. And everybody loves ice cream."

"Okay." Robbie finished his own float. "Like . . . how were you so brave? That guy could have had a knife or something?"

"Oh, he did. I know the guy."

"You know him?"

"Yes, his name is Eddie. He's Mrs. Watt's nephew. I babysat him a few times when he was little."

"What? Why was he hurting his own aunt?"

Tim tim sighed. "Well, he has some problems. Drugs. Alcohol. Debts to some guys, probably."

Robbie was incredulous. "Why didn't you call him out and tell him off? Is being nice to bad guys part of the mission?"

Tim tim chuckled. "I never looked at it that way!" He sighed again. "Well, I was glad that he hid his identity from his aunt, because it would have broken her heart. Thank God for small favors."

Tim tim sensed the confusion. "You won't believe this, but Eddie is actually a pretty nice guy. He just has a lot of problems. It's made him do some bad things. Some dumb choices. I'm hoping he can turn it all around soon."

Robbie shook his head. He was probably never going to understand tim tim.

. . .

The drive back to Catonsville was quiet, as usual. Robbie would typically keep his nose in his comics. This time he was looking straight ahead, engrossed in the incident.

"Tim tim. How did you know when to get involved? I mean, like, to actually stop the guy. Not just dial 9-1-1 or something. You said the guy had a knife. How did you know you could take him?"

Tim tim chuckled. "Take him. Well, you could call it that, I guess."

He paused. "But how to know when to act? Yes." This was another tricky part. "Well, there will be a feeling. You'll know."

"A feeling? Like, what kind of feeling?"

He sighed again. "Well, it's really hard to describe. And it's different for each person, apparently. But I get a feeling of something like an adrenaline kick. But not quite. It's more. It's like a mixture of fear, but mostly exhilaration." He corrected himself. "No, more like . . . Like a feeling of happiness. Like suddenly you're energized by happiness. A slightly scary happiness. Like a ride at an amusement park. Sort of? But actually, much better. Happiness, basically."

"Okay?"

"And timing is very important. I only have so much energy. My own fault. I'm a little out of shape. You have to make sure you keep enough energy to complete the given mission." He would explain later that the older you get, the less energy you have. And that's the reason for turning the reigns over to your nephew. "Oh. And always breathe. It's critical. If you start feeling less good or slightly less certain, you just have to breathe. No matter where you are or what you are doing, breathe. It always works." But it was time to mention the other thing.

"And, there's another thing. Like, just out of the corner of your eye, you might see a glimpse. You know, you might catch a 'thumbs-up.' Or an 'atta boy!' . . . something like that."

Robbie was perplexed. "By who? Somebody who happens to be there?"

Tim tim scowled. "Well, sort of. It's a glimpse. And you quickly look around, and then the guy's gone. That fast. But that person is there, for sure."

"A person? Do you ever figure out who it is?"

He sighed again. "Well, for me it's, like, a guy. Always the same guy. Like a friendly, encouraging guy, I guess."

"And you don't recognize him?"

The Corolla was at the destination. Tim tim wheeled the car over in front of Will and Megan's home.

"Well, it's a super quick glimpse. And it may be different for everyone. That's just me. But, you'll see for yourself. You'll put together those feelings of happiness and your encouraging glance and you will know yourself you are good to go. Time to move that mountain."

Tim tim figured he'd relayed enough information. He'd dropped sufficient hints. He didn't want to frighten or overload Robbie at this point. There'd be plenty more training in the future.

. . .

She was getting tired of religious discussions with Robbie. Will said he had drawn the line with Tim; the religious talk had to stop, or Robbie's visits would be cut off. Or so Will had said. She was wondering. Will was such a softie when it came to his crazy brother.

"Robbie, no. You need to just ignore Uncle Tim. Your Dad is too nice and loves Tim so much. We all do. But you have to realize that everything Tim tells you is a fantasy. Fairy tales. Impossible things. He does not have any superpowers. Think about it. What 'super' thing has he actually done?"

"Well, he helped an old lady when a guy was stealing her purse."

"He did? Well that shows what a good guy he is. But a lot of people help others in need. That's what good people do. It doesn't require any superpowers or any religion."

Robbie wanted to explain the rest of it, but it wouldn't make any sense.

"You know, Uncle Tim is not your only uncle. You've got Roy and Roland. And Stefan! Think of how much fun you'll have hanging out with those guys in London?" She didn't think it possible, but she was now actually glad that Robbie would be away for that long weekend. Any break from Tim was a gift.

Robbie heard his mom saying some more stuff, but he had tuned out. There would be a way to take a bus to tim tim's house. After school, almost anytime, he could simply take a bus. And there would be some walking involved, too. But not too much. Doyle wouldn't even notice he was gone.

"Did you hear me? Are you listening to me, Robbie?" She felt exasperated.

"Yes, ma'am. All good." He turned and sulked back to his bedroom. Megan watched the forlorn-looking child slump his way down the hallway. *This is getting to be too much,* she thought. *Forbes is not cutting it. We're going to have to find another professional.*

. . .

"Arman Brigand. Very nice to meet you both!" He extended his hand first to Megan and then Will.

Will spoke first. "Yes, very nice to meet you, Doctor Brigand."

Megan chimed in, "Yes, thanks so much for seeing us, Doctor. Your reputation precedes you. We could really use your help." They had absolutely struck out with the first so-called doctor. Doctor Forbes with his dual PhDs in Economics and Divinity. An epic fail.

The doctor nodded. "Yes, from what you told me, Ms. Elders, we have a classic case of youth indoctrination. Children just entering their teen years are particularly susceptible to indoctrination. Cults and similar groups thrive on young minds. It's an unfortunate thing, but it's something we can deal with."

"Can you help?"

"Yes. Certainly. The key is adjusting your son's behavior. Just tweaking it a bit. You want a son that can go about his day, normally by all appearances. You want him to fit in with his schoolmates and friends such that a disinterested observer would find nothing but a well-adjusted and happy teen."

Megan nodded in agreement. "Yes, we want our son to be seen as well-adjusted and independent thinking. To think for himself."

Will nodded along. "Yes, I love—we love—my brother Tim, dearly, but Tim just can't seem to stop drowning Robbie with a lot of

79

pseudo-religious fantasy. It's not healthy, and we think it's going to damage our son permanently."

Megan agreed. "Yes. Robbie's a good boy, but he's beginning to act like Tim in his thinking and behavior."

"Of course! And the key will be minor behavioral tweaks. I've had great success before."

Brigand thought back to his most stunning success: Helping the schizophrenic population within the ranks of the great urban homeless. He was able to turn the problem around for the Town of Glenhaven, Connecticut—a landmark study. The Glenhaven Town Council had become troubled by the increasing number of schizophrenic homeless persons who wandered their usually tourist-filled streets, incessantly talking or yelling to themselves. The disturbances were alarming and troubling to the tourists. He successfully demonstrated to the Town Council that distributing dummy cell phones to its schizophrenic population would transform the population's seemingly bizarre rants into typical, everyday cell phone conversations. Tourists would believe that the given schizophrenic was simply a person engaged in an animated cell phone conversation. No different than any other cell phone user one may encounter. Problem solved.

"That's wonderful, Doctor. We can't wait to see what you have in mind!"

. . .

The breeze blew wildly through Robbie's hair. He loved it. Doyle had called "shotgun," as usual, and sat in the front next to Desales. Desales had pushed the Mustang's sound system to full blast. Doyle was tapping his fingers against the outside of the door panel in rhythm to "Immigrant Song." He had heard of Led Zeppelin but had never heard that song before.

"There's one."

Desales decelerated and pulled the Mustang over to the edge of the manicured lawn of the office park. The breaks squealed. "I can't believe that people fall for this shit." He grabbed his Sharpie pen. The rectangular yellow sign said "Mattress Sale" and "Truckload!" An 800 phone number was handwritten below. Desales hopped out of the idling convertible while Doyle and Robbie looked on. He stooped down to the sign and added, in neat block lettering, the word "Used" in front of "mattress" and the words "Nearly Urine Free" below. He stood and examined his work, clicking the top back onto his Sharpie. "What do you think, numb nuts? Can you read it?"

Doyle looked over his shades. "Not bad. You made it bigger this time."

Desales hopped back into the driver's side. "Good! Let's find a few more!"

They drove around the office park roads and then back onto York Road. "There's one!"

Desales pulled the Mustang into a store parking lot. The sign along the sidewalk said "We Buy Houses" and included an 800 number. Desales unlocked the tiny trunk of the Mustang. He walked over to the sign and yanked it out of the turf. He held it over his head in celebration, "whooped" a few times, and then dumped it into the trunk with the other signs.

Robbie heard the clattering noise and the sound of the trunk being slammed shut. He looked at his watch. They'd have to get back now or face the wrath of their mom. "I think we should be getting home now, Desales. Mom will be mad at us."

Desales shrugged. "Sorry, dickhead. I have to drop these off at my guy's, first. You'll have to wait." He looked over to Doyle. "Are you in a big hurry too, pecker face?"

Doyle shrugged. "Nope." He didn't particularly mind getting home late. He would just blame Desales. "How many do you have in there?"

"Five, I think. I already had a couple when I picked you turds up. Should be about ten bucks. It's a 'win-win.' We shut down some of these rip-off artists, and we make a few bucks selling scrap."

"Does your dad know you do this?"

"Royal? Of course not! But Roy wouldn't mind."

Doyle was thinking their dad would kill them. Robbie spoke loud enough to be heard from the back, "Why do you call your dad Roy or Royal? Why not Dad?"

"Because that's his name, dickhead."

"But our dad wouldn't want us to call him Will or William? We always call him Dad."

"I don't know, dummy. Roy doesn't care. I almost never call him Dad." He gunned the Mustang along the ramp and onto the Beltway.

"So, Roy showed me his new suit." He barked out a laugh. "That's what you get for going to that crappy Sears Discount place. You two dumbasses are going to look ridiculous. Bad enough for Roy. I mean, he's an old guy and will look normal in that geezer suit. But you two? Like twins? I'm going to take a lot of photos. You better be nice to me, or I'll make sure everyone gets photos of you two dipshits!" He laughed again.

Doyle shook his head. "Not my fault, man. I told your dad it would be better for us to get something different, but Robbie said he wanted one too. So we both got stuck with them."

Desales laughed again. "Well, getting a different suit wouldn't have helped you, douchebag. Don't you know? Every suit you buy from Sears is a 'Sears sucker' suit." He laughed again.

. . .

Roland wheeled his ridiculously overfilled small cart to the parking lot. He was thinking about his upcoming trip. There was still a lot to do. Things to organize. He was going over his mental list as he approached his car. Suddenly, he heard a woman's voice, close behind him.

"Sir? Sir?" He turned around, startled. That woman again. Her small cart was overfilled nearly to the point of tipping over. Even worse than his.

"Oh? Is that you, Karen?" He noticed her tee shirt. It said "Make America Great Again!"

"No. Remember, I'm a Brenda, not a Karen."

"Oh yes. Of course, dear. My bad!"

"So, my husband said there might be something to your idea about using the smaller cart. See. I've taken your advice!"

Roland choked back a guffaw. "Oh, that's wonderful, Brenda! Your husband is a very astute individual! Bravo!"

"Thank you!" She smiled gratefully. "You know, I never got your name, though?"

Roland pivoted. "Oh, yes. My name is Hugh Jackman." He was trying desperately not to smile.

"Hugh Jackman? Like the actor?"

"Yes. Exactly. Same name. Everyone says there's a resemblance, too. It's crazy." Roland smiled suavely.

Brenda looked up and down, sizing up the girthsome man. She couldn't see it. Not even close. She looked puzzled.

"Oh yes, by way of ankle size. Ankle circumference. The other Hugh Jackman and I have identical ankle sizes." He stifled a laugh and quickly looked away to his car.

"Oh, okay. I think I couldn't tell that because you're wearing socks."

"Yes, of course, dear." He had to turn his head again. He quickly composed himself and turned back around. "So, that's a lovely tee shirt, Brenda. But may I ask, do you not believe that our country is already 'great?' I believe America is great, myself. The greatest."

Brenda looked flummoxed. "Oh, of course, Hugh! Of course I believe this country is the greatest!"

"Yes! Yes! The greatest, Brenda! But, your shirt implies that America is not the greatest. In fact, it implies that we are not even 'great' at all, now. Because it requests that we make America great, again? That means we are not great now. Do you see?"

Brenda looked on, puzzled. "Well, I don't really know about that. They gave these shirts out after church services last week. The Iron Christ Christian Church in Perry Hall. Do you know it?"

Roland had to look away again. "Well, gosh, no dear. I'm not familiar with that particular congregation. You see, I was baptized Catholic, not Christian." He nodded his head, knowingly, stifling a smile.

"Oh. Well thank God you are at least baptized, Hugh! That's good!"

"Yes, Brenda! So true. Now, sadly, I must toddle off before these items spoil. But remember to tell them at the Iron church to fix that shirt, because you and I are proud Americans who both believe that America is already great—the greatest! Oh, and next time you see me, just yell 'yoo hoo, Hugh!' And I'll know it's you!"

"I will, Hugh! I will. Thank you, and have a blessed day!"

. . .

He approached his apartment building with a bold idea: a flanking maneuver! He avoided the usually overcrowded rear lot—under the constant patrol of Mrs. Barnwhistle—and rolled the Corolla into the tiny side lot. The side lot held only two parking spaces—for the Manager and Property Manager. He saw Mrs. Barnwhistle's ancient green Ford Fiesta parked in the Property Manager's spot. But he had never once seen any car parked in the Manager's spot. Ever. The weather-worn sign said "Reserved for Mr. Sykes, Manager." Who the hell was this "Sykes"? He had never seen Sykes or his car. Judging from the age of the sign, Sykes was probably dead by now. He took a chance and pulled into the spot.

He approached the side entrance door holding four particularly painful plastic bags. The metal door flew open.

"Mr. Biv. There's no parking there. That spot is reserved for our manager. That is not a tenant loading zone. You'll have to move your car, now, or it will be towed."

Roland gritted his teeth. He responded calmly. "Now, Mrs. Barnwhistle. How do you know that Mr. Sykes did not expressly authorize my use of this space?"

She looked on suspiciously. "You're telling me Mr. Sykes gave you permission to use his spot? And without informing me? Seriously?" She chuckled. "Really, Mr. Biv?"

Roland placed the plastic bags onto the ground. He rubbed his sore hands. "Well, I'm not saying that he did, but suppose he had? You'd be running afoul of the desires of your boss. Had you considered that?"

Mrs. Barnwhistle clenched at the neck of her muted pink housecoat. "Well, then, if that's so, why didn't Mr. Sykes call me. And in lieu of such, where is your placard? Do you see my car there?" She pointed to the Fiesta. "Look at the rearview mirror. Do you see that hanging placard? That means I am authorized to park there. Mr. Sykes did not contact me, and you have no placard and are therefore not authorized. So, I'm sorry Mr. Biv. Please move your car, now, or it will be towed."

Roland sighed. "Okay. Okay. You win. May I bring these in, at least?" He nodded toward the bags on the ground.

"Well, of course, Mr. Biv. Hand them to me, and I'll drop them off by the elevator for you."

He handed them over glumly. He thought to himself, *Have a nice peep.*

The metal door closed behind her. She couldn't wait to take a look through the bags. Mr. Biv purchased so many unusual and surprising things. Shocking things. She also enjoyed recycling day.

Mr. Biv always took his weekly selection of newspapers and tabloids to the trash room early. Plenty of time for her to retrieve them before the trash men came. Besides the good reading, she enjoyed checking which ads or coupons he had clipped.

. . .

Roland heard his door buzz. He wasn't expecting a visitor at eleven a.m. on a Saturday. He placed his eye against the peephole. *Great,* he thought. *Mrs. Barnwhistle in her most fetching turquoise house coat and a uniformed delivery man.* He slid the chain latch and opened his door.

"Mr. Biv, this man has a delivery for you. It requires your signature. Also, I need to check what's in that package for security purposes." Mrs. Barnwhistle nodded, assertively.

Roland sighed. He saw the Bonded Couriers logo on the man's hat and uniform jacket. "So, let me get this straight, Mrs. Barnwhistle. You want to peek inside my personal correspondence?"

She nodded again. "Yes, for security purposes, Mr. Biv. This man said that the package originated from a non-US source. I am authorized under the terms of your lease to inspect any and all packages that may contain dangerous, toxic, or hazardous materials." She glanced toward the courier. "Consider how easy it would be for anthrax or ricin or Legionnaire's Disease or any of those to be placed inside an envelope." She continued nodding.

The uniform man shrugged. "Ma'am, I can assure you that there are no dangerous substances in the envelope. We screen all the packages. And we know our customers very well and can vouch for this particular source. We are an authorized contractor for the US State Department. We handle packages for all governments with which the US has diplomatic relations. We do not deliver dangerous or hazardous materials."

Mrs. Barnwhistle stood her ground. "Well, that's fine for you, sir, but I answer to a higher power: our manager, Mr. Melvin Sykes, and all of our residents who depend on me as gatekeeper for their safety and security." She nodded her head again, several times, forcefully. She really wanted to see what was in that envelope.

The courier looked over to Roland pleadingly. He needed to get moving.

"Okay, Mrs. Barnwhistle. How about a compromise? I will sign for this package and open it in front of you so that you will see its contents. I predict correspondence, an airplane ticket, and an itinerary. However, I am not authorized to permit you to read the correspondence for yourself due to various international confidentiality treaties and protocols."

He nodded, gravely, and looked over to the courier for affirmation. The courier looked on blankly.

"I will review the contents for compliance with governmental standards and, if appropriate, I will relay the contents to you, aloud. Such, I believe, would not violate interagency charters. Do we have an agreement?" Roland licked his lips, savoring the moment.

Mrs. Barnwhistle's eyes had gone full saucer. She feigned nonchalance. "Uh, yes, Mr. Biv. That may suffice."

The courier then clicked a button on his handheld tracker. He handed it over to Roland. Roland signed with his pinkie, adding a squiggly flourish for dramatic effect. The courier nodded. "Thank you, sir, and have a pleasant day." He handed over the cardboard envelope and exited, hurriedly.

Roland slowly opened the package, savoring Mrs. Barnwhistle's reaction to the painful striptease. He gently removed the gilded business-sized envelope from the package and turned it over, front to back, before Mrs. Barnwhistle's eager eyes. She saw the scarlet sealing wax on the back.

"Hold this please." He tersely handed over the empty cardboard envelope to Mrs. Barnwhistle. She studied the return address closely. She gazed at the capital letters E R with the Roman numeral two sitting in between. She saw the tiny crown sitting atop the letters. She gasped. The round mark said "Buckingham Palace" with a bunch of letters and numbers. She wasn't sure what they meant.

Roland slowly broke the red seal of the business envelope. He withdrew the folded letter and lackadaisically tossed the empty envelope over his shoulder, backward into his apartment. He watched Mrs. Barnwhistle's eager eyes greedily follow the trajectory. He placed the predicted flight confirmation and hand-typed itinerary into his breast pocket. He slowly unfolded the accompanying letter and cleared his throat, dramatically. He pretended to read:

"Hear ye, hear ye. To all whom these presents shall come—greetings—and now, hearken, thusly!"

He waited a moment and glared earnestly at Mrs. Barnwhistle. She was positively stunned. He looked back down at the letter and continued.

"Please acknowledge, immediately, that Roland Biv, Esquire, has been afforded full diplomatic and consular privileges and immunities by this United Kingdom and our gracious and dear friends, the United States of America!"

He waited another few seconds for Mrs. Barnwhistle's reaction. She was utterly thunderstruck.

"This designation shall continue in perpetuity for the duration of the British Monarchy, present and in futuro." He cleared his throat, loudly, again. He was now salivating. "To that end, please provide Chancellor Biv with all available and possible civil accommodations and immunities, including, but not limited to, all parking and transportation privileges, of every kind and nature, unlimited in scope, location, and duration."

He had voiced the word "parking" with particular emphasis. He refolded the letter and placed it, stiffly, into his breast pocket. Mrs. Barnwhistle was flabbergasted. This changed everything.

"So, Mrs. Barnwhistle. What do you make of that? Should we inform Mr. Sykes? Should we have Mr. Syke's sign changed to 'diplomatic missions only'?"

Mrs. Barnwhistle caught her breath. "Well . . . Probably so . . . I would think so. Of course, I'll have to inform Mr. Sykes about this immediately, though."

Roland slowly retreated behind his closing door. He needed to get inside before his laughing jag began. He could only stifle it for so long. "Yes, that sounds appropriate and in conformity with my formal consular designation. Thank you, Mrs. Barnwhistle. And our United States government and the British Crown, jointly and severally, thank you, also!"

. . .

Etta's eyes followed the man and his stylist back to the salon chair. Men seldom booked appointments at the salon, and she always wondered about these men. This one was not very manly and not great looking. Huge and way overweight. And he hardly had any hair worth cutting. And that frightening mustache.

Morris carefully placed his stylist's cape around his most humorous, yet annoying customer. Not actually his favorite customer, though. And, *surprise*, his customer was agitated, as usual.

"Okay, Morris. Zhuzh me. Zhuzh me good, brother, like you've never zhuzhed before!"

"Becalm yourself, Roland. You're so not chill. Do you want a gummy . . . maybe two?"

"Yes. Two. The good ones from the back, please."

Morris sighed and headed to the rear of the salon. He opened the tiny closet holding his and his coworkers' belongings. It was a pharmacy of sorts. He found the green tin and plucked two burnt orange-looking objects.

"Here you go, dear. Chew two. These will give you some peace. Let's get you to your happy place."

"Thank you, Morris! You're a lifesaver!"

"De nada!"

Roland began chewing furiously. "You know, we live in an enlightened age. No need to smoke and ruin your lungs when you can nibble on good old full-spectrum CBDs. So natural! And legal now, too."

Morris was thinking that the compound was probably a little more Ecstasy than CBD, but he let it pass. "Yes, Love. Now, what's troubling you, and may I first say that your hair is looking fabulous!" He began tousling Roland's hair with his hands. Roland eagerly watched the performance in the mirror.

"Fabulous, really? No bullshit? I keep thinking it's getting thinner and thinner. I keep trying everything!"

"It's fine." Morris corrected himself. "I mean it's 'fine' as in 'fine looking,' not 'fine hair' per se." He began moving the natural boar bristle brush through Roland's hair. "Looks quite healthy!" He didn't enjoy lying to customers, but he thought to himself, *A boy has to earn a living.* The whole toothbrush mustache thing was just plain off-putting though. And Roland's part was dropping farther and farther down the left side of his head. Almost to ear level. Not a good look. At least he had dropped the sad, raggedy-assed excuse for a soul patch.

"Phew. Okay. I feel better."

"You're still applying the Minoxidil? Or were you onto Finasteride? I've lost track?"

"Well, I told you that the damned Minoxidil made my scalp sore as hell. So I moved on. I've been taking one milligram of Finasteride daily. Can you believe that crap is still prescription? Expensive. Should be OTC."

"Oh, really?"

"Yes, and besides shrinking my balls—and I haven't even had a look down there for a while, thanks to this damn weight gain due to my Seasonal Affective Disorder—I don't know if it's really done anything at all. They could be sugar pills for all I know."

Morris put the brush down and sprayed Roland's scalp with hemp oil lotion. He began gently massaging Roland's pink scalp. Roland gazed on, dreamily. He loved the scalp massage.

"Did you buy the Finasteride from that pharmacy in Cancun? Or was that something else?"

"Good Lord. Don't mention Cancun. Never again! I peeled for a month. No. I'm still peeling. And, no, that wasn't Finasteride. It was some naughty thing. I can't even remember. This Finasteride is legit, straight from the boring old supermarket." He was thinking of Mrs. Barnwhistle snooping through his bag. She had seen both his prescription Finasteride and two containers of personal lubricant. *Bitch.*

"Well, you know Finasteride is a generic. Why don't you get Propecia? That's the real deal. Not a cheap knockoff. You can't trust cheap knockoffs. You don't know where they've been."

"Really? It would make a difference?"

"Guy on YouTube says so. I think he was a doctor or researcher. Maybe an influencer. But it made sense, whatever it was he was saying."

"Hmm. I can try that. Good suggestion. But what else have you got? I need some help, Morris. I absolutely must retain a good zhuzh during travel. If you can believe it, your favorite customer is flying out tonight to 'Merry ole England' to attend a royal wedding!"

Morris realized that Roland was speaking about himself and not Justin, his actual favorite customer. "Whoa, Roland! Shut that front door, guy!"

"Yes! I know! Crazy! My little brother Stef is engaged to some relative of the Queen, and it's a BFD event at St. Paul's Cathedral. Media and everything. Paparazzi, for sure. I'm the best man, so I need to look totally perfect and put together. Especially my hair. So, once we establish a good zhuzh, I'll take my seat in Business Class, British Air, and try not to lean back in the seat, which would mess up the back. It's a long flight, but if I can preserve my hair until the wedding the next day, I will be a very happy camper."

"When will you sleep, dear?"

"Well, I'll be too excited to sleep anyway, so no biggie on that. I'll just sit up in a chair in my hotel room. Probably a suite, actually."

"Okay."

Morris was curious about the mustache. "May I inquire about this?" He ran his forefinger across his own face. "What are we doing, here?"

"Ah. Well, it's the damn graying. I must have the worst genes, hair-wise. The hair right below my nose stays pretty dark. Salt and pepper. But the stuff growing more along the edges of my mouth comes in almost white." Roland ran his index finger against his face along his mouth. "I just got sick of using mascara to darken it all the time. I said to myself, 'I shall not be a slave to this' and cut those parts off. Yes, what I'm left with is a little old school, but at least it's dark." He was also thinking that he did not miss swallowing mascara bits with his food.

"Okay. Certainly. And you've dumped that soul patch?"

"Soul patch? That was a beard, my friend. Again, cursed genes. I identify as a bear, and it takes me like a year to grow anything close to a proper beard. But with the wedding coming up, I decided to just go clean-shaven except for the mustache for photos. My bears will just have to accept me the way I am."

"Of course. Of course. I'm sure they will."

Morris began carefully snipping Roland's split ends. He produced a lot of snipping sounds but didn't do a lot of actual cutting. There just wasn't much to work with.

"So, is the Queen going to attend this extravaganza?"

"Well, just the 'Queen of '19.' Not the boring one."

"Weren't you also the Queen of '17 and '18?"

"Of course! And I shall ascend my royal throne next year in 2020 and thereafter!"

"What will we do when it's 2020? It won't rhyme?"

"Well, I plan to exercise a lot of twenty-twenty hindsight, so I'll let you know, then."

Morris chuckled, "Yes, my lord!"

He thought it was time to reveal his secret weapon. "Okay, big guy. I have a little surprise for you. Now, this is just an experiment. But I think it will work perfectly. And pricing is reasonable. Incredibly reasonable."

"What? Do spill!"

Morris sighed, dramatically. "Okay. Suppose there was a potion that was healthy for your hair, actually cleansing. But it would thicken the follicles, producing the maximum presentation of fullness. Are you interested? Are you in?"

"Well, of course, my good man! What is this miracle?"

"Okay. You won't believe it. Waterless shampoo, with a hint of color, in a convenient spray bottle."

"What? How does it work?"

"Okay. Now, it won't do much for the forehead area. But it will virtually eliminate any perceived 'weak areas' on the crown." Morris always shied away from the word "baldness." The B word was bad for business.

"Really? Well, sure! Do you have some to try?"

Morris opened the top drawer of his station and produced an aerosol bottle. "Ta-da!" He handed it to an eager Roland.

Roland looked at the bottle in awe. "Fletcher's Dry Shampoo – Hint of Almond." He looked over the directions and ingredients on the back. "Wow! It's gluten-free and approved by PETA, too!" He handed back the bottle, gingerly, as though it were an egg.

"Yes! So, I'll get things started, today, but when you use it, remember to follow the instructions carefully. You have to shake the thing like a bastard."

He pulled off the top cap and shook the bottle frantically.

"Okay, shield your eyes with your hands, Roland."

Morris began carefully spraying the bald spot. The bottle produced several quick spurts—the initial "targeting" move. He then pulled the can back several inches and sprayed in a wider arc, slowly filling in the surrounding areas. Excess brown powder fell gently onto the cape; iron filings mixed with cinnamon.

"Yes, there we go! Success! Let me give it a brush-through and a good zhuzh!"

Morris began to carefully run the boar's hairbrush through the mixture of hair and powdered shampoo. There was that one tricky area, so he gave it another quick blast with the aerosol can. He completed brushing and found the most optimal place for the all-important part. Something natural. Avoiding the comb-over effect was difficult. *Balance . . . balance . . .*

He then gave Roland's hair a quick blast with the hair dryer. Not too much, as there was not much to dry. The shampoo had absorbed most of the hemp oil treatment. He put the dryer aside and gave Roland's hair a two-handed, final zhuzh. He spun the chair around, dramatically, and placed a hand mirror in front of Roland's face so that he could check out the back.

"Looky loo, Sir Roland! Nary a hint of . . . deficiency!"

Roland looked with disbelief. He no longer had that bald spot! It was gone!

"Oh dear Lord, Morris! You are a genius! Look at this! Michelangelo!" He handed back the mirror, stunned.

"Thank you, thank you!" Morris took a quick bow and rapidly turned the chair back around, causing Roland some dizziness. "Now, let me hit you with a finishing spray to hold everything in place!"

He dramatically removed the top of the hairspray aerosol and shook the can furiously. He sprayed the mist in a near random fashion near the scalp and then away from the scalp and then back toward and quickly away again—a symphony conductor of a twelve-tone sound poem.

He spun Roland around again and thrust the mirror before his face. "What do you think?!"

"Yes, yes, Morris, this is perfect! This is what I've been waiting for . . . dreaming about!"

"Thank you, Roland! Now, here's the thing, we have this miracle product available to our most beloved clients—that would be you—but we are required by the bastard owner to significantly mark the price up over our acquisition cost. But I can provide you the rest of this bottle as a 'sampler,' and the markup will be much more reasonable. Sound good?"

"Yes, of course, Morris! That's very kind!"

"And, here's the good thing, this product is manufactured in the UK, so should you run low while engaging the queued masses of fans and paparazzi, you could toddle on over to one of those Boots stores, or whatever they have over there now, and pick up more!"

"Yes! Excellent thinking! You are a life saver!"

Morris removed the cape, dramatically, and walked a somewhat wobbly Roland to the cashier's station. The gummies had kicked in. Morris gave Roland a gentle hug.

"Godspeed, Sir Roland! Break a leg!"

As he watched Roland settle up with the cashier, Gillian, he couldn't help but think, *You absolutely must lose that mustache, dear.*

. . .

Desales pulled the Mustang up to Will and Megan's. Roy got out, too, so that Doyle and Robbie could get in the back. Like Roy, Doyle and Robbie were wearing their matching seersucker suits and clip-on ties. They each carried small wicker suitcases. Doyle looked disgusted. Will and Megan followed them out.

"Hey, big brother! Thanks for doing this!" Megan and Roy hugged warmly.

"Yeppers! Me 'n Sonny 'r happy to be doin' the chaperonin'!' Gone ta be fun!"

Will shook Roy's hand warmly. "Yes, thank you, Roy!"

"So, like you said, Sissy, I got us all dressed up so's we won't hafta worry 'bout changin' for the weddin.' Cuz, once we land, that'll be the weddin' day. That night, I mean. An we'll look good 'n fancy for the plane ride, right, Sonny?"

Desales was busy checking his phone. He was dressed in a stylish gray business suit with a modest club necktie. "Oh yeah. Sure, Royal."

Roy opened the trunk. Will and Megan saw a backpack, a bright orange Orioles fanny pack, and two green plastic trash bags with black twist ties. Roy placed the two wicker suitcases next to the trash bags.

"Roy, didn't you bring luggage?" Will couldn't imagine . . .

"Yep. Right there!" He pointed to the trash bags.

"Ah. Okay." Will looked over to Desales for help. Desales shrugged his shoulders.

. . .

Desales had navigated the Mustang into a decent spot in the BWI garage. Roy was astonished at the size of the garage. "Go to war, Miss Agnes! This is a confusin' place, ain't it? All kinda walkways all over? Trickier than a bumped beehive!"

They made their way along the people movers connecting the garage with the terminal. "Boys, this is like a escalator that don't go up 'r down! Just goes flat!"

They found their way to ticketing at British Air. The line was enormous.

Fellow travelers were astonished at the group's matching seersucker outfits. A few wondered if the group was trying to make some sort of "artistic statement" with the trash bag luggage. The younger, well-dressed man was likely their PR. A swarm of cell phones pointed toward the group as they moved along in line. Just the stuff to go viral!

Finally, they made it to the counter. The clerk saw the trash bags. "Sir, I'm afraid that we can't allow those onto the flight. They don't meet FAA stability requirements." Roy looked puzzled. He had even gotten the Xtra Sturdy ones from the dollar store. Desales moved forward politely. "Ma'am, on your website, you mention that garment bags are allowed. These are essentially garment bags. My dad's garments are in the bags."

Roy figured this would not be the time to mention the chicken necks.

The clerk was conscious of the many cell phones pointed her way. "One moment. Let me make a call." A few moments later, she returned. "Okay, you simply need to sign this form. It's a waiver of liability should your bags or anything in your bags be damaged in flight or cause damage in flight."

Desales looked it over. It also included an indemnity clause. Mock trial coach Tom Crowder had explained those. But Desales figured, *Blood from a stone*. "All good." He handed it back to Roy to sign.

They made their way through security. Desales had warned Roy back home about having to take his shoes, pouch, and suit jacket off. But it was still puzzling. "This place is smellin' worse than Back River at high tide on a Monday mornin'. Lotsa stinky ole feet out!" He looked down at his own. Somehow his best pair of socks managed to have holes.

. . .

Special Constable Corbin knew that this was going to be an unusual day. As he glanced around for an empty seat, he saw the commander by the podium speaking earnestly with fellow officers. He had never seen the commander attend morning roll call. Usually, it would be the superintendent or more frequently just the chief inspector. And more surprising were the two uniformed members of the MPS. He had never seen a Met officer attend one of their roll calls.

Corbin saw Police Constable Williston and waved him over. Williston took the adjoining seat.

"What do you make of this, sir?" Corbin motioned toward the front of the conference room.

Williston grimaced. "Well, lucky us, lad. Looks like a banner day."

The room had filled up. Superintendent Drew rapped on the podium with her mechanical pencil. The noise continued, and she rapped a few times more, saying, "Please." The room then fell silent.

"You see that our commander and chief super are present today. Also attending at our invitation are Inspectors Roberta Donovan and Martin Broyle of the Metropolitan Service. Obviously, there is much going on today in our Square Mile. Let me turn these proceedings directly over to Commander Ableson. Commander?"

Ableson moved to the microphone. "Thank you, Superintendent Drew." He looked around the room solemnly. "Officers, today will pose many challenges to our City of London force. No doubt you are well aware of our environmentally conscious friends who call themselves the Insular Rebellion."

Several officers nodded. A few groaned.

"As you know, our force and the Met share credible intel regarding threats and potential instances of civil disobedience."

Ableson glanced over to Broyle and Donovan who nodded back in return.

"We are given to understand that the IR has chosen today to hold massive demonstrations throughout London. Why today? Today is the rescheduled trial date for the French IR organizer. According to Met intel, we can expect a series of sit-ins and obstructionist demonstrations around town. We don't suspect any particular disturbance at court, this time, because their antics outside Old Bailey backfired last time. The trial was postponed for another three months, assuring continued incarceration for their leader. Not quite what they had in mind."

Ableson smirked as several officers chuckled.

"But, we are hearing that IR will be targeting both public transportation and public venues. We understand IR will be staging a sit-down to block off portions of M25."

Several officers in attendance groaned, and a few looked up, puzzled.

"Yes, M25 traffic is not our problem but for the consequence that the blockages will likely create undue traffic on our City thoroughfares." Ableson looked up toward the ceiling in annoyance. He shook his head.

"Likewise, our French colleagues at Eurotunnel have shared their concerns. Those authorities are preparing for blockages of the Chunnel. Yes, the usual IR antics—gluing themselves to accessways, sit-downs, handcuffing themselves to train cars to prevent movement." He rolled his eyes. "Again, the Chunnel is not our particular problem, but it will mean more calls to us from UK citizens complaining about delays and missing persons, etc."

Officers in the room nodded in agreement.

"But, more apropos, we are looking for IR groups to infiltrate local museums today, either en masse or as ordinary tourists. More of the same techniques. Gluing hands to artwork, walls, floors, etc.

Our joint intel suggests that the group will be assembling in Trafalgar Square by midday. Thereafter, we believe the crowd will attempt to converge upon the National Gallery, which, by the way, we have ordered closed for the day, unbeknownst to IR." Abelson stifled a smile. "But that won't keep them out of the Tate or V & A or any other one in or about our Square Mile. We can't shut down every museum or public facility today. And there's an additional complication." He paused dramatically. "Inspector Donovan, could you?"

Inspector Donovan nodded and moved to the podium next to Ableson. "Thank you, Commander. Yes. Our intel suggests that the IR has gotten into bed with the local branch of the neo-Nazi party."

Several officers mumbled puzzledly.

"Yes. How or why an allegedly pacifist group decided to link up with violent neo-Nazis is a mystery. However, that particular mystery is not our concern. Our concern, today, is public safety and facing the challenges posed by these groups."

Ableson moved back to the microphone. "Yes, we have been working with the Met to develop a workable strategy for handling these challenges. So, please listen up. First, we have called up all available personnel to handle processing of the arrests we will make today. But, to that end, we will not and cannot arrest every single demonstrator we encounter. Unless a demonstrator has used violence or displayed a weapon, leave them be. Met will be handling assigned public venues and arrest and interrogation—and ungluing—of any demonstrators within those public museums or other public spaces."

Several officers chuckled at the absurdity. Ableson smirked and continued.

"We will handle the rest. Your commanding officer will make appropriate assignments. Notwithstanding this division of labor, we presume that our lock-up resources will be greatly burdened. For overflow, we have obtained the usual access to Old Bailey. But, to the point, be discrete in handling the typical minor offenses like public intoxication, pub fights, vagrancy, rough sleeping, etc. If you can avoid an arrest for one of those, please do, as long as the perpetrator has credible ID and is not an apparent menace to themselves or others. Arrestees with credible ID will be processed immediately as 'own recognizance' and released. Those without will be held in lockup for twenty-four or until someone can ID them for their own recog. Actual offenders requiring bail will be handled through Somerset today to reduce stress at our stations." Several officers in the room nodded in confirmation.

"Lastly, as regards the fascist groups—several of you with undercover experience will be stationed in known neo-Nazi hangouts. Take this seriously. Their leader, Klaus Rötger-Dieter, is a dangerous man. Yes, we may laugh at his ridiculous 'dress-up' in a Nazi uniform and nonsense that he spews, but his followers are quite serious. And dangerous. Your role will be as collectors of intel—plans, movements, names. Collection and timely delivery of intel will be vital."

Most officers in the room nodded in agreement. Ableson nodded over to Donovan and Broyle, who both nodded back.

"I believe that covers everything. Please be aware and on your guard. If you learn of something relevant to these disturbances, communicate it to your superior immediately. Your patience and hard work today will be key."

Several officers nodded and a few began to stand.

"Oh, nearly forgot. Of all things, we also have a royal wedding tonight at St. Paul's at six p.m. Fortunately, the Windsor entourage will not be in attendance, but we will have many of our minor royals in town this evening. So, again, discretion and courtesy for our visitors at all times, please."

. . .

Bertram Dixon had completed his promotional "couture tour" of Boston, Philadelphia, and D.C. He had let his younger brother, Teddy, snag New York. It was the right thing to do. Yes, he had founded the company. But Teddy's work at New York Fashion Week that past December was quite remarkable. Business had increased threefold.

He couldn't wait to get back home to London. He had booked the aisle seat as per usual for hassle-free treks to the loo. He glanced at the embarking travelers moving their way down the aisle—a sordid mass of humanity. With some exceptions. He had noticed the style-conscious entourage in the concourse earlier: the older, rugged-looking chap with the two young men, each wearing matching light blue seersucker suits and striped ties. Brilliant marketing. He wanted to find out more. Seersucker was so alarmingly "out" as to now be "in." He hadn't seen them making the rounds in D.C. but figured they must have attached themselves to the small boutique networking party the night before that he'd simply not had time to attend.

He was particularly impressed with the older model. *What a PR master stroke. Seen by all in the departure area multi-purposing utilitarian green sacks as luggage. That's how you get noticed,* he thought. *What a socially conscious and yet potentially politically relevant statement.* He'd look for it later on IG.

And as luck would have it, the very same entourage was finding their way to their seats in close proximity to his. Perhaps he could find a way to chat up the older gent at some point? He was curious as to the sponsoring house. *Had to be Thom Browne.* The ultra-tight, deliberately shrunken fit of the jacket on the older model was the giveaway. *Then again, Kiton was always a possibility. Good use of the plus size model, too.*

Desales had managed to scoop the solo ticket farthest away from the others. "Roy, here's the layout. There's one seat, right here, that

I'll take. See, three rows down are those two open seats." He pointed. The crowd of passengers behind the group was waiting impatiently behind the clog. Several were grumbling. They wanted so badly to "hurry up and wait."

"And then right behind them is that single seat next to that man. Those are your seats to work out however you want. I'll stay up here so that you guys can be together."

"Okay, Sonny! That's good." Roy had to figure out the rest. Two in front and a single in back. "So, d'you boys want ta sit together in them seats in front and Uncle Roy sit behind yous next to that man with them white things in his ears?"

Robbie answered. "We'll sit together, Uncle Roy." He was glad that Desales was sitting three rows away. *Perfect.*

"Okay, Robbie. There ya go, right there for yous." He pointed at the open row. The two boys took their seats. They had never flown before and were impressed with how much room they had. And each a separate TV screen, right there in front of them in the seat! The screen was showing the local news. But they couldn't hear anything. Robbie looked around for a volume control. He found none. He'd have to figure out how to get *Young Justice* or at least *Peppa Pig.*

Roy saw the man smiling at him. Seemed like a nice guy to sit next to. Nicer than the milling crowd nearly pushing him down the aisle. The man nodded in a friendly manner and stood to let Roy pass into the window seat. Roy bounced his way over the armrests.

"Phew! Place's busier than a set 'a jumper cables at a Dundalk funeral! Jeez 'n crackers!"

The man pulled out his earbuds. "Did you say Dundalk?"

"Dundalk? Yep. D'ya know it?"

"Certainly. Wife and I haven't been there for years. Heard it's still quite lovely, though. Blackrock Beach is wonderful."

Roy thought that the guy was a little confused. "D'ya mean Blackrock Run, up near Belfast?"

Bertram calculated. "Yes, that sounds right. Blackrock's not far from Belfast."

"Yeppers. Our Daddy took us out to YMCA camp out there when we was little. Beauteous place."

"Oh. Didn't realize YMCA had a facility there."

"Yep. But then they shut it down in the '70s. Probly sold it."

"Ah. Of course."

He was thinking that the man's accent could be Irish. But more Cockney, almost. Odd. He saw the man thrust his hand forward.

"Name's Roy." He shook Roy's hand, earnestly.

"Name's Dixon. Pleasure to meet you." He glanced over at Roy's suit. "Nice couture! A refreshing play on seersucker! 'Maison Dixon' is mine. Curious to hear about yours!"

Roy felt a bit confused. He had already introduced himself. He figured maybe those white things were hearing aids. And he had a crazy name. "Ya said yours is Mason Dixon?"

"Yes!"

"Like your Mason-Dixon line?"

"Well, thank you, Roy! Which particular line do you favor?"

Roy felt confused again. "Favor? Well, I was thinkin' of the long one? The old one?"

Bertram nodded, knowingly. *Nice to know the "Smart Man" line was still revered.* Teddy had been encouraging him to drop it. "Yes, Smart Man, a long and successful line."

Roy nodded. "Why, thanks, Mr. Dixon. But I would reckon everbody 'roun here's heard of it. Don't take too much brains. Historical, like."

"Brilliant! Thanks, Roy. That's my job. To keep those lines out in the public's mind."

Roy scratched at his rusty beard stubble. "So, like, ya do surveys, still? Ta mark the lines?"

"Well, certainly. But those are a little old school. We don't always attach a survey to each line we produce. We get things done more with social media. Influencers, mainly. Good judges of the zeitgeist."

Roy was thinking that surveyors setting lines without surveys didn't sound very safe. And he wasn't sure about the rest. "Ya done anything here in Bawlmer? Any new ones?" Roy had been shopping at that new supermarket in Middle River. He wanted to make sure the building was safe. He was hoping Mr. Dixon's company was not involved.

"Baltimore, Maryland? No, not specifically, but we definitely are hitting the East Coast hard."

"Oh. Okay." Roy felt relieved, somewhat.

Dixon moved his head closer to Roy's, conspiratorially. "So, if I may ask, whose house are you working for?"

"Whose house? Well, I guess my own house. Waterman. For many years now. Been puttin' food on the table, but it's gettin' harder 'n harder, cuz of all the rules."

Bertram nodded. He hadn't heard of the "Wooderman" house before. Obviously an independent too. "Yes, we indies face such bureaucracy. Tariffs. Regulations. They never help us little guys."

"Yep. Hard ta catch anything but a cold these days."

"Yes. What's your line like?"

Roy stroked his beard again. "Well, twine. Good 'n strong. Sturdy. Don't want 'em ta get stuck on sumpthin' when yer pullin' 'em in."

"Ah. Well that's quite fascinating. Impressive!" He was thinking that fabric twine used in couture would be quite unique. Proletarian. A little retro, too, like the seersucker. Roy was onto something. And, yes, the material would have to be quite sturdy to make it through the pull of a single jersey machine, let alone a double.

Roy figured that if Mr. Dixon thought his crab lines were interesting, he might really enjoy hearing about the chicken necks.

He was about to mention them, when he noticed the ruckus in the row ahead. Robbie was pushing at Doyle. They were slapping at each other. He stuck his head forward, between the two seats.

"Now, boys, settle down up there for Unca Roy! What you boys fightin' 'bout?"

"Doyle keeps turning my TV off, but I want to watch it!"

"You want to watch that baby show, *Peppa Pig*! That's why!"

"I do not!" He really wished he had found it, though.

Roy sighed. "Now fellers, be good and stop all that roughhousin', or I'll have to separate ya! I'll have Sonny sit back here with one a ya and th'other'll be stuck up there by their lonesome!

Doyle looked back and responded. "Okay, Uncle Roy. Sorry. We'll stop." He did not want to get stuck with Desales.

Dixon had placed his earbuds back in his ears and was relaxing, reading his tablet. The horde of passengers had subsided. He was keeping an eye out for the flight attendant. He looked forward to a pre-takeoff beverage. He saw the attendant moving slowly down the aisle, row by row, taking drink orders.

Finally, the flight attendant arrived at their row. "Care for a complimentary drink or beverage? We have bottled water and a selection of juices, cocktails, wine, or beer?"

Dixon removed his earbuds. "Yes, thanks, I'll have a Stella Artois, please." Roy looked on in wonder.

"You sir? Complimentary water, juice, cocktail, wine, beer?"

He scratched his beard. "Well, do yous have Natty Boh? Could use a nice cold one!"

"What was that, sir?"

"National Bohemian beer? Not the National Premium, though. Too durn bitter. Gives me the gawks."

"Beer, sir? Our selections are Stella Artois, Guinness, and our newest, JetStream, a delightful pale ale. And I believe we have some Budweiser in too, today."

Roy was a little disappointed about the Natty Boh, especially since they were sitting right there in Baltimore. Except for Bud, he didn't really know the others. He knew Guinness a little. He remembered it was never cold enough. "Well, just to be on the safe side, how 'bout a nice Budweiser?"

"Yes, sir."

A few minutes later, the attendant returned with a tray holding two transparent plastic cups. Roy was delighted. "Go to war, Miss Agnes! Ain't the beer cold!"

The flight attendant handed one to Dixon and then the other to Roy. Dixon nodded and held his cup aloft. "Cheers, mate!"

"'N cheers ta ya, too!"

Dixon placed his earbuds back in and went back to reading his tablet. Roy took a healthy sip. His face puckered. The beer was definitely not cold. Warm! And definitely not a Bud. He licked his lips.

"Cheese 'n crackers! What the heck kinda beer is this? All warm and doesn't taste anything like Bud!"

Dixon looked over and pulled out an earbud. "Sorry. Couldn't hear you. Did you say the beer's no good? I see the flight attendant just up ahead? Shall I fetch him?"

A few minutes later, the flight attendant stopped by.

"Mister, this is some funny tastin' kinda Budweiser."

"You didn't enjoy the Budweiser? It's a German import. But maybe not to everyone's taste."

"German? I'm purdy sure it's from the U.S. of A. But why's it so daggone warm? Ice box on the fritz?" He had taken a few more sips trying to get accustomed to the taste.

"The refrigerator? No, sir. Most of our travelers prefer their beer that way. I could bring you a cup of crushed ice and a spoon? Many of our American customers ask for ice to put in their beer. Or I could bring you a different beverage?"

"Ice cubes, in a beer? Never heard 'a that. That'll just make it taste worse. No thanky! I'll just finish this warm one."

"Yes, sir."

Roy dipped below his seat for his last-minute carry-on. He bought them in a shop in the concourse. Utz potato chips with Old Bay seasoning. He munched away and secretly yearned for a nice cold one.

Bertram noticed Roy eating crisps. He glanced at the bag. He figured the "Old Bay" must be Dundalk Bay but wasn't sure of the significance. He thought, *That's the Irish for you.*

. . .

Dixon was enjoying the in-flight supper: Trout Provençale with baby tomatoes and haricot verts accompanied by a delicious glass of Côtes du Rhône. He noticed that Roy had chosen the Beef Steak with carrots and potatoes. And he figured that Roy had apparently gotten used to the beer because he had ordered a second glass of the same beer.

Dixon replaced his ear buds and settled back to watch the world news. The headline story featured interviews with two "modern social activists." The lead story was how Klaus Rötger-Dieter, unofficial leader of the UK neo-Nazi party, had come to team up with the French Socialist Environmental group, La Rébellion Insulaire. Rötger-Dieter was shown in one frame sitting placidly at his office desk chair. He was dressed in a brownshirt replica uniform, complete with swastika armbands and an iron cross pinned to his shirt pocket. Behind him were two large flags on poles: the British Union Jack and the Nazi Swastika. He wore his thinning and well-dyed black hair in the greasy style reminiscent of the Fuhrer. Completing the image was an attempt at a complementary mustache, sitting slightly askew, a touch lopsided. His pasty white face peered over his rimless glasses into the camera.

Claude-François Lamarche, the Vice Chair of the La Rébellion Insulaire, stood in the other frame. He wore a plain white tee shirt with a blue-gray, double-breasted blazer and dark green trousers. His hair was impeccably manicured: a carefully trimmed lion's mane stylishly draped over his left shoulder. His healthily tanned face bore a stylish two-day stubble. Behind Lamarche was a flickering screen, a slowly changing collage of environmental disasters: oil rig fires and spills, oil-soaked fish kills, tire yard fires, congested motorways, and aerial views of choking smog.

The birdlike face of Cynthia Jerome of Global News Services nested in its own smaller cut-in frame. The story began with a prerecorded narrative and video featuring Ms. Jerome:

"Earthshaking geopolitical history was made less than forty-eight hours ago when the UK Nazi party announced that it had joined forces with the popular French Socialist Environmental group, the Insular Rebellion. The press release indicated that the two groups would begin their work together this very weekend in the City of London. Although the announcement provided no details, we have heard through a variety of sources that members of the Insular Rebellion will be staging a series of protests around London in honor of their imprisoned leader, Gerard Giroux. Giroux has been held in prison in the UK for nearly nine months following last November's demonstration within the British Museum. Various legal motions, counter motions, Parliamentary actions, and protests have led to a series of postponements. Today, Giroux finally stands trial."

The static messianic shot of Giroux's upturned face was replaced with video footage. Dixon scowled. He had seen the same file footage run many times before on that network and with always the same sequences edited and looped together: the Insular Rebellion members glued to the walls chanting and singing protest songs; the crazy Frenchman with his loudhailer bellowing out missives against

Big Oil and Environmental Criminals; the silly protesters dancing about in their sunflower costumes; and then the denouement—the unfurling of the infamous Oil Can monster.

Ms. Jerome's narration continued: "Monsieur Giroux will be represented at trial today in London's Central Criminal Court by his very famous but reclusive free speech avocat." The backdrop footage changed to a scene featuring the back of a shadowy figure in a black raincoat, collar upturned, walking up the stairs of la Cour de Cassation in France.

Just then Dixon saw the flight attendant standing next to him. He quickly withdrew his ear buds.

"Yes, sorry to disturb you, sir. Just wanted to see if you'd like any additional drinks or snacks at this time?"

"For me? Oh, no thank you!"

They both looked over to Roy, who was now fast asleep.

"We'll leave him be. Thanks."

Dixon replaced his earbuds. The narrative portion had ended. Cynthia Jerome began her interview by addressing Rötger-Dieter first. "Mr. Rötger-Dieter . . . may I call you 'Klaus'? . . . could you tell us a little bit about your decision to team up with the . . . may I say . . . rather liberal French environmental organization, the Insular Rebellion? What are your feelings on that . . . your perceptions?"

Rötger-Dieter cleared his throat. "Firstly, you may address me as Chancellor Rötger-Dieter. Or, if you prefer, Professor Rötger-Dieter is acceptable." He nodded several times creating multiple double chins.

Dixon thought it odd that the man was affecting a German accent of sorts, even though he had read somewhere that the man was actually British.

"As for 'liberal' I don't really understand what you mean. The Insular Rebellion speaks for the People. That is why our Party is quite content to join forces with theirs. We, too, speak for the People. We have the same goals . . . the same desires . . ."

Dixon noticed the Frenchman in his frame waving desperately, trying to get an opportunity to speak. His microphone was muted. Ms. Jerome saw the movement in her monitor and responded, "Yes, Monsieur Lamarche. 'Oui.' You will have an opportunity to speak in just one moment. Please hang on." She continued her interview. "Now, . . . Professor, your neo-Nazi party is known for its desire to, shall we say . . . take over the British government, to put it simply. Your party platform also mentions the 'consolidation and concentration of British assets within the Party for proper disposition and exploitation.'"

"That is correct."

"Could you explain that?"

"Well, yes. We seek to nationalize all natural resource assets, just as do our brothers and sisters of the Insular Rebellion."

"Do they? I mean . . . I believe that the Insular Rebellion seeks environmental goals. You know, to move the Euro and UK economies away from Big Oil towards solar and alternative sources of fuel?"

Ms. Jerome nodded emphatically several times. Dixon recalled the silly Yank dance of the '70s, the Funky Chicken.

"Yes, we agree with the concept of solar and other alternative sources of power. Provided those resources are also nationalized." The Professor nodded again, placidly. "Let the People have their solar, and our Party will deal with the remnants of the so-called Big Oil industry. We will make certain it is duly dismantled following its very proper and complete economic exploitation for the benefit of the Nazi Party and, commensurately, the People. Power to the People."

Ms. Jerome shook her head, almost defiantly. "But are you aware of the . . . say . . . 'objections' of your partner? I don't necessarily think that the Insular Rebellion agrees with the entirety of your proposed agenda?"

The Chancellor leaned back in his chair and stroked his squared-off mustache. "Hmm . . . I couldn't say. There is certainly no objection on our part."

Dixon was not paying all that much attention to the foolish Charlie in the Hitler suit. His eyes were peeled on the other box, the one featuring the man performing near jumping jacks, desperately waving both arms, over and over.

"For instance, your views on ethnic purity and ethnic cleansing?"

The Professor looked on, wistfully. "Hmm. Nothing new there. Every government engages in some form of that. Some variation. A certain amount of ethnic purification is required in every governmental transition, in every transfer of power, whether such occurs peacefully or not. Our Party has been slandered in the past by intimations that we have, perhaps, pursued those otherwise routine goals too vigorously . . . too zealously for some tastes. As my brother Monsieuer Lamarche might say, 'comme ci, comme ça.' 'Each to their own.'" Rötger-Dieter shrugged his shoulders, nonchalantly.

Finally, Ms. Jerome relented. Monsieur Lamarche's microphone was summarily unmuted. The audience was immediately treated to the strident remnants of Lamarche's ongoing verbal tirade.

"Monsieur Lamarche, Monsieur Lamarche?" She tried to get her guest's attention.

Lamarche composed himself. He repositioned his earpiece in his ear. "Oui Oui?"

"Do you hear me?"

"Oui, yes!"

"Monsieur, may I call you Claude-François?"

"Yes, you may."

"So, Claude-François, tell me a little bit about your feelings, your emotions about teaming up with the British neo-Nazi party? Were there any compromises to make? Were those compromises difficult?" Lamarche had been breathing in deeply to regain calmness and decorum. But his eyes betrayed a brewing fury. He spat out, "Mademoiselle! La Rébellion Insulaire has absolutely nothing to do with that group of Fascists! We emphatically deny any connection! We disavow any nexus, whatsoever! We would never consider working with those criminals in any fashion!" He breathed out and folded his arms defiantly.

"So, let me get this correct, if I may. Are you now saying you have no alliance with the Professor's group?"

Lamarche looked to the ceiling in frustration. "Oui! Yes! Yes!"

"You're saying, 'yes,' there is an alliance?"

Lamarche took a deep breath. "Non! No! No alliance! No! We deny them! We reject them!"

Rötger-Dieter was smiling, looking on with amusement.

"Now, then, for the record, you are saying that your group has not aligned with the Nazi group, even for this weekend? Even for the planned demonstrations?"

Lamarche exhaled in frustration. "La Rébellion Insulaire has absolutely no connection to that man's group, whatsoever. Neither now, nor the past, nor the future! His press announcement is a fabrication. A falsehood! We are Socialists! What possible connection could our organization have with totalitarian Fascists!" He practically spat out the words.

The Professor interrupted. "Monsieur . . . if I may say, for the record, we, too, are Socialists. National Socialists." He smiled and nodded demurely.

Bertram heard no more. He had nodded off.

. . .

Roland had been checking his hair in the reflection of the transport van window, but he couldn't really tell. He didn't dare give it a zhuzh without a proper mirror. And he didn't want his fellow passengers to see him fussing over his hair. *Embarrassing.* The driver had dropped off all of the others at hotels in the center of town and other spots in the West End. He was the last fare. Finally, the driver pulled over and double-parked on Wellington Street in Covent Garden. Roland looked up at the dingy sign: The Saveloy. The transport driver unceremoniously unloaded Roland's massive suitcase and bloated carry-on from the van and dropped them onto the pavement a few yards from the entrance. He waited.

Roland noticed. "Sir, wasn't a tip included in the fare?" Roland recalled that it was.

The driver shrugged. "Somewhat, sir." He frowned.

Roland quickly reached into his pocket and handed over a one-pound coin. "Here you go, sir."

The driver gingerly fingered the lone coin between his thumb and forefinger. He stared at the coin as though doing so would make it multiply, magically. It did not. He placed the coin in his pants pocket and moaned, sullenly. "Cheers, mate."

"Yes, you too! Oh, are you going to see my bags into the lobby?" He drove away.

Roland groaned. He positioned his carry-on on top of his enormous suitcase, grabbed the two handles, and cautiously rolled the luggage to the front of the hotel. They had certainly given him enough crap about the carry-on at the airport. He had struggled to force the damned thing into the bag measuring rack. And then, when it got stuck, he had to face the further indignity of unzipping the bag while it was jammed to remove enough stuff to free it up. Personal stuff, too. Some of his better pomades and several pair of underpants. And a couple people waiting in line behind him actually complained about it. One of them said "Could you move it along, buddy? You're holding everyone up." He shook his head in recollection. *People.*

He knew he'd never get the damned bags through the tiny revolving door, so he pushed the assemblage up against the closed double doors and manhandled the massive load through. Immediately, the carry-on dropped to the floor and the suitcase toppled over. He bent over and reassembled the load to the expressionless stare of the bellman.

The clerk at the reception desk greeted him, pleasantly, and found his reservation in the system. "You're in luck, Mr. Biv. Your room is ready."

As the clerk clacked away on his keyboard, Roland noticed his image in the mirror along the lobby wall. *Not good!* Despite every effort, he had somehow fallen asleep during the flight. His hair was an absolute disaster! He walked over to the mirror for a closer examination. He was mortified. And he must have also drooled while sleeping because his sports coat now featured a dried, chalky white streak on the lapel. *Great.* He tried to rub the dried effluence away with his thumb, with limited success.

"Sir? I'm all finished here. Perhaps you'd like some assistance from our bellman?"

The clerk handed over an electronic key and paperwork, including a coupon for one free bottle of water from the hotel lounge.

"Oh. Yes. I could use some help, thank you."

"Brilliant. I'll get our man."

. . .

He tipped the bellman with a five-pound note. His luggage barely fit into the cramped, monastic chamber. The room's lone window looked out onto a filthy alley running along the rear of the building—a gloomy view of mangled rubbish bins and dented green dumpsters. Grimy rooftop air conditioning units sat upon the decaying building across the alley. Roland heard the humming sounds of the units. He bumped past his suitcase and pushed the dingy lace curtain aside for a glance. He quickly drew it back into place. *Lovely.*

He moved his carry-on from the twin-sized bed to the floor. He tested the mattress with his hands. Serviceable, provided he could fit onto the tiny thing. He squeezed himself into the bathroom. A plexiglass shower stall was jammed up against an ancient pedestal sink. The sink featuring a leaky faucet and rusty drip stains. A tiny white toilet took its place next to the shower. He noticed the lone glass shelf fastened above the sink. It held a single worn hand towel and a sliver of pink soap wrapped in plastic. He moved the towel aside and noticed that the glass was cracked. He glanced at the rounded curves of the sink. He would have to place all of his toiletries on the one skinny, cracked shelf or the unpleasant toilet tank lid. Everything would otherwise roll off of the surface of the sink. He stooped down a bit to see his face in the mottled bathroom mirror. He straightened back up. An utter horror.

He grasped the worn faux gold handle of the shower door. The handle had long ago ceded away much of its precious fool's gold, exposing bruised aluminum underneath. He felt the plexiglass door immediately bump against the side of the toilet. He glanced inside the shower. He would barely fit. He inspected the floor of the shower. Someone else's gray hair had accumulated in the drain strainer. Mildly nauseated, he inched his way out of the bathroom, backward, in escape.

He spied the spare vinyl pullback door of the closet. The door fought valiantly, so he wrenched it across with a violent tug. The effort pulled it free of its runner. He pushed at the now limp, disconnected door and looked in. *Great. No hangers.* He'd have to carefully remove his tux from his suitcase and spread it out over the tiny bed to prevent creases.

He sat himself on the tiny bed and stared forlornly at the worn mahogany dresser. It was adorned with a Victorian-era, white-lace bureau scarf, yellow with age. He was mulling over whether to risk opening a dresser drawer, when he heard a knock at the door. He looked warily through the peephole. "Gremlin!" He quickly drew back the latch and opened the door.

"Teddy Bear! Gimme a hug!" The two brothers embraced warmly.

"I wasn't expecting you in person, Stef! I thought you'd send over one of your manservants in the royal horse-drawn carriage!"

"Manservants. Ha! Yeah, that would be me!" They both laughed. "Yeah, I could have used a courier, but I figured I would just walk on over and see my best man in person!"

"Isn't that considered bad luck? Best man shouldn't see the groom before the wedding?"

"No, Rol. You're thinking of the bride and groom."

"Oh. Okay. I knew there was something like that."

"Yeah, if you can believe it, they gave us two separate rooms at the Charing Cross. A standard one for me that I used last night and, like, a honeymoon suite that Flo's in and I'll move into tonight."

"Sounds very proper!" Roland looked around the room. "Speaking of proper, I'd offer you a place to sit, Gremmie, but this is it." He pointed to the spartan bed.

"Wow. What a dump! I'm really sorry about this, Rol. Flo's people took care of all this shit. Her crazy Aunt Philomena scarfed up all the good rooms in the best hotels. Our side got the dregs, apparently."

They both sat. The springs of the tiny mattress creaked in protest. Stef reached into his coat pocket. "Okay, here it is." He snapped opened the black velvet ring box. He gently removed the precious object, holding it in his palm before Roland. "Look at this thing. It's ancient."

Roland gently plucked the ring from Stef's palm. He held it up toward the yellow light of the ceiling bulb. He noticed the desiccated corpse of a moth trapped inside the fixture bowl. He ignored it and studied the ring.

"Wow. It's quite amazing. Very lovely, Stef. Really shiny, too!"

"Yes. It's some kind of special Welsh gold that you can hardly get anymore. Flo said the ring is over three hundred years old!"

"Holy shit! That's crazy!"

"Yeah, I know! Because of her family, she was entitled to pick out a ring from a pile of ancient ones that they keep in the family vault somewhere. Check out the inscription."

Roland studied the inner surface of the ring, moving it around in his palm. "I see, like, wavy lines and some writing. I see 'Stour.' What's the other word say?"

"It's 'constantia.' Latin for 'being constant.' You know, like 'being steadfast.' The British 'stiff upper lip' and all that."

"Oh. Okay."

"And the wavy lines are for the Stour River."

"Got it! Wow. That's quite amazing!"

"Yeah. It's priceless. This thing is worth about a thousand of my weak-assed engagement rings."

"Wow. Yes. I will be, like, super careful with it." Stef handed the box over to Roland and watched him put the ring back in place. Roland clicked the box shut dramatically.

Stef stood up. "Thanks Rol! So, I've got a bunch more things to do this morning into the afternoon. And then they start the big motorcade over to St. Paul's. We'll pick you and the gang up here from the lobby around 4:30. Or as close to that as traffic permits. There's apparently a lot of shit going on in town today so traffic may be tough." He paused. "And I'm scared shitless. 'WTF?' Crazy enough getting married. But into a royal family? I have no idea what the 'blank' I've gotten myself into, man. But I love Flo, so much.

It's not even funny how much I love her. She's my everything." He paused again. "Am I nuts?"

Roland looked back up to the moth. "Gremmie, calm down. We're all crazy, okay? Welcome aboard. Sometimes it's best to roll with it. To go with the flow, okay?... Oh, was that clever?"

Stef shook his head. "Yeah, big bro. That was! Thank God you're my best man. This will all work out." He took a breath.

"Amen. No worries, Gremlin. We've got this!"

Stefan took another breath and composed himself. "Okay. Did Roy and the kids check in yet?"

Roland took a breath too. "Not as far as I know. But I literally just got in here."

"Okay. Text or phone me if there are any problems. I'm in your contacts, right?"

"Sure, sure."

"You got yourself the SIM card, right?"

"What?"

"You know, the little chip thing in your mobile phone? You have to remove yours and stick a different one in so it works over here?"

"Of course, of course." He remembered reading something about that at the end of the itinerary. He hadn't gotten around to it, but he figured he could always borrow Desales's phone.

"Or, you might be able to use roaming if there's a problem with whatever SIM card they sold you."

"Yes, of course." He wasn't exactly sure what "roaming" meant.

"And you reminded Desales about the SIM card, right, like I put in the itinerary? I don't think Roy even has a mobile phone."

"I believe so."

"Alright, big bro! Gotta bounce. Tell the gang I'll see them later!"

Roland stood and they hugged again. The door closed. Roland sat back down and gently wept.

...

Roy put his matching green plastic luggage onto the ground and withdrew his half-rim glasses from the breast pocket of his seersucker suit. He pushed them a little farther down the bridge of his nose and squinted at the printed text. "Says here, the Sav . . . Savoy? Can you read that, Sonny? I've got old eyes."

Desales glanced over at the piece of paper and turned away. "Yes, Royal, that's what you told the driver. That's why he dropped us here."

Desales then made a sweeping motion with his arm. "Voila!" He pointed to the huge glass "Savoy" sign proudly crowned above the entrance doors. He snickered to himself. *This is going to be fun!* No one in the group had noticed that the reservation was actually for a much more rustic hotel, a bit farther down the Strand: the glorious "Saveloy"—not the "Savoy." Desales had spotted the dingy place as they passed through Covent Garden.

"Well, go to war, Miss Agnes, that there Savoy is a helluva big place! Fancy looking, too, ain't it? I can't believe little Stefan and his girl scraped up the 'dough re mi' to get us inna this kinda place! Geezy Christmas!"

"Well, Uncle Stef's betrothed is royalty, so it makes perfect sense that they would put us up at a place befitting our station." Desales nodded proudly to Doyle and Robbie, who looked on, confused.

"Which station would that be, Sonny?"

"Never mind, Roy. So, shall we make our regal entrance—see if our special suites are ready?" He was doing all he could to refrain from chuckling.

Roy looked at his wristwatch. It had stopped. "Sonny, what time ya got?"

"It's a little before ten a.m."

"Geezy. Ten a.m.? Doesn't feel like it. That plane ride seemed ta take forever. An when we started, it was lighty out, and now it's still lighty out. It's broad daylight here! But, tell ya what? I ain't never stayed in a motel that let ya check in before lunchtime. All the ones downy ocean make you wait. Used to make ya wait 'til one or two. Last time me 'n Mardi went downear, they said four p.m.! Can you b'lieve that? Mardi had saved up ta get us into that Ho Jo, you know, cuz they have that pool right there on the Boardwalk? Real fancy. But they didn't treat us very special. Made us wait 'til four! So, whad'ya think, Sonny? I'm thinkin' it's too daggone early ta check in."

Desales nodded earnestly. "You're probably right, Roy. But, you know, why don't we give it a try, just to see what happens?" He was smirking again.

"Naw. Tell ya somethin'. I been a little worried about them chicken necks. Good they get a little ripe, but I'm thinkin' I should get my lines out before they get a little too ripe."

"Absolutely, Roy!"

"So, which way ya think is the wooder? That map you showed me before made it look like someairs back there, behind the motel." He pointed to the Savoy sign. "Should be some path er somethin' to cut through. You showed a park, like, on that map?"

"Yes. Let's enter the Savoy and find the cut through!"

Doyle and Robbie picked up their miniature wicker suitcases and Roy his matching green luggage.

"These dang twisties hurt yer hands. Gotta be careful how ya hoist these fellers up onta yer shoulders!"

Desales led the way past the uniformed doormen and through the glass doors. They passed through the lobby over the checkerboard-patterned floor. Roy looked around. "Makes ya feel like playin' checkers!" Their stroll prompted curious looks from several guests, apparently unused to seeing either seersuckers or Roy's particular brand of luggage. Desales noticed the concierge's desk.

"Wait here, I'll find out about the cut through."

Doyle and Robbie looked on as Desales chatted with the Concierge. They watched the concierge nod and point toward a bank of elevators. They saw Desales nod in response.

Robbie was noticing that there was definitely a stinky smell coming from Uncle Roy's luggage.

. . .

The seersucker parade made its way through Victoria Embankment Gardens. They were passed by several dark-suited business persons making their way over to the coffee stand in the park. The weather could not have been more beautiful.

"Sonny, this here's a fine park! Look at all the purdy flairs, boys!"

They worked their way through the park to a lane leading to the embankment road. Desales looked up toward the massive Waterloo Bridge and over to the Savoy pier.

"Wow! Look, Roy, just along this road. That's the River Thames!"

They crossed the road to the pedestrian walk along the Thames bank. Roy looked up at the sign. "Yer mispronouncin' the name, Sonny. It's not 'tems.'"

"Okay, Roy, sure."

"Okay, fellers. Right near that big monament's got a little tiny beach. Let's see if we can jump downear."

Desales read the plaque as they passed. He made a quick check of his guidebook.

"That's Cleopatra's Needle, Roy."

Roy nodded. "Yep. Look at them E-gyptian lions there!"

They found a safe spot, and Roy tossed his bags onto the mucky shore below. He stepped down from the walkway, carefully.

"It's a mite slippy down 'ere, boys. Be careful of yer footin.'"

The three followed Roy down to the narrow stretch of silt.

Roy found a dry spot on the shoreline next to the embankment wall. "This here's good a place as any for droppin' my lines. Nice spot. Not too deep."

He reached into his right suitcoat pocket and removed his makeshift "seat," an abandoned newspaper liberated from the departure lounge at BWI. He spread it down carefully on the silt. He pulled his bags over and undid the black twist tie from the aroma-producing bag.

Robbie spoke up. "That reeks, Uncle Roy."

"Oh, that's okay, Robbie! I'm used to it. If there's any crabs to be had here, nothin's better'n some ripened chicken necks!"

The three watched as Roy withdrew his ball of twine from the bag. He bit off two separate lengths of cord and tied a chicken neck to each. Roy gently swung each line out a few yards from shore. He jammed two wooden clothespins into the mucky shore, one on each side of his makeshift seat. He attached a line to each clothespin, making sure he could easily feel the lines rub against his legs, should there be any "bites."

"Did you bring a net, Uncle Roy?"

"Sure did, Robbie." He reached into the bag and pulled out a homemade net made from a metal coat hanger with cheesecloth appropriately stapled onto the wire.

"Wow. That's pretty cool, Uncle Roy."

"Yep, Robbie. I had ta impervise since I couldn't pack ma big net."

Roy leaned back against the embankment wall and relaxed. The others stood around, taking in the Thames scene, mostly tourist boats.

"Wow! Way over there is a giant Ferris wheel! Can we get on it, Uncle Roy?"

"I'm sure we can, Robbie! Maybe tomorrow after that breakfast we're supposed ta go to. How's that sound?"

"Cool!"

Doyle finally spoke up. "Uncle Roy, I'm kind of hungry. I was asleep on the plane when they served the main meal."

"Oh, okay, Doyle. How 'bout yous, Sonny and Robbie? D'jeet?"

Robbie shrugged. "I ate. I'm okay."

Desales spoke up. "You know, I could use a bite, Roy."

"Okay. So, how 'bout you boys go off an find somethin' ta eat from up the road or maybe in that nice park? I don't need nuthin' cuz I ate good at dinnertime on the plane ride. I asked the lady for seconds, and she brought back a whole second meal! Was suprised! I thought she'd just bring back a couple pots and servin' spoons. But she brought a whole daggone second meal! I ate it all. Dern good! Gramaw always said, 'Waste not, want not.'"

"Okay, Roy. I'll take Doyle and Robbie and get us something to eat. We'll meet you back here in a little while. But I have no cash. Could you give us some money?"

Roy looked down at his Orioles fanny pack. "Sure 'nuff. Sonny, why don't you just take the whole O-reos pouch? Safer that way. I don't need nuthin' from it right now." He also figured he might take a snooze after enjoying those two free beers and didn't want it to get stolen.

"Sure, Roy."

The three looked on as Roy groaned and grimaced, performing an ersatz contortionist act with the Velcro belt. "Hard ta get the dang thing off from the sittin' position. Now you fellers run off and have a good lunch or whatever. I'll be here!"

He handed the fanny pack up to Desales.

"Thanks, Roy!"

They climbed back onto the pedestrian walk and began to backtrack to the garden.

"Here, Doyle, you get to wear the fanny pack!" Desales was thinking that he would not be caught dead in it.

"No way, Desales! It's Robbie's turn."

Robbie looked on, perplexed. He'd gladly wear the fanny pack. He loved the Os. "Okay."

. . .

They had walked back through the park toward the Savoy. "Okay, guys, before we get food, I think we should surprise Uncle Roy by getting checked into our hotel."

"No way, Desales. We need an adult with us." Robbie looked over to Doyle for affirmation.

"He's right, Desales."

"Ridiculous. First, I am considered an adult. I'm seventeen with my own voter's registration card. Second, you guys have all the paperwork right there." He pointed to Robbie's Orioles fanny pack. "Third, checking in will be the fastest way for us to get food. Why? Because I know for a fact that there will be food already waiting for us in our rooms. That's how they do over here at the fancy hotels. So, why spend your money on food when you'll get it free? And fourth, you don't want to be carrying around those dorky picnic basket suitcases all over London while you look for food, right?"

Doyle and Robbie looked from one to the other. "Okay, Desales. We can try it since you'll be there." Robbie nodded in agreement.

"Perfect!"

They arrived at the Savoy lobby. Even though there were three reception clerks, the reception line to the reception desk was long and snaked back nearly to the revolving entrance doors. A convoy of six limousines had just pulled in.

Desales pointed. "See. I told you they would let people check in."

The three took their places at the end of the line. Soon, others took their places behind the three as the line increased and slowly moved forward.

Desales whispered, "Guys, I have to take a whiz, and it can't wait. So just keep moving with this line, and I'll be back in a minute." He could barely hide his smile.

"Okay, but hurry!" Robbie looked over to Doyle.

The line was making progress. Robbie and Doyle kept looking over to the restroom alcove, hoping to see Desales emerge. They hadn't noticed that his visit was momentary. Desales had carefully and quickly made his way in and out of the restroom and over to one of two dramatic staircases leading down to the lobby. There he could get a good look at the front desk, while avoiding his cousins' line of sight.

Assistant Hospitality Host Reg Pemberton was up for the task. Manning the reception desk during busy times was anathema to some of his fellow clerks. But he enjoyed it, especially on "big event" weekends. He loved chance meetings with celebrities and particularly royals, major or minor. He adored his Queen and the British Monarchy. He often felt that Parliament was a nuisance. The old ways were, perhaps, the better ways.

The chief had put the entire staff on notice. There would be many royals today. Absolute decorum was required of all and at all times. And, just like that, Reg spotted several in his line! Lady Bentwillow and her clan from Hertfordshire. And of course, there was Ms. Margaret Stanhouse. She was a personal assistant and chaperone to the extended Percival clan. He remembered seeing her with several of the Percival youngsters. That meant to be on the lookout for the Youngley-Hough troop, too. And, sure enough, yes, those had to be the two boys. Well dressed in seersucker traveling suits. *Smart. Close relatives of Lady Florence, our gem of East Anglia!*

Doyle looked over to Robbie. "Where the hell is Desales! He sucks!"

Robbie wasn't paying attention. He was listening to what that lady just ahead of him with that pile of kids was saying.

"These are Peters from Sunningdale." She patted each child on the head. "And these are Percivals from Hemingford Abbots." The kids squirmed under Ms. Stanhouse's heavy hands.

"Yes, very good, Ms. Stanhouse! And may I say what a delight it is to see you all again."

"Thank you, Mr. Pemberton. It's always so very fine to see you here at the Savoy. Such a dear old friend you and this fine hotel have been over all these wonderful years."

"The pleasure is mine!" Pemberton checked his screen and entered the necessary data. He handed over the key cards to Ms. Stanhouse.

He saw the nicely attired boys. The smaller one had a fanciful orange pack around his waist. Quite adorable! A happy, smiling bird. *A young ornithologist, no doubt!*

Doyle pushed Robbie forward. Robbie looked around for Desales. Desales was still hiding, doubled over at the base of the stairs, nearly urinating himself in his effort not to laugh.

Robbie felt Doyle's nudge forward. He approached the reception desk. "We're Royal's from Essex."

"Yes, you are! And I cannot tell you how pleased we are to have you here as our honored guests at the Savoy!"

Pemberton began clicking away, confirming the suite reserved to the Youngley-Houghs.

"Room 1245, young men! And I'll make sure to tell the rest of your party that you've checked in!" He handed Robbie two key cards. Robbie wasn't sure what they were. But he took them.

"One moment, and I'll summon our bellman, Romney, to help you with your bags and introduce you to your suite." Pemberton looked slyly at Robbie and Doyle. "Not that you lads are strangers to the suite, eh?"

Robbie felt confused and said, "Okay."

Instantly, Romney appeared and grabbed their bags, quickly escorting them to a bank of elevators.

Desales had stopped laughing. He could not believe what he was witnessing. The two donkey heads being admitted into the hotel? And a bellman to assist them? He quickly left his hiding place on the staircase and caught up just in time to make it into their elevator.

"Oh, hi, guys. Sorry for the bathroom holdup. I'm here."

Romney turned around. "Nice to meet you, sir. I was just telling the lads that your family has been provided one of the premier suites in our Savoy. I hope you will be satisfied."

Desales took over. "Why thank you. We're greatly looking forward to this stay."

Romney ceremoniously opened the door. Desales's jaw dropped. They entered, spellbound. They had never seen a hotel room like this! Multiple sofas and overstuffed chairs surrounded an enormous television screen. A second set of sofas and chairs were drawn cozily in front of an ornate gas fireplace. Fresh cut flowers had been carefully placed in antique-looking vases. They watched as Romney pulled aside the curtains adorning the massive picture window. They felt the blinding light of the sun.

"I've always loved pulling these curtains back for our honored guests! Look at our beautiful Thames!"

The three looked out the enormous window to the breathtaking view of Victoria Embankment Gardens and the Thames. They saw the bridges over the Thames and an enormous Ferris wheel in the distance. They didn't know where to begin to even look.

Robbie looked to Doyle. "Wow!"

Doyle chimed in. "Yes, double wow!"

Desales looked out and feigned nonchalance. "Agreed. Quite acceptable, Romney."

"Excellent, gents!" Romney carefully placed the two suitcases and Desales's backpack in the enormous luggage closet. The three continued to glance around the suite, dumbstruck.

Romney provided a quick tour of the suite: the multiple bedrooms, the three separate baths, the individual thermostats, the stocked bar, the safe, the snack foods and fruit, the mini refrigerators, the dry cleaning and shoe polishing service bags, the Savoy bathrobes and umbrellas. The experience was mind-numbing! There was so much to see and absorb!

Romney completed the tour and walked to the door. "As you can see, the suite is equipped with all mod cons. Now, remember, if there is anything that you lads need, just dial 1-4, and we will assist immediately!" He stood, waiting.

Desales ambled over. "Romney, thank you so much for the tour." He then whispered, "Our dad will be taking care of all gratuities upon arrival."

Romney responded, sotto voce, "Sir, gratuities are not required here. But I appreciate your kind consideration." Romney thought, *bollocks*. He'd give it another go, later, when the dad arrived.

Once Romney had departed, Desales grabbed a bag of crisps from the snack bowl and plopped himself on the sofa in front of the enormous television. Doyle and Robbie stood behind the sofa and watched as Desales fiddled with the remote control. The screen came to life. "Welcome, Youngley-Houghs."

Desales turned to the two. He pointed at the screen. "Can you believe that? They still have the names of the prior occupants on our screen. I would have expected better. I'll have to let Romney know." Desales stifled his smile.

The three lost interest in the endless television menu and began to individually explore the oddities of the suite. The bathrooms were unlike any they had known. The showers had no doors! But they had multiple metal hoses and push-button controls. And somebody had left real live orchids in the bathrooms by mistake!

They looked at the section of the wall next to the luggage closet. "What's that?" Robbie was pointing to a flat, rectangular metallic object, artfully exposed in its custom mounting. Desales saw that it was a stylish clothes iron. The accompanying ironing board would fold out cleverly from its slot by a mere button push. Robbie and Doyle had never actually seen an iron and ironing board, except on TV.

"Oh, that's the sandwich maker that's included in each room." He pulled the iron out of its mounting and held it upside down to expose its flat metal ironing surface. "See. You place your sandwich on the metal heating plate. It gets hot quickly. Non-stick. Really perfect for grilled cheese sandwiches."

"How does it stand up so you can cook on it?" Robbie was puzzled.

"Oh, well usually there are special stands, like a frame so that you can set the temperature and then turn it over to cook on. You'd place it in the frame."

Robbie and Doyle looked on, inquisitively.

"You know, I think our man Romney slipped up again. I don't see the frame here? But, no worries. You just need a couple sufficient blocks to support it. One on each side. Preferably bricks. Four would do. Two on each side. I've also seen piles of hardback books, shoe boxes, and other stable objects used. Robbie, you didn't happen to notice any bricks lying around when we were walking to the hotel?" Desales had watched Robbie's bewilderment at seeing the streetside newspaper vendor. The vendor had seven different piles of newspapers laid out on the sidewalk with a brick on each pile to prevent the papers from blowing away.

"Yes! When we were walking here, I saw a man on the sidewalk with a bunch of bricks! I wonder if he'd lend us some?" He was starting to get hungry for a grilled cheese. He really wanted to see the sandwich maker in action.

"Oh, you wouldn't even need to ask him. Bricks in England are just like ordinary rocks or stones you'd find somewhere back home. Rocks and stones don't belong to anyone in particular. Same thing with the bricks here." Desales nodded, confidently. Doyle was suspicious. But he wanted a grilled cheese too.

"Okay, so here's the plan. I'll run out and get us some nice cheese and white bread and meet you guys back here. You guys go ahead and look for maybe four good bricks. Use this key. I have the other one." He grabbed his backpack from the closet. "Let me show you how the key works."

Robbie and Doyle enjoyed trying out the key. Robbie began laughing watching Doyle quickly lock and unlock the door with the card—hearing the clicking and buzzing sounds of the latch opening and closing electronically.

"Okay! You guys know how to get in and out. Remember, it's suite 1245. See you guys in a little while with the bread and cheese. Don't forget the bricks!"

Desales made his way through the lobby and gave a friendly "thumbs up" to Romney who was struggling with a lopsided carrier full of luggage. Romney waved back, weakly. Desales figured he'd better get over to the Saveloy to check it out. He couldn't believe their good luck in scoring the suite at the Savoy. But he figured their luck could turn should the Youngley-Houghs make an appearance. *So far, so good.* He would check in on Uncle Roland, too. Then he'd grab some sandwiches for the three of them from a Pret A Manger on the way back to the Savoy.

. . .

Roland was beside himself. He had performed several good zhuzhes while hunched over the sink of his tiny bathroom. *Not good enough!* Particularly the crown area. He had turned his back to the

131

bathroom mirror and was now bending backward, painfully trying to navigate a good look at the back and top of his head with his hand mirror. The Michelangelo experience was a lot more agony than ecstasy.

He didn't want to, but he realized that he would have to use more of his precious Fletcher's Hint of Almond dry shampoo. He shook the can fiercely. He shook it again. He began to carefully spray the shampoo onto the top and back of his head, approximating the areas based on "feel." He believed he had made some progress when the can ceased delivering its powder. *Crap!* He shook the can again, furiously. He carefully positioned the spray nozzle over his scalp and pushed in the applicator button. He heard the weak sounds of the propellant giving out. The can was empty!

"Life's not fair!" And he wondered about his dear friend, Morris. Did Morris deliberately charge him for a nearly empty "tester" bottle? *No,* he thought. He was Morris's favorite customer. But he remembered Morris's advice about going to the Boots store and picking up another can. He would do that immediately. And maybe take a look around for a place where he could get an early lunch. He was starving, as usual.

He heard a knock at his door. He looked out the peep hole. *Oh joy.* Desales. He pulled back the latch chain and opened the door.

"Hey, Uncle Roland. The guy at the desk said you were in. How's it going? How was your flight?"

Roland sighed. "The flight was miserable. I mistakenly fell asleep and . . . caused some wrinkles in my sports coat." He wasn't going to discuss his hair problems with Sonny. Desales noticed the drool stain.

"Oh, too bad. Ours was okay."

Desales entered and looked at the atrocious hotel room. "Holy crap, Batman! This is it?"

Roland sighed, despondently. "Yes. Quite lovely accommodations, eh? Are your rooms any nicer?"

"Uh, well, yes. We're checked in over at the Savoy. Decent hotel just a few blocks from here."

"The Savoy? You mean like the 'Savoy' Savoy with the afternoon tea and theatre and all that?"

"Probably."

Roland wondered how the hell that could be, but his thoughts were consumed with his rather urgent need to get to the nearest Boots. And to someplace for food. "Okay. Sounds nice." Then he remembered. "By chance, does your room have its own safe?"

"Yes, it definitely does."

"Thank God! Help a brother out." He walked two short paces to the dresser, bumping his bulging suitcase along the way. "Look at this. The wedding ring." He opened the box. "It's gold from Wales. Apparently, that's a big deal. Can you believe that? And the ring is, like, anciently old!"

Desales held the ring and looked it over. "Wow! How did Uncle Stef score this?"

"Well, his betrothed, Lady Flo, was given access to the Royal Vaults of Essex. Her family gave it to her." Roland couldn't help but think, *And they will pull it from her dry, shriveled hand, once she's kicked the bucket.*

"Wow! Impressive! I see, like, wavy lines on the inside."

"Yes. That's the family river, the Stour. They even have their own river if you can believe it."

"Amazing!"

"So, here's my problem. This absolute dump has no safe, of course. In fact, nothing is 'safe' here, except obviously for the dumpsters in the back alley, which seem to be emptied every fifteen minutes."

"Okay. You'd like me to keep it in our safe at the Savoy? And then bring it up here when we get picked up later?"

"Yes! That's exactly it. Can you handle it, bro?"

"Yep! You bet!"

Roland handed him the ring box. "Okay. Tell your dad and the others I said 'hi.' And Godspeed, young Desales!" Roland provided an absurd salute.

"Got it, Uncle Roland! See you later!"

As he left the stench of the Saveloy, Desales thought to himself, *There's no way in hell I'm going to stay at that dump.*

. . .

The two young men in seersuckers left the lobby and wandered down toward the paper peddler's spot by the road. They spied the stacks of papers splayed out upon the sidewalk. Each boy grabbed two bricks and calmly headed back toward the Savoy. Immediately, the gentle London breeze swirled to a mad frenzy, blowing newspapers apart in every direction. The vendor could not believe what he had just witnessed. Scoundrels of all stripes tried to steal coins from his box. Some swiped a paper, now or then. But no one had ever stolen his fucking paperweights before! He began yelling, "Oi! Bring back me fowkin' bricks you fowkin' young twats!" But they had disappeared.

Back in room 1245, Doyle and Robbie began experimenting with the sandwich maker. The bricks worked out, perfectly, just like Desales had said. They moved the sandwich maker out of its holder and onto the floor of one of the massive bathrooms. They didn't want to make a mess in the main room. The cord would just barely stretch to the crazy electrical outlet unlike anything they had ever seen. They considered turning it on to get it preheated, but figured it would be better to wait for Desales.

. . .

THE BIG COMB OVER

Roland was glad to have turned over the ring to Desales. Now he could go out on safari to track down the Fletcher's Dry Shampoo. He wandered through Covent Garden and spied a Boots just a half block away. He entered and found his way back to the hair products. They had dry shampoo, but it was a different brand and without any color, "hint" or otherwise. He wandered down to the Strand and figured he'd have better luck there. Sure enough, he found another Boots, entered, and checked the racks of beauty products. Another strike!

He was getting tired of searching. His hunger alarm had sounded. He found another Boots just a block or two closer to Trafalgar Square. He noticed that the traffic was crazy and that there were an awful lot of people milling around in the Square. He entered the Boots. *Yes!* There it was, finally. But this Fletcher's had "A Hint of Ebony," not a "Hint of Almond." Would it make much difference? He figured not. Some people already believed he had dark hair. That was the thing about his hair shade, it could pass for brunette or dark blonde. Some even thought it was red. He paid for the shampoo and headed back to the hotel to begin the process.

. . .

He began with a good zhuzh. Not much help there. His hair had dried out during his breezy safari. He decided a little of the hemp oil follicle treatment could help. He applied the oil generously and gave himself a scalp massage. *Not nearly as nice as Morris.* But good enough. He gave the new can a hellish shake and bent his head over the sink. He pushed the applicator button. The powder blew out quickly, a mini cyclone. At least this bottle had plenty of life in it! He ran the brush through his hair, turned around and positioned his hand mirror so that he could check out the back and top. *Not bad,* he thought. But, perhaps, a bit darker than he had expected.

He brushed some more and decided to give it one more shot. The spray hit his scalp like tiny BBs. *Better,* he thought. But the dryness of the shampoo called for another quick round of the hemp oil. He carefully worked more hemp oil onto his scalp. Maybe a touch oilier than he'd like, but not bad. *Lustrous, actually.* He was about to give it some finishing spray, when he noticed that his mustache was looking a little gray. He held the mirror, closely. Too gray. He hated using mascara, but c'est la vie. As he carefully applied the mascara, he realized that he was absolutely and utterly famished.

. . .

The two playing snooker saw the big guy enter the Dog and Fish. They watched him standing at the bar, looking hapless, confused. The barman saw him, but was in no great hurry. He continued drying pint glasses with his towel. It was early. Way too early for the usual lunch crowd. *Tourist. Make him wait.*

Two other patrons wearing leather biker jackets watched from a pub table. They noticed Roland's black, greasy hair and odd mustache and looked from one to the other.

Roland presumed that the barman had not noticed him enter. "Oh, barkeep?" He made a waving motion.

The barman looked up, unamused.

"Hi! Do you have a lunch menu?"

The barman couldn't believe it. The menu was right there on the chalkboard. He thought, *Typical Yank, thinking there's a menu handed out in a pub.* He pointed at the chalkboard and scowled, "Right there, mate."

"Oh! Thanks! I should have looked there!"

The barman went back to drying his glasses.

Roland ran through the menu: Bangers/Mash, Mex-style Burrito, Am. Cheeseburger, Scotched Eggs (2), Ploughman's. There were Sides: Mushy Peas, Chips.

He figured it was safer to stay with the burger. "I'd like the cheeseburger please, with chips."

The barman did not look up. "Comes with crisps. Still want chips?"

"Yes!" Roland wasn't exactly sure about all that, but he could eat almost anything.

Just then, one of the two young men playing snooker spoke loudly, "Hey, fat poofster."

Roland turned to the sound.

"Yeah, you, fatty. Why don't you go the fuck back home where you came from. Get the fuck out of our pub."

Roland sized up the two snooker players. Skinny children. He could pick one up in each arm if he had too. He responded, "Are you addressing me?"

"Addressing you? No, fat queer, I'm not addressing you. I'm directing you. Get the fuck out of our pub!"

Roland turned to the other two bar patrons, as though performing. He held his arms out dramatically. "They're not being very inclusive, now, are they?" He turned back to the men playing snooker. "Sticks and stones, fellows! Sticks and stones!"

With that, the one who had been speaking began marching his way over toward Roland, cue in hand. As he walked, he waved the stick as a club. "Here's your stick, queer!"

The taller of the two pub patrons stood up quickly, knocking over his stool. It clanged loudly against the floor. He held up his hand to the approaching man.

"He's with us kid, so back off!" The other guy in the leather jacket stood in solidarity.

The barman returned from the kitchen in time to see the ruckus. "Hey! Piss off, everyone, or I'll clear everybody out!" He waved his mobile phone over his head.

The man with the cue stick stopped in his tracks. He wanted to finish his pint and was not going to mess with the bikers. He stood foolishly for a moment. "Okay, not this time, queer. But look out." He went back to his snooker table.

Roland took a seat with the bikers. "Well, thank you for the hospitality, gentlemen! I'm Roland. And proud to be here in London for a very special event!" He shook hands with the two. He noticed that they were a bit more "Village People" and less real biker. He had known many from both circles. He could always tell the posers.

"Good to meet you, Roland. I'm Vic, and that's Tony. Yeah, we're here for the same thing."

"Really? That's wonderful! Do you fellows know the star of our show?"

Tony looked over to Vic. "Yes, very well. You too, obviously?"

"Oh yes! He's my brother! I'm his best man."

The two nodded. "He's a brother to us, too."

Roland nodded back, appreciatively. "Can I buy you boys a couple beers? What are they called here—pints?"

Special Constable Vic Corbin looked over to Police Constable Tony Williston. They were not allowed to drink on the job, but being undercover meant that certain deviations would be required.

Williston responded, "Ah, yes, Roland. We'll have a pint with you."

Roland waved over to the barman, dramatically. "Sir, three pints of whatever kind of a nice beer you have on tap. Something good!"

He looked up from his Sudoku. "Pilsner or lager?"

"Lager sounds fine!"

Moments later, the barman arrived with the beers.

"So, I was just hanging out with my brother for a bit, but he had to go and get himself ready for later. What's he been up to these days?"

Vic looked again toward Tony. "Ah, good things. Good things. Trying to bring some order around here. We need it." Vic scowled and took a sip.

"Yes! He's a fanatic. I thought I was compulsive, but he can clean up a place like nobody's business!" Roland was not surprised that Stefan's friends had figured him to be a neat freak.

Corbin finished his sip. "Yes. Cleaning up around here is what we need. It's all about the PM, now. Remains to be seen what will happen." Vic figured that Rötger-Dieter's henchman certainly would know about Boris Johnson's recent election.

Roland took a sip. "Yes, the whole p.m. thing was a little crazy. Caught us all off guard. We're all going to need to stay alert." Roland was thinking that the idea of an evening wedding was a little nuts and that he should really be drinking coffee, not beer, because he needed to stay wide awake. An evening wedding combined with jet lag could be disastrous. He had to at least be alert through the photo sessions. He could mentally check out afterward.

Tony Williston was efficiently working his way through his pint. He nodded in agreement. "Brilliant. Yes. We need to be alert. So, Roland, if you are at liberty, give us the rundown. How can we best show our support? Where should we station ourselves today?"

Roland finished off his pint. "Well, of course, I'm in the party, and I'll be front and center. Otherwise, I'm not a hundred percent sure where everybody else will be. But Stefan will have his guys usher people around once they get there. I would just follow whatever directions are given." He figured that Stefan's biker friends were really good guys. They didn't just want to attend. They wanted to be involved. To be helpful.

Corbin spoke up. "We're in the Party too." He waved his hand toward Williston and finished his pint, slapping it down on the table as an exclamation point.

"Wow! That's fantastic. Really glad you guys are with us!" Roland figured the wedding party was going to be pretty large. But that was okay, because he was still the best man. Plenty of photo ops no matter how large the wedding party would be.

Williston made a mental note about the insider's name being Stefan. Now they were making progress.

A thick paper plate with a cheeseburger, dill slice, and crisps arrived. A moment later, the barman returned, placing a large bowl of chips onto the table, along with unmarked squeeze bottles of vinegar and ketchup.

"Good Lord, look at all this! I'm going to need some help. Feel free to take some fries, guys!" Roland bit into the burger hungrily. "Not bad!" He called out to the retreating barman. "Sir, could you please bring us another round of beers?"

Moments later, three new pints arrived. Vic and Tony sipped their beers and helped Roland out with the chips. And then Roland remembered something. He felt his pants pockets. He had left the hotel without his wallet! He had no way to pay for the meal and the beers! *Crap!* He had only a single pound coin! That would never be enough. He began to sweat. He calmed himself. He'd think of something. He'd stall with some small talk.

"So, guys, how did you all meet?"

Corbin looked over to Williston for help. Williston responded. "Well, yes. At one of the rallies. We've been to the rallies. Plenty of mates there." He quickly took a sip of beer.

Roland remembered that Stef met Flo at a PETA rally. "Yes. Great cause! Good people. They've really been pushing spaying and neutering to cut down on the unwanted population. Too many unwelcome and unwanted creatures wandering around this poor old earth these days."

Corbin looked over to Williston. That was enough. He wanted to punch Roland out. Listening to the filthy Nazi talk about human beings as though they were animals made his blood boil. It made him sick. But he reigned it in. He had a job to do. He took a deep breath and drained the last of the beer from his glass.

Roland noticed and figured he'd get another round going. He didn't see the barman but figured he'd catch up with him on the way to the men's room. "More beers coming. I'll find the barkeep."

Once Roland left the table, Corbin complained, bitterly. "Jesus, Tony. I've had enough of that bloke. Why don't we just arrest him and be done with it. He's a falkin' menace!"

"No. No. We have to keep cool. We're starting to get somewhere." As senior officer, Tony was also not opposed to having a third round. And the chips were quite good.

Inside the cramped men's room, Roland stared at his face in the ancient, speckled mirror. He was horror struck. His hair was an absolute mess. He tried giving it a good zhuzh, but the hemp oil was not playing nicely with the Hint of Ebony dry shampoo. He noticed that several clumps of now greasy shampoo powder had landed on his shoulders. He brushed them off, carefully, so as not to stain. And then he saw that damned saliva stain again.

This was an absolute disaster. A cluster bomb! He looked at the delicate part he had so carefully established for his hair. It was a "fail." Blown to bits in the London wind. He hated to admit it. He was going to have to regroup back at the hotel and perform his "go to" tried and true: the comb over. His greatest, most important, biggest comb over, ever. It would be the only way to save some degree of dignity. He would also need to turn his face at just the right angle for the wedding photos. Tricky, but nothing he hadn't done before. He sighed. He was an actor. He could do it. But it was depressing as hell. *If only I hadn't fallen asleep on the damn flight!*

And then his thoughts turned to his dilemma. He slapped his pockets again, instinctively, wishing to feel his wallet. There was no wallet. Just the one-pound coin. Time to plot an escape route.

He left the men's room and looked farther down the dark corridor. He saw a door. An exit. He walked toward the door through the long-tenured stench of urine and bleach. The sign on the door said "Fire Exit Only. Alarm Will Sound." He grimaced to himself. *Crap!*

He backtracked toward the bar and spied a jukebox. He wandered over and checked out the discs. *Bingo!* That could work. And a pound per play. He had just enough.

He headed back to the table and saw the barman. "Oh, sir? Could we have another round please?"

"Sure, mate."

"And, sir, by chance do you carry a very nice Scotch Whiskey called Ox Loin?"

The barman did a double take. "Ox Loin! Most certainly! It's one of Scotland's finest. Not well known, mind you, but a damned fine malt! Make it right out of Glasgow. I know the maker. Good family."

"You're kidding? My bears and I drink that stuff like water!"

The barman wasn't that sure about the Yank's "bears" but nodded in appreciation. "Really? Well that's brilliant, mate!"

"Thank you! So, yes. We'd like a bottle of Ox Loin and three glasses. And the round of beers, too, please!"

Roland rejoined his new friends Tony and Vic. Moments later, the barman swept by, dropping off three drafts and the bottle and shot glasses.

Tony couldn't believe his eyes. "Look at this, Vic! Ox Loin! Have you had a shot of the Loin, before, lad?

Vic was still smoldering. But seeing the Ox Loin cheered him up a bit. "Yep. My dad loved the stuff. Good choice."

Tony distributed the drafts and shot glasses about the pub table.

The pub door opened. Two tough-looking skinheads entered. The tall one had a scorpion tattoo on his neck. A swastika was razor cut into his close-cropped hair. Blurry prison tats were etched onto his scalp, barely visible through his hair. The shorter, dark-haired one had a scar running along his face from his left eye socket to his lip. Purple tats covered the bottom of his neck. Rough prison tats were etched into the back of his hands. They saw the two guys using the snooker table. The tall one yelled as the two walked back toward the table, "Hey, you two twats. Get the fuck off our table. Fuck off, now."

The two young men looked from one to the other. They knew of these two. Carlo and Pug. You did not fuck with them. Ever. They began easing away from the table.

Roland heard the ruckus and stood up. He spoke calmly, like a patient parent. "Sirs, those boys are using the table, now. So you'll have to please wait your turn!"

Pug and Carlo turned to the sound in disbelief.

Corbin looked over to Williston. He was feeling a little dazed from the beers and wasn't sure what to do.

Carlo, the taller one, yelled angrily, "Just who the fuck do you think you are, you fat wanker! This is our fuckin' pub, so you and your twat boyfriends should get the fuck out of here, now!"

Roland stood his ground. "I don't think so, sir. Last time I checked the Magna Carta, anyone may enter an English public house!" Roland nodded expressively, to further make the point.

The two young snooker players stood in shock. They had never heard anyone fuck with Carlo and Pug. And they had never witnessed an actual murder before.

Carlo's jaw dropped. "What the fock! You miserable focking sod-off! I'll get you out of my pub, you focking Yank!"

Carlo began walking, menacingly, over toward Roland. Pug followed behind.

Williston glanced over toward the barman for help.

The barman raised his mobile over his head and began waving it broadly. "Lads, lads, that's enough. I won't allow any trouble here. Best you two get on out of here, now!"

Carlo stopped in his tracks. "What the fock? You're telling me what to do in my pub? You gonna throw that mobile at me? I'll make you eat that phone, champ!"

The barman raised his voice, "No, I'm just goin' to make a call to the right people. You don't want that, friend. Believe me."

"Cops? Who the fock cares about the cops! This is our pub! My mate Tick should be tendin' this bar, and I don't know you or what the fock you're doing here. Tick runs this place, not you!"

The barman yelled back, louder, "Tick? That was my tenant! I let this place to him, and the falkin' twit couldn't pay his rent, so I'm here now. I own this place, mate, so you two falkin' Nazis get the falk out of my pub, now!"

Carlo began marching toward the bar. "You fockin' bog roll. I'm gonna enjoy punchin' out your face. Nobody tells me to leave!"

With that, the bartender bent down behind the bar and emerged with a sawed-off shotgun. He pointed it squarely at Carlo.

"Oh really? I make the rules here in my house, so you two pieces of Nazi dog shite get out of here, now, before I take a shot or two. Because I falkin' will!"

Staring down the barrel, Carlo lost some enthusiasm. He and Pug headed for the door. "We'll be back for you, twat. And that gun won't help you then!" They slammed the door shut behind them.

The barman put the shotgun back behind the bar. "Sorry for that fracas, men. Those two criminals are the kind of shite that sent my people to death camps not that many years ago, and I sure as hell won't have them drink in my pub. Oh, and the gun's not loaded. Usually does the trick, though."

Tony and Vic were still in shock, as were the two young snooker players. The older of the two looked over to Roland. "You are one fat, brave motherfucker!"

Roland had sat back down and was chewing through a mouthful of crisps. He mumbled and waved the two over. "Sit with us, boys.

Drinks on us!" Roland figured that two extra people for the game would be perfect.

The two put their cues back in the wall rack and wandered over. They each pulled up a pub stool.

"Sir, could you please bring two more beers and two shot glasses?"

. . .

She hadn't seen Mr. Biv around for a few days now. Mr. Sykes said that Mr. Biv needed to provide some additional proof of his diplomatic credentials in order to obtain the parking space. She was a little insulted. Apparently, her word was not good enough! The housing industry was another male bastion. A chauvinist fiefdom. She couldn't wait for Mr. Biv to produce the evidence. She would delight in putting Mr. Sykes in his place!

But Mr. Biv was off somewhere. She hadn't had a chance to read through his last pile of recycled papers. Maybe there was a clue there? She thumbed through the pile next to Bijoux's litter box. She was looking for something clipped. And then she saw it! Something cut from a tabloid. A British tabloid! *The Sunday Mirror*? Mr. Biv had never recycled a British tabloid before!

She grabbed the paper and took it over to her PC. She went online to the Sunday Mirror's website. She'd seek out the online version of the paper and see what had been cut! She found it! The headline read "Lady Florence Stour, The Jewel of East Anglia!" She began reading the article, eagerly.

"Who said Essex is all Flitch Trials and Southend Holidays? We East Anglians are chuffed with pride for our own Lady Flo Stour. Royal? Yes! But also one of us. Young Lady Flo has made her voice heard as a strong supporter of PETA. Her ancient Essex family estate along the Stour has gone fully meatless. Yes, she's taken over the family farm and supports vegetarianism and veganism. Grain only, non-GMO, and completely up to snuff in all things organic and all methods biodegradable. Pesticide-free and utilizing no-till agriculture only.

"But did we mention she's a beauty? Yes, her male Oxford classmates swoon, but now she is leaving the free and happy single life and tying down with a lovely young Yank by the name of Biv . . ."

Suddenly, a flag came up on Mrs. Barnwhistle's screen. To continue reading required a subscription to the tabloid! She angrily clicked off of the site. She'd try again later. Maybe she'd try to read faster next time. But, if nothing else, she could tell Mr. Sykes to see for himself. Mr. Biv was engaged to a royal, from Essex!

. . .

"Sir. Wake up, sir." Officer Elise Donegan tapped Roy's foot gently with the toe of her boot. Roy continued snoring. Quite loudly. She looked around at the scene. Poor old guy. Two rubbish bags holding all his worldly possessions. One of them was partially submerged in the muck of the Thames. The other was partially opened, exposing horribly shabby clothes. And wearing that terribly outdated seersucker suit. Probably given to him at a shelter. And a poor fit. She felt bad for him. Reduced to rough sleeping in public places. All of his life's efforts summarized in a couple bags of rubbish. She reached down and gently jostled his shoulder. "Sir, sir. There's no sleeping here. And this is not a public access area. You can't stay here."

Roy awoke and blinked. He looked to each side. His lines had gotten free and drifted away! He'd have to find them and pull them out of the shallow water. And then he saw the shadow and realized there was a person standing over him. "Sonny?"

"Sir, as I said, this is not a public place. There's no trespass allowed. And no sleeping. And you can't sleep in the park, either."

He shielded his eyes from the sun and looked up to see a uniformed officer. "I'm sorry, ma'am. Was just doin' some crabbin' here. Didn't know about the rules. Ya know we got a beach like this in Middle River. Skinny little patch, but crabs run good there in the shallows. Thought I'd try it out here."

Officer Donegan had no idea what the man was talking about. She was having trouble getting past the odd Cockney accent.

"Are you able to stand, sir?"

"Well. Sure! Just gotta give muhself a boost. Might take a second. Ya know my 'get up 'n go' has got up 'n went."

She shook her head. She figured he was saying "yes."

Roy grabbed onto the barrier wall and hoisted himself up. He steadied himself with both hands on the wall. "Go to war, Miss Agnes. Gettin' old ain't no fun!"

"Okay, sir. Steady on. Have you been drinking?"

"Drinkin'? Well, just them two beers on the plane ride. They said they was Budweisers but tasted nothin' like Budweiser to me. Warm, too."

"Okay. Plane ride?" *Poor guy might need a psych eval.*

"Yep. Comin' over for the royal weddin'. Gone ta be a big shindig!"

She shook her head. "Of course, sir. What's your name, sir? Could you show me your ID?"

Roy had steadied himself. He reached out his hand in greeting. "Yep! Name's Roy. Roy Biv. Pleasure to meet ya. What's your name, Ma'am?"

She declined the handshake. "I'm Officer Donegan. City of London Police. Just show me your ID, sir."

Roy was thinking that she didn't seem all that friendly. He looked down for his Orioles fanny pack and realized he'd given it to Sonny. "Crap. Muh boy's got muh driver's license. Was in the O-reos pouch. Dang. But Sonny'll be along soon. He went up off the beach to get him and the boys a nice lunch. That's why he has the pouch."

Officer Donegan figured he was saying he had no ID. "So, you have absolutely no ID with you, now, sir? You said another man has your ID?"

"Yep. Muh boy, Sonny. Good boy. Smart like his momma. Should be along soon. Did you see what happened to muh crabbin' lines?"

More nonsense. She could barely understand him. "No, sir. Now, what is your full name?"

"Well, it's Roy G. Biv. 'Royal,' actually, is my o-fficial name, but I just go by Roy. Less snooty tooty. And the G's for Gamaliel."

"Did you say your name is Roy G. Biv? Really, sir?"

Roy was surprised. "Yes, ma'am. Why? Ya heard o' me? Got lotsa folks back home that know ole Roy. Maybe even a few over here?"

She grumbled to herself. *Cheeky old nutter.* She pulled out her mobile. She pointed at Roy. "Stay right there, sir." She punched in the number for her ranking officer and turned her back for privacy.

"Phil. Elise. Got a rough sleeper. Old bloke with no ID . . . Yes. Usual patrol. He's at Thames Embankment near Waterloo. By Victoria Gardens . . . You'll like it. Cheeky old sod. Says it's Roy G. Biv . . . You don't get it? You know, the colors of the spectrum, red, orange, yellow, green, blue, and so forth?"

She chuckled back. "Yes. Likely. Said he had a couple beers on his flight. As though he'd flown over here as a tourist. Said he's here to attend a royal wedding."

She chuckled again. "No chance. He's a local for certain. Cockney thick as Hackney. But I don't recall arresting him before."

"Yes, probably so we don't pull up his record."

She turned back around to check on Roy. He had wandered over to the shoreline. He was peering over his half rims.

"Sir! Please step back from there and stand back by the wall!" She pointed tersely.

"Okay, ma'am. Sorry. Just lookin' for my lines." He wandered back to the wall. Donegan turned back around.

"Yeah. Wandered off a little."

She listened. "No. Probably more the drink than mental condition. Yes. I agree. He's docile and no threat to anyone. Yes. Not much choice since he won't tell us his real name or give us an ID."

. . .

Roland poured the Ox Loin into Trevor and Burns's shot glasses. Trevor held his up and yelled, "Cheers!"

The rest joined in. "Cheers," and clicked shot glasses.

"Look, man. Sorry for calling you a queer. I don't care what the fuck you are, actually." He remembered that his dad, who had long ago abandoned the family, would do shit like that.

"Perfectly okay, Trevor! People say a lot of mean things, but they usually don't mean them, right?"

Tony said, "Amen, Roland. So, you lads know those two skinheads?"

Burns said, "Yeah. Those guys are for real. Some bad shit."

Vic looked inquisitively at the two. "Are you guys eighteen yet? For drinking?"

Trevor laughed, "We are now. But believe me, it never made no difference in most pubs. We been sneakin' in for years. Only place to play darts and snooker. We got shit. We both livin' with me dad's third wife who he left three falkin' years ago."

Roland chimed in, "Aren't there any youth clubs around to join? You know, for sports and stuff?"

Burns looked at Trevor. "Youth clubs? No, mate. Not at council flat. Got gangs if ya want 'em, though."

Corbin was feeling a bit woozy. "You know, there's a great club a bunch of us coppers started a couple years ago for young guys. Listen—three dart boards, snooker table, two foosball tables. And a regulation football field next door. Costs nuthin' to join. Pub two doors down. Good fun. Chance to hang out with some other lads and some cops that give a shit."

Tony realized that Vic had just blown their cover. *Oh well.* At least they had gotten some intel.

Burns said, "No charge?"

"No charge."

"Shit. I'd go ta that."

Roland stepped away and headed back to the jukebox. He fished his coin out of his pocket. It clinked in, successfully. He pushed in "Roxanne" by the Police.

He rejoined the table quickly. "Okay, guys. We're playing 'Roxanne.' Two teams—youth vs. old. Youth is 'Roxanne.' Old is 'red light.' I'll sit out the first one." He poured another round of Ox Loin for the four, just a finger each. "Start now!"

Vic and Tony heard "Roxanne" and downed a preliminary shot. Then "Roxanne," again. They quickly repoured. Then all four had to really start pouring and pounding them down when the chorus came in.

Roland wandered off toward the men's room. He knew the words "Roxanne" and "red light" would repeat about twenty-five times each. A great distraction and plenty of time for an escape. He felt a little guilty about running out on the tab, but he would apologize to Stef's two policemen friends at the wedding tonight. He'd have his wallet and would reimburse them. Perhaps he'd even counsel them on the risks of excessive day drinking? He pushed open the rear exit to the sound of a ringing alarm. He felt the blazing London sunlight.

. . .

Donegan was glad that Roy did as told and walked back with her to the embankment road. He had hauled his matching luggage with him. If he wanted to bring his rubbish, she wasn't going to stop him. She certainly was not going to touch it. She had decided against placing the daft old guy in restraints. *He's not going anywhere.* They walked a short distance to the crossroad and waited. Within minutes, the blue and yellow London Police van arrived. The escort officer disembarked. They both helped Roy onto the seat bench within the rear caged portion of the van.

Escort Officer Parker helped Roy with the seat belt. "There you go, sir. For your safety." Parker used his feet to push the plastic garbage bags toward the metal divider behind the driver. He wanted to avoid unnecessary contact.

"Are yous takin' me back to the motel? Ya know I could just as easily walk? Ain't far." Roy pointed toward the Savoy. "Don't need ta bother ya for a ride, if that's what yer doin'?"

Officer Donegan looked blankly at Roy. "You're staying at a hotel around here, sir? Which one would that be?"

Roy pointed again, toward the park. "That one right through there. There's a cut through Sonny found. Gotta big sign, says the 'Sa-voy.' Looks real fancy, but I ain't checked in yet, cuz it's too darn early 'n they'd just shoo us away, just like they do at other fancy places, like that Ho Jo downy ocean. Well, our ocean, I mean. But, you know how they make ya check in ta them fancy places late as hell, now."

Donegan and Parker stepped away from the back of the van. She murmured, "Poor old guy thinks he's staying at the Savoy. Like I said, a little delusional, but harmless. I truly feel sorry for him. You can tell by his face that he's had a hard life."

Parker nodded in agreement. The old guy kind of reminded him of one of his crazy uncles. "Don't worry, Officer. We'll be nice to old pop."

Parker stuck his head back inside the rear of the van momentarily. "Won't be long, sir."

Roy was beginning to feel a little leery about this. He tried to get the officers' attention, but they were busy speaking a few yards away. "Ya know, my Sonny'll be lookin' for me? Spects me ta be right downear by the shore." Roy pointed toward the Thames. "He won't know I was drived back to the motel?"

They ignored him and continued their conversation.

Roy tried to engage the driver. "Mister, 'r you 'n charge a this?" The driver looked into the rearview glass.

"No, sir. I'm just helping out as a driver today. Shorthanded everywhere."

"Are you a po-lice, too?"

"Well, yes. But I'm PCSO. Community Support only."

"Oh, like a helper?"

"Yes, sir. Where you from, sir?"

"Essex. Do you know it?"

"Know it well. Was born 'n raised there, myself. I thought you might be from there cuz of your accent."

Roy was puzzled. "Accent? Didn't think I had one. Maybe I do?"

"Yes. Some people look down on us East Anglians. Think we are all pumpkin bumpkins with funny accents."

Roy wasn't quite sure what the driver meant but figured he meant he was an Anglican who grew pumpkins. Figured he'd leave the religious talk alone.

"Well, Essex is doin' okay, I guess. Feel more sorry for the Dundalkers. They take a lot 'a guff. You know, not as so-phisti-cated as us 'n so forth." He was hoping the policeman wouldn't raise the topic of duckpin bowling though.

"Dundalk? Haven't been there in years. Gone downhill, I hear."

"Yep, was talkin' to a nice feller on the plane ride. You probly know him. Name ya can't forgit, Mason Dixon. Says he thinks Dundalk is fine 'n dandy. Don't know. Hard to b'lieve. Some parts, maybe. Like near the country club at Sparrows Point. Fancy. But I think he was just jealous cuz I was from Essex."

"Yep, mate. The Irish got nuthin' on us."

"Fighting Arsh? Yep. They got nuthin' on our Navy."

"Amen to that, sir. God bless our Jacks."

. . .

"Got room back there for these?" Parker was handling the two garbage bags with gloved hands. He hoisted them over the rail of the property clerk.

"Sure, Officer. We've seen worse. What's his name?"

Parker looked over at Roy. He was seated on the wooden bench inside a cell in the Old Bailey lockup. He had just been processed by the Security Office.

"Well, just put him down as 'Biv.' It's a false name, anyway. No ID, so we had to bring him in. He was sleeping out near Victoria Embankment. Need to keep him for the full twenty-four unless someone responsible comes by to claim him. He won't face charges. Just need to keep him off the streets."

"Yes, sir. That's what they told us, too."

Roy noticed Parker looking back his way. "Officer, could ya at least let my Sonny know ya got me in the hoosegow? He ain't goin' to know where I am?"

Parker walked over to the cell. "Sir, if anyone inquires of the patrolling officer in that area, they'll be advised. Otherwise, we're required to keep you here for twenty-four hours."

"Twenty-four hours? A whole day? How'm I supposed ta go ta the royal weddin'? Got Sonny and two young boys, muh nephews, ta take?"

Parker sighed to himself. *Poor old pop.* "Well, if any of your entourage stops by to see you, we can release you to them. Perhaps they'll pay you a royal visit?"

. . .

Desales returned to suite 1245 with a plastic bag filled with four sandwiches and paper napkins. Doyle and Robbie had turned on the television. They were watching *Clangers*. They had never seen it before.

"Bad news, tumble turds. Couldn't find any bread and cheese. But I bought us each a sandwich. Two tuna salad and two ham and cheese." He noticed the iron propped up between the two sets of bricks on the bathroom floor. "Nice work, boys. Looks functional. We could always use it to warm our sandwiches."

He brought the sandwiches over to the sofa. "Here you go. Take your pick. And there's plenty of soda over there."

Doyle grabbed into the bag for a tuna. "Thanks, Desales. I'm starving!"

Desales sought out the safe. "Robbie, hand me the passports from Roy's pouch." Desales placed the ring and the passports inside the safe. "Hey, dipshits. I'm putting our passports and Uncle Stef's ring in here. We're keeping it for Uncle Roland. He said it was super valuable. It's made of gold from Wales. The combination is the year. 2019. I'm hanging onto Roy's wallet."

"Okay, Desales."

"Okay, while you idiots stuff your faces and stare at the TV, I'm going to run a sandwich down to Roy. I'll be right back. Don't go anywhere."

"Okay, Desales."

. . .

Desales trotted back to Roy's crabbing beachhead. He was shocked. The tide had submerged most of the tiny patch. And Roy was gone! *Shit!*

He looked around trying to see if he had just moved to another spot. He had not. He looked back up to the park. He couldn't make out the telltale sign of Roy's robin's-egg blue seersucker. He wandered into the park and began looking around. He was starting to feel panicked. A man in a dark business suit noted his distress.

"Sir, are you okay? Are you looking for someone?"

"Yes, my dad! He's missing. He was just down there." He pointed back toward the beach area.

They both saw a uniformed police officer patrolling on foot. The businessman said. "Oh. Look, there's someone you could see. I, unfortunately, must get back to my work now."

"Okay. Thanks, anyway!"

Desales jogged over to the officer. He didn't notice that the businessman still lingered, just out of sight.

"Ma'am, I'm looking for my father. He was just down there along that barrier wall on a little patch of beach. Did you see him by chance?"

She stopped in her tracks. "Was the man wearing a seersucker blue suit? Homeless with some rubbish bags?"

Desales exhaled. "Yes. I mean no. Yes, that was him, but he's not homeless. Do you know where he went?"

Officer Donegan sighed. "Yes, I do. He refused to provide an ID and would not give me his real name. He said his name was Roy G. Biv, like the colors of the spectrum. So we knew it was false."

"False? No. That is his name. It's Royal G. Biv. G is for Gamaliel. My name is Desales M.G. Biv. M.G. is for Mardi Gras. My mother's name."

She was puzzled. "Do you have ID?"

"Yes. Here." He showed her his wallet with a Maryland driver's license. She couldn't believe it. The old guy's name might actually have been Roy G. Biv.

"What happened to his ID?"

"Oh, I had to borrow his wallet for money to get us sandwiches." He jiggled the plastic Pret A Manger bag. "Ah. I still have it. Hang on." He put the bag down and pulled Roy's wallet out of his breast pocket and handed it over. She read the name on the license. *Shit.*

155

"Okay. So, because we had no proper ID on him, we had to run him up to Old Bailey. He's safely in . . . protective custody. So he'd have a place to rest whilst we figured it all out. He's okay."

"How can I bail him out? We have a wedding we're going to this evening at St. Paul's."

"Okay. Easy. Just go up to Old Bailey. They will release him to you on his own recognizance. He's not charged with any crime."

"Phew! Okay. Thanks, officer."

She wanted to ask if their room was at the Savoy, but figured, *best not to ask.*

. . .

"What's keeping Desales?" They had both bored of watching TV.

"I don't know. He's such a dick!"

"I think we should go back out and hang out with Uncle Roy? That would be fun, at least."

"Me too, Robbie. This is bullshit."

They made their way down the side street past the paper vendor. He saw the two seersucker suits flash by. He jumped up from his tattered lawn chair. "Hey! Hey! You two boys! Where's my falkin' bricks?" But they were long gone. *The little buggers!*

Doyle and Robbie made it down to the barrier wall. Roy was gone without a trace. And there was no sign of Desales.

"Crap! What do you think happened?"

"I don't know. Do you think we passed them on the way down here? Maybe they were taking a different elevator up?"

"Maybe."

A man in a business suit ambled by. "Hello lads. Any trouble?"

Robbie spoke. "Yeah. We can't find our uncle and our cousin! They should be right here!"

The businessman responded sadly. "Oh yes. I do know something of that. I happened to be by here, between office appointments, of course. I love nature, you see. I happened to learn that your poor Uncle was taken into custody by the Police. He is, unfortunately, in jail now. As for your cousin, I would not know." The businessman looked positively cherublike.

"In jail? How? Do you know what happened?"

The businessman became serious. Quite concerned. "Well, there was some problem with his identification. His wallet was missing apparently."

Robbie brightened. "We have it! We have it in the safe with the ring!"

"Oh! Brilliant! Now you'll be able to bail him out. You'll just need to pull one hundred pounds from his wallet in the safe and take it to the right place!"

Doyle said, "No, Robbie. Desales has Roy's wallet. And all of the money!"

Robbie went sullen. "Crap!" They both looked down at the ground distraught.

The businessman rubbed his chin, trying to think up any possible solution. He rubbed some more. They watched.

"Hmm. Well, there is one rather simple solution."

. . .

He checked his tourist map. This was definitely the Old Bailey. He approached the two police officers in SWAT gear guarding an entranceway.

"Sirs, I'm here to bail out someone who's in the lockup. Is there a particular entrance to go through?"

The larger officer spoke. "Are you a solicitor, sir?" He thought it possible because the man was wearing a proper business suit and tie. And they were churning them out younger and younger these days.

"No, sir. Does it matter?"

"Well, we can allow solicitors and barristers in with valid ID, but to establish bail, everyone else must go to Somerset House." He pointed generally toward the West End. "They'll phone it over and let your man out once you handle it there."

"Uh, okay, thank you."

That didn't sound quite as simple as the officer had suggested. Traffic was bad enough getting to Old Bailey. There was no time to find another taxi and wait in line at some office and then get back again. He walked around the side of the building and found the visitors' entrance on Newgate Street. He had read in the tour book that people could sit in on trials from courtroom galleries. *Good enough.* He took his place in the line. He figured once in, he'd improvise.

Time was ticking by, but his group of six tourists received their visitor badges and were allowed inside. Once in, he dawdled a bit to let the other tourists ahead. They turned a corridor, and he broke off from his group, allowing the others to continue. He wasn't noticed.

He wandered down the hall and happened upon an Exhibition Room. The placard on the wall stated "Forensics Demonstration." He entered the room but was immediately confronted by a guide.

"Sorry, sir, you're a bit early for the 13:00 demonstration. They're still cycling through the last group. But I can take your name in the meantime."

"Certainly. Desales Biv. How long is the demonstration?"

"Well, it's interactive, of course, so the amount of time varies, but most of the groups take about thirty or forty minutes. Not too long. It begins in the courtroom, not here. This is where you check in and later collect your things at the end." He was thinking that the students and pensioners in these tour groups usually got bored by the time they got to "trace fibre evidence" and couldn't wait to leave. But they all seemed to love the initial courtroom tour and film on demonstrative evidence.

Desales thought that forty minutes was about the normal amount of time for a mock trial type of forensics demonstration:

fifteen or twenty minutes for each side. It struck him that he could actually participate in the contest and still get Roy out of detention in plenty of time to get back to the Savoy and over to St. Paul's for the six p.m. wedding. He enjoyed participating in mock trials. He could practice his skills in an incredibly novel environment. He knew he could handle it. Yes, he was in.

"Yes, I'd like to participate, but I'm trying to meet up with my uncle. May I sign up here and get to the courtroom by 1300?"

"Certainly, sir. I will sign you up and check in your backpack and mobile phone."

"Excellent. Thank you. Are the issues or discussion points set?"

"Written materials? Yes, we provide those in the courtroom."

"Perfect. Now, by chance, do you know of an elevator or stairs that leads to the holding cells?"

"The lift? Yes. Straight down that corridor and then left right there, and then you'll need to take the half stairs you'll see down to the mezzanine. Then, straight ahead that way to the lift." The man was pointing in several directions as he spoke.

"Thank you!"

Desales checked his watch. He wandered down the corridor as directed and then looked for the left turn leading to the stairs. He was hoping for a sign or placard that would lead him in the right direction. There was none.

They saw the man in the well-cut, dark-gray business suit walking hurriedly down the hallway past the robing room. Then the man stopped and peered back down the hallway he had just traveled. The man began walking away from the robing room, looking a bit confused.

Solicitor Sammie Evans squinted over his bifocals. "Do you think that's him?"

Geoffrey Taliaferro, Junior Barrister, stared at the figure in the hallway. "Could be, Sammie. I've never actually met the man, and

I'm not quite sure what he looks like. No one around here does, I suspect. I'll call out."

"Sir? Sir? Are you by chance Monsieur DeSalés?"

Desales stopped and looked back. Someone must have gotten his name from the list. Mispronounced, but otherwise perfect timing.

"Yes. I'm Desales."

"Oh, thank God! Or should I say, Dieu merci!"

Desales was wondering how they could tell that quickly that he was part Creole. He figured it was a Brit thing.

"Bonswa. Komon ou ye?"

"Pardon?" Taliaferro looked confused.

"Oh, I was saying 'hi' and 'how are you.'" He had learned his Creole from Mardi.

"Oh yes, of course. My apologies. I am barely adequate in the French tongue."

"Well, English is always fine with me. It's what my mom mostly spoke in our home."

Taliaferro was quite surprised, but glad to hear it. They would not have to rely upon the court-appointed translator who was already a no-show. He placed his briefcase on the ground. The three shook hands, warmly.

"I'm looking for the lockup and then the courtroom for the demonstration trial?"

Taliaferro's eyes lit up. "Yes, of course! You made it just in time, Monsieur. So, you haven't had a chance to see our man below? They brought him in a few hours ago."

Desales thought that a client interview before a mock trial was a nice touch. Problem solved. He'd be able to check in on Roy, too. And if by chance Taliaferro happened to be a solicitor, maybe he could arrange the bail that way.

"No, sir. Shall we do so?"

Evans glanced at his watch. "Geoffrey, there's really no time. We literally must get Mr. DeSalés robed and to the courtroom, post haste."

"Yes, yes. Thank you, Sammie. Mr. DeSalés, let's get you to the robing room. There should be a few minutes in which to chat with the client in the dock before the entrance of his Lordship. I've got your brief here." He pointed to his briefcase.

"Sammie, could you run this up for me? Thank you, and I'll see you back in Chambers."

"Yes, sir."

Desales and Taliaferro strode quickly toward the robing room for the male barristers. As Taliaferro walked, he took stock of the situation. He was damned glad that DeSalés had made it through the Chunnel cock-up this morning. And he felt gratefully surprised at DeSalés command of the English language. Not only spot on, but absolutely no trace of a French accent when speaking English. And there was that very slight adoption—that hint—of a cockney accent. Unexpected. But otherwise a perfect speaker of the Queen's English. He thought it appropriate to make further small talk.

"Mr. DeSalés, I understand that your family is from Le Havre?"

"Le Havre de Grace?"

"Yes."

"Well, our family is actually just a little down the river from there."

"Seine?"

Desales chuckled. "Far from it. Not even close." He figured Taliaferro would soon understand his family's lack of sanity once he met Roy.

Taliaferro was a bit embarrassed. He had thought that Monsieur DeSalés was from the heart of Le Havre. Surprised to learn his home was much farther down river.

They continued walking briskly. Desales added to the small talk. "You know, the Marquis de Lafayette named the town."

Taliaferro was puzzled. He had never heard of that. "Why, no, that's quite interesting."

"Yes. And you won't believe it, but the locals there pronounce the name as 'have a disgrace.' Ridiculous. And they constantly complain about the Dutch Navy coming in on weekends."

"Really? That's quite surprising! Very unexpected." Taliaferro was unaware of any present tensions between France and the Netherlands. There was much to learn from Monsieur DeSalés.

Sylvester Montclare-Twigg, QC was admiring his robed appearance in the floor-length mirror. He saw the two enter the room.

"About time. You know we go off in about five." He glared at DeSalés. Certainly younger than he had expected, based on the media nonsense. Looked more Algerian than French.

He glowered at the two and smirked to himself. *Bravo, young fool. We'll soon find out whether you were worth the trouble of the private Parliamentary Act passed to permit you, the great "free speech" champion, Avocat Pascale DeSalés to defend this common criminal pretending to be an environmentalist. What a load of rubbish and waste of Parliamentary resources. I do hope you have learned English High Court procedures because Calvin will carve you up and serve you for Sunday roast if you slip up . . . or, rather, when you slip up. And I do hope that you are familiar with the Queen's English.* He admired himself, again, in the mirror. *What a sharp figure, still, for a man my age.* He smiled to himself and ignored the two as they got DeSalés robed and wigged.

"See you in Court, gentlemen." Montclare-Twigg, QC made his exit, dramatically.

Desales didn't notice. He was enjoying the costuming and adjusting his wig in the mirror. Unbelievable! If Roy could see him now!

Taliaferro spoke, sotto voce, "Glad he's gone. You know, we've been imprisoned now for over eight months awaiting trial, thanks to the Crown's delay tactics. Unconscionable. Really an unfair treatment of Zshrah Zshrooh."

"God bless you."

"Pardon?"

"You sneezed?"

"Sneezed?" And then he immediately felt embarrassed. He had mispronounced the name of the client, Gerard Giroux, beyond recognition of even his own avocat.

"Pardon, my French is a bit deficient, Mr. DeSalés."

"That's perfectly okay! I have many 'pardon my French' moments too."

Taliaferro looked on blankly. There were obviously some language barriers at work. But he thought, notwithstanding, what a damned decent young barrister Monsieur DeSalés would have made, had he only had the good fortune to have been born British.

. . .

Montclare-Twigg sat at the trial table with arms crossed while his clerk, Martha, methodically emptied his briefcase and arranged the file brief materials before him. Sections of the paginated bundle were meticulously numbered with additional sticky notes. The notes were emblazoned with initials, "M.T. – Q.C." in a stylish rococo typeface. His junior, Maurice Fables, joined him at the trial table.

"Mr. Montclare-Twigg, how are we today, sir? Is there anything else you may need?"

"No, Fables. I've been living this brief for nearly nine months. It's time to give it birth, wouldn't you say?"

"Ha ha, yes, sir! Very good!"

Fables produced a nosegay of flowers from his own briefcase. He chuckled, "For you, sir. Our best defense against this particular defendant."

Montclare-Twigg took the bouquet and laughed, "Oh, very good, Fables! Singular!"

They watched as Taliaferro and DeSalés took their places at the defense's side of the trial table. Taliaferro unpacked his briefcase and set the paginated bundle of court documents before DeSalés.

Suddenly they heard a disturbance. Giroux was being escorted up the stairs leading from the holding cell to the dock, accompanied by a custody officer. Giroux was speaking loudly, objecting to having had his sunflower pin confiscated by the officer before ascending the stairs. He swore at the officer in French. The officer ignored him. Giroux looked over to the trial table and saw Taliaferro beckoning for him to quiet down. He took his seat and stared icily out at the courtroom.

"Now's a good time to confer with our man. The jury's not been seated yet."

They left the trial table and walked a few paces over to the dock. Giroux watched blankly as the officer admitted the two. Giroux knew Taliaferro from the initial meeting. But he stared at Desales, wondering who the hell this person was. Where was his chosen avocat, the great DeSalés? He was beginning to think it was another British trick. Some young, last-minute amateur sent in to replace DeSalés.

He pointed at Desales. "Qui es-tu? Comment tu t'appelles?"

Desales thought it odd that everyone here wanted to try out Creole when they met him. Strangers at home never seemed to guess that he was part Creole, but here they all seemed to just be able to look at him and tell. *Crazy.* And the guy's "how are you" in Creole was way off. He corrected him and responded back, "Ah, yes, 'Koman ou ye?' Mwen trè byen, mèsi."

Giroux thought, *Great, glad to know he's well, but who is he and why the hell is he here?* "Okay, tu vas bien. Mais pourquoi es-tu là?"

"Pouki sa ou là?" Desales hated to continually correct the guy. He would respond that he was his attorney for the mock trial. Hopefully that would do it, and the guy would drop the Creole thing. It was getting a little annoying. The whole separate "dock" thing in the courtroom was crazy, though. "Mwen se avoka pou demonstrasyon jijman."

Giroux's face went ashen. His worst fear had come true. This child with atrocious grammar and a bizarre accent was going to be his avocat, not DeSalés. This ruined everything.

The court usher entered the courtroom. Taliaferro and Desales quickly returned to the trial table. All immediately stood, expecting the entrance of his Lordship. But the usher waved them down.

"Please remain seated. I'm just here to announce that his Lordship has been unavoidably delayed due to . . . traffic issues and that another Justice shall be serving in his Lordship's stead. There will be a very short delay. Perhaps ten to twenty minutes. Thank you."

The usher was glad he did not slip up and mention the reason for the delay, the M-25 seize-up. Mentioning such may have been considered as prejudicial to the defense. One had to be careful.

Montclare-Twigg grimaced at Fables. "You've got to be kidding! What the hell has happened to Calvin? Fables, quickly. Find out who the hell is taking this trial."

"Yes, sir, I'll seek out the usher."

"Dear God, let's hope it's not the bitch recorder."

"I don't think they'd give her a case this big. I'll find out."

Desales looked toward Taliaferro. "Is this part of the exercise?"

"Ha. Yes, I suppose. British trials can be a bit of a crapshoot. But, on the whole, this is probably good for us. The Prosecution has been particularly cozy with his Lordship, so any other judge may be beneficial."

Giroux began yelling something in French. Taliaferro quickly looked over and motioned for him to be quiet.

Desales began his review of the paginated bundle. He was shocked at the size of the document. It seemed extraordinarily detailed for a mock trial exercise. This would be a challenge. But he remembered what his coach, History teacher Tom Crowder, always said: "Don't freak out at the amount of paper. It's a head game. The true issues will jump out at you." Desales steeled himself and began to skim through the materials. The facts and witness statements outlined in the brief were fascinating.

Montclare-Twigg spoke loudly enough to be overheard by Taliaferro and DeSalés. "Fables, I don't see any silk over there, do you?"

"Why, no sir."

"Yes, thought not." Montclare-Twigg folded his hands and looked over toward Taliaferro, smugly.

Desales looked up. "What is he saying?"

"Oh, he's just rubbing in my face that I am a junior. His wearing silk is an acknowledgment of an elevated status. I have not taken silk, which means I am a junior, but at least I am a bona fide senior junior."

"Really? Back home, I'm the reverse. I'm a junior senior because of my curriculum. We don't have any special fabrics. But successful juniors and seniors sometimes get a cloth letter to wear."

Taliaferro thought, *Another oddity of the French legal system.* He pictured senior attorneys wearing cloth letters on their robes. *Peculiar.*

Desales figured that Taliaferro must have been taking some kind of post-grad classes because he was definitely beyond college age. And the opponents were pretty old-looking too. Then again, Coach Crowder did say that a lot of people enter the legal profession as a second career. He resumed his review of the bundle.

It seemed fairly simple. The hypothetical defendant was named Gerard Giroux, the French leader of an environmental group called the Insular Rebellion. The IR had been calling for the UK to immediately divest and disengage from its associations with the oil industry and turn to solar energy. Giroux had organized a protest with local IR members, targeting the British Museum. The protest had begun peacefully. The busload of demonstrators with signs and placards arrived at a rear entrance of the museum. Many were dressed in elaborate sunflower costumes. Their faces formed the center of the flower, surrounded by large floppy yellow petals. The group had conspired with a sympathetic museum guard to let them enter. Other demonstrators wearing sunflower buttons and badges entered the museum as paying visitors and joined the protesters. Once admitted, they assembled in the main lobby, the Great Court.

Giroux then began a boisterous chant, "Fuck big oil. Solar forever!" with the help of a loudhailer, surreptitiously supplied by the same guard. Demonstrators in the sunflower costumes blocked access to works of art by performing dances they called their "opening to the sun ritual." Several glued their hands to the works of art and the walls and floors of the museum to avoid being removed bodily. Other protesters split off, assigned to various wings.

The police called to the scene tried to grab Giroux, who eluded capture by running through the crowds. He eventually worked his way to one of the staircases in the Great Court for his denouement: the unfurling of a large tapestry. The tapestry depicted a monstrous metallic oil can creature urinating oil onto the British Union Jack. The arrest of a boisterous Giroux and his compatriots soon followed. Giroux was charged with the offense of committing and inciting an affray.

Fables returned to the trial table. "Disturbing news, sir. It's going to be the Recorder, Rebecca Davenport-Bligh."

Montclare-Twigg threw his pen down onto the table. "Oh, fuck all! Of all the rum luck! She hates me, you know, Fables. We went to Uni together. I've never understood why she's harbored such ill will."

Fables thought to himself, *Well, but for your calling her a "nasty bitch" publicly, on several occasions, no reason at all.*

Montclare-Twigg regrouped. In the big picture, nothing changed. The case would be in the hands of a jury. A jury of hardworking Brits whose passions he would inflame, quite easily. He had a plan, and he would stick to it. But it would have been a lot easier if Calvin was sitting on that bench.

Desales was still working his way through the bundle. He now understood that the guy playing Giroux was trying to speak French. The moot court people had actually arranged for a French speaking actor to play the hypothetical French defendant. *Awesome!* He looked over to Taliaferro. "I need to look a few things up online if that's allowed. I don't have my phone. Do you have web access on your laptop? Can I use it?"

"Yes. Certainly! Here you go." He pushed the laptop over.

"Thanks." He checked online to confirm a few things. Coach Crowder said to "always, and I mean always, be prepared." He also said to "keep it simple, stupid. No one wants to hear a lot of hot air."

The jury had been seated. The court usher rose. "Be upstanding in court." The judge, dressed in a red robe with white fur cuffs, entered and took her seat at the bench. As the jury was sworn in, Desales felt a flutter of excitement. This was going to be an incredibly realistic mock trial!

Montclare-Twigg received a "go ahead" glance from the judge and began to speak. "May it please the Court, I prosecute this case, R. v. Giroux, on behalf of the Crown—my learned friend Mr. DeSalés defends."

Desales heard the sounds of the gallery and participants taking their seats. He saw Taliaferro sit down, so he took his seat too.

Montclare-Twigg continued standing and addressed the jury. "Members of the jury, I would like to take this opportunity to explain what this case is about. The Defendant has been charged the offense of criminal affray. On Friday 16th of November last year at about noon, our national institution, the British Museum, was set upon by the defendant, Gerard Giroux, a French citizen, then illegally on our shores." He spoke sneeringly and pointed back to the man in the dock. "And what did this Frenchman do?" Montclare-Twigg had emphasized the word Frenchman, contemptuously, rolling his eyes, dramatically. "The evidence you will hear today from eyewitnesses will describe the riotous affray caused by that man and his agents. You will hear evidence of how that Frenchman sent his minions, many clothed in preposterous costumes, to meet with him to provoke public outrage and terror at the museum. You will hear evidence of his followers gluing themselves to our national treasures, our British art, in destructive acts of desecration and violence. Lastly, you will learn of the great outrage committed against the British people—the unfurling of an obscene and disgraceful tapestry, so distasteful in its disrespect to the British people as to prevent me from describing such in detail. But, and my apologies to you members of the jury, the evidence will be shown, and witnesses will attest to the specifics of that violent act against Britannia."

Judge Davenport-Bligh was biting her tongue. As usual, the pompous ass was taking his statement of the case just to the edge of propriety's limits, nearly testifying himself, potentially prejudicing the jury. She smoldered quietly.

"And, what was the result of these violent attacks on Great Britain and her hallowed artistic and cultural institution? Chaos. A riotous and damaging affray causing personal and monetary injury to the museum and its innocent patrons as well as to Great Britain, herself!"

He glanced smugly at the jury and took his seat proudly.

Desales realized it was his turn. He stood, facing the jury. "Good afternoon. How are you folks doing today?"

Montclare-Twigg immediately rose to his feet. "My Lady, my learned friend seems under the impression that he can have a nice chat with the jurors in High Court?"

He sat back down. Desales looked up to the judge, confusedly. She responded. "Yes, that is correct. You may not engage in conversation with a jury in a British criminal court. I do understand that you are from a foreign land, but you must please adhere to our Rules of Court."

Montclare-Twigg smirked and looked over to Fables, rolling his eyes.

"Yes, your Honor! My apologies, ma'am!"

Montclare-Twigg's eyes lit up in delight. He whispered to Fables, "oh . . . here we go again. Wait for it!"

Judge Davenport-Bligh sighed and shook her head. "And, although it is clear that you are trying to address me in a respectful manner, please understand that you are to address me as My Lady, as I am sitting as a Red Judge."

"Yes, ma'am—I mean yes, My Lady! My apologies!"

Taliaferro looked down at the table, sheepishly. He should have coached DeSalés on a few of these subtleties. He might have guessed that a French avocat would be in the dark on some of the local peculiarities.

Desales took a breath. *Strike two.* He turned back to the jury and regrouped. "Ladies and gentlemen of the jury, the evidence you will hear today will prove that the defendant did not commit the offense with which he is charged." He nodded to the judge and sat back down.

The judge was stunned. And pleasantly surprised. She had been warned that DeSalés was a rambling gobby, a gasbag, a speechmaker, who never knew when to quit. She was prepared to sanction him publicly, if necessary. This was quite the opposite of what she expected. But how welcome! Plus, he had very little French accent. Perhaps just a touch. And he was a decent looking young man. Nicely dressed. Olive skinned. *Mediterranean. Probably from the South of France.*

Montclare-Twigg looked over to Fables, in surprise. They too had been expecting a mind-numbing monologue. Montclare-Twigg shrugged and called his first witness.

"I call Detective Constable Samuel Corson."

The DC was duly sworn in by the usher. Desales sat ready with notepaper and pencil.

Montclare-Twigg began his examination of the witness with the usual preliminaries, such as identifying the witness and establishing his rank and office within the Metropolitan Police. "DC Corson, would you describe the scene and events that occurred at the British Museum on 16 November 2018 and your response to those events?"

"Yes. At or about noon that day I received a communication from Headquarters advising of a serious row taking place at the British Museum. I was directed to muster a TSG of eight, which means a territorial support group, to respond and report back. I did so, and our unit arrived a few minutes after noon."

"Continue please, Detective Constable."

"I found the museum in a state of chaos. Various individuals had assembled in the Great Court, which is the large entry gallery of the museum, and within other galleries. These individuals were chanting slogans, performing some sort of dance, and disrupting the business of the museum and disturbing the museum visitors."

"Approximately how many of these individuals did you see engaging in this behavior in the Great Court?"

"I recall approximately twenty who were disguised in costumes and performing some sort of dance. I saw approximately another twenty criminals holding signs and chanting loud slogans."

Desales rose to his feet, "Objection."

Montclare-Twigg smirked and looked over to the jury, knowingly, waiting for the next round of fireworks.

Judge Davenport-Bligh glared at Desales. "Counsel, it is not necessary to make an 'objection' in this court. We don't recognize that term here. If you would like to raise a point of contention with QC Montclare-Twigg's direct examination of the witness, please simply stand and make your point, politely."

Desales thought, *whoops, foul tip.* "Yes, My Lady. My apologies, again."

She nodded in acknowledgment. "And the witness will please refrain from making conclusory statements about whether any individual you witnessed was a criminal."

"Yes, My Lady."

"Now, please continue."

Montclare-Twigg nodded. "Thank you, My Lady. Now, DC Corson, describe your next actions with respect to these individuals."

"When I arrived and after witnessing the aforementioned individuals, I met with the Museum's Acting Curator in Charge, Ms. Martha Mayhew, and the Museum's Director of Security, Mr. Robert Dawes. Ms. Mayhew and Mr. Dawes confirmed that the individuals at issue were deemed trespassers who refused to quit the premises. She requested our assistance in expelling the individuals from the museum. She told me that there were other groups assembling in several of the other galleries."

"What did you do next?"

"I contacted Headquarters advising of the situation and requesting additional backup and vans with which to make arrests. Two more TSGs of eight each and six Met vans. I then directed the officers of my TSG to begin requesting the trespassers quit the premises or be arrested. I myself confronted a sign carrier and directed them to leave the premises. Rather than doing so, the sign carrier sat down and glued themselves to the museum floor. Apparently, this prompted similar behavior from several of the other sign carriers. Approximately half glued themselves to the floor."

"Yes, thank you, DC Corson." Montclare-Twigg looked to the judge and then the jury with a dramatically lugubrious expression. "Now, unfortunately, I must ask you what particular slogan you were hearing being made by the trespassers throughout this . . . event. And my apologies to My Lady and our jury in advance."

"Yes, they were all yelling, 'Fuck big oil. Solar energy forever.' And they kept at it throughout."

Montclare-Twigg shook his head as though deeply offended. "Thank you, DC Corson. Now, you had mentioned dancers in some sort of costumes. Could you elaborate?"

"Yes, roughly twenty individuals disguised themselves as flowers, I believe."

Desales stood. Montclare-Twigg scowled and made a pretense of sitting down without actually doing so. "Pardon me, My Lady, but no evidence has been put forward indicating that the so-called costumes were intended as disguises, as opposed to simply being costumes."

He quickly sat down and Montclare-Twigg straightened back up.

"Yes, DC Corson. Again, I must caution you about conclusory testimony."

"Yes, My Lady."

Montclare-Twigg continued. "Now, My Lady and members of the jury, I would like to direct your attention to the bundles with which you have been provided and the screens located before you. These represent evidence agreed to in advance prior hereto by the Crown and Defense. I direct your attention to the photograph on tab 16 of your packet, which shall be projected onto the screens."

The evidence monitors clicked on showing a still color photo of protestors sitting on the floor and a group of dancers dressed in sunflower costumes.

"Who took this photograph, DC Corson?"

"I took that photo with my mobile phone, sir."

"Does the photo accurately depict the individuals you have just testified about?"

"It does, sir."

"Thank you. Now please describe your interactions with such costumed individuals."

"I got the attention of one of the dancers and told the individual to cease or they would be arrested as a trespasser."

"How did they respond?"

"The individual refused to quit the premises. They continued their dancing."

"Thank you." The screens flickered off.

"Now, DC Corson, are you familiar with the Defendant, Mr. Gerard Giroux?"

"I am."

"Is he present in this courtroom?"

"Yes sir, he is sitting back there in the dock." He pointed to Giroux.

Giroux stood and began pointing and yelling, "Trou du cul!"

The judge spoke. "Counsel. Please know that if your client makes further outbursts, he will be taken back to his holding cell."

Taliaferro responded. "Yes, My Lady." Taliaferro turned around and motioned for Giroux to sit down.

"Now, did you see that man at the museum that day?"

"Yes. A moment or two following my directing a dancer to quit the premises, he appeared at the top of the right staircase in the Grand Court. He had a loudhailer and was yelling that same slogan."

"Did he take any further actions?"

"Yes, he put the loudhailer down, and he and another individual walked down the stairs to about halfway down. There they unfurled a very large cloth sheet containing a drawing."

Montclare-Twigg again assumed a mournful expression. "Now, My Lady and members of the jury, please know that it offends me to have to expose you to a certain image, but justice requires that I do so. From tab 42 in the packet." The screen lights flicked on to reveal a photo of the infamous oil can monster urinating oil onto the Union Jack.

Several members of the gallery gasped.

"Now, DC Corson, does this photo correspond with the image you saw that day?"

"It does."

"Did you have any further interactions with the Defendant?"

"Yes, I and two other officers climbed the stairs in order to make an arrest. But the defendant and his associate ran back up the stairs away from us. I called out for two other officers to assist, and before long, we four were able to subdue and arrest the defendant."

"How would you describe the scene in the Great Court, thereafter?"

"Chaos, sir. The protesters on the floor continued chanting the . . . slogan, and the dancers became even more . . . energetic in their dancing. The additional units arrived, and we began making arrests. The noise level was quite extreme, as you can imagine. Several of the museum visitors had rolled their guide maps into tubes and began striking at the demonstrators as we took them away."

"My Lady, no further questions for this witness." Montclare-Twigg sat and looked on, smugly.

Desales rose. "Officer, you stated that you called for backup. You must have had some fear that the Defendant and the protesters would attack or injure you or your unit, correct? Isn't that why you asked for backup?"

DC Corson looked puzzled. He glared back, angrily. "Fear? Seriously? Absolutely not. But we did want to restore order, effectively and quickly. That is why I called for backup!" He nodded firmly to the jury.

"You mentioned interacting with the dancing protesters, asking one or more to leave the premises. Is that correct?"

He scowled again. "Yes. As I just testified."

"Do you recall what any of these individuals said to you in response?"

Corson sighed. He knew what was coming. "Well. Some just cursed at me and continued chanting."

"Any others?"

He sighed again. "Yes. Several asked if I would like to dance with them."

The jury began chuckling. Desales had noticed it in the bundle. He figured *quit while you're ahead.* "Nothing further, My Lady."

Montclare-Twigg called his next witness. "I call Mrs. Martha Mayhew."

A dowdy looking woman in a conservative tweed skirt and blazer took the stand. Her blue-gray hair bore all the signs of a recent and unfortunate homemade dyeing event. After establishing her identity as Curator in Charge that day, Montclare-Twigg began his examination.

"Mrs. Mayhew, we have heard testimony from DC Corson about the antics of the defendant and his henchmen . . ."

Desales began to stand, but sat back down when the Judge stated, "Counsel is cautioned against using prejudicial characterizations of the defendant."

Montclare-Twigg scowled. *Bitch!* "Yes, My Lady. Now, Mrs. Mayhew, we have heard testimony of DC Corson as to the events of that day. Did the museum suffer damage?"

She nodded vigorously. "Yes, of course. The frames and cover plates of seventeen paintings had to be restored due to the glue, the cements used by the individuals. Likewise, we had to remove glue and cement from areas of the floor and surfaces of walls throughout several galleries and the Great Court. One of the museum patrons suffered a fall in the confusion and has filed a claim against the museum. And there was the general cleanup required following such commotion."

"Was there a specific number representing these damages?"

"Yes. Excluding the claim by the visitor, which damages have not yet been adjudicated, Seventy-Eight Thousand, Five Hundred Twenty-One pounds sterling. And this, of course, does not represent the injury suffered by the museum for the indignity caused by the Defendant and the demonstrators. The tapestry in particular was an abomination and an insult to both our institution and our British people, everywhere."

Members of the jury nodded sternly in agreement.

Montclare-Twigg began to sit down, expecting the Avocat to jump to his feet to protest. But surprisingly, he did not.

"Mrs. Mayhew, does the accounting reproduced on pages 51 and 52 of the Exhibit bundle accurately represent those calculations?" The jurors turned to the pages.

"It does."

"Thank you, Mrs. Mayhew. My learned friend may have a few questions for you."

Desales stood. "Mrs. Mayhew, describe your feelings when you encountered the demonstrators and demanded they leave."

"Feelings? Well, feelings any sensible person would feel—outrage, displeasure, disgust."

"Were you afraid for the safety of the artwork, as we've had testimony on the cementing?"

"Well, fortunately, we use state of the art protection for our works of art. The trespassers may have thought they were destroying those artworks, but in fact the works were protected by special glass surfaces. We had no concerns but for the expense of replacement and repair."

"Were you fearful for your own safety due to the protesters?"

"Well, no. Certainly not. They may have wanted to provoke fear, but I rather think that the silly flower costumes were a bad choice."

Several members of the jury nodded and laughed.

"Thank you. No further questions."

Fables looked over to Montclare-Twigg, trying to get his attention. He wrote a large question mark on his legal pad and pushed it over. He was concerned about the avocat's seeming lack of fight. It seemed too easy. Montclare-Twigg saw it and pushed it back.

"I call Robert Dawes."

After running down preliminaries, Montclare-Twigg began his examination. "Mr. Dawes, please describe the scene on that day."

"Great confusion. The trespassers were loud, riotous, and destructive."

"What was your response to this behavior?"

"Well, I rallied the museum's security staff and told them to assemble in the Great Court and to begin expelling the trespassers. But it was soon obvious that police intervention was required. That's the point where I contacted the Metropolitan Police."

"You described the scene as riotous. Could you elaborate?"

"Yes. The protesters were extremely boisterous with their chanting. The defendant was yelling through a loudhailer. We were running after the dancing people, but they quickly sat down on the ground and glued themselves, making removal impossible. We were trying to direct ordinary museum visitors to the exits, but some of those also turned out to be protesters and continued to move about, evading our efforts to remove them. The vile tapestry was the worst of it. It was an insult. A slap in the face of all British people. Reprehensible conduct that should be harshly punished."

Several jurors nodded sympathetically. Montclaire-Twigg winced, expecting the avocat or even the judge to protest the prejudicial statements. But they did not. "No further questions, but please stand by for my learned friend."

Desales had been looking at his watch. He was making good time. The exercise would be over soon, and he'd be able to bail Roy out. This fit one of Tom Crowder's Top Ten mock trial scenarios. He stood. "Mr. Dawes, you described the scene as riotous. Were you fearful that things had gotten out of control? Perhaps even concerned for your own safety or the safety of your staff?"

Dawes huffed. "Absolutely not. We were not going to let ourselves be bullied by a Frenchman with a loudhailer. We Brits do not scare that easily. But, we are pretty good at offering an appropriate comeuppance when and as required." He nodded sternly and several members of the jury did likewise.

"No further questions."

Montclare-Twigg had three additional witnesses at the ready. But he felt he had done all he needed. The jury was clearly on his side. He was quite certain that any weak-willed member of the jury would be duly convinced by their stronger peers. The pathetic cross-examination by the great avocat gave him sufficient confidence to rest the case for the Prosecution.

"My Lady, that is the case for the Crown." He nodded and took his seat.

Desales looked over his notes and stood. "My Lady, I would like to submit that there is no case to answer here." He quoted from his notes. "Section 3 of the Public Order Act provides that a person is guilty of affray 'if the conduct of that person is such as would cause a person of reasonable firmness present at the scene to fear for their personal safety.' Each of the Prosecution witnesses testified that they experienced no fear with regards to their personal safety. Thus, although, no doubt, the scene at the museum may have been chaotic and confused, no witness who testified was actually afraid. There is no prima facie case before the Court." He sat back down.

Montclare-Twigg immediately took to his feet. "Preposterous! My Lady, with all due respect, this case is suitable for submission to this jury. We have heard the testimony of the riotous and ugly fracas at the museum that day. We have heard of the significant damage and injuries caused by the Defendant. Undoubtedly, every museum patron present that day was actually or constructively terrorized by these acts and certainly in fear of their personal safety. And I am certainly willing to submit reopening the Crown's case to further establish such, if such is even deemed necessary under the circumstances." He shook his head in disgust and looked over to Fables smugly.

Judge Rebecca Davenport-Bligh smiled to herself. She could now finally turn the tables on her old Uni "friend." "Thank you. Having considered the submission of Defense and response by the Crown, I am prepared to rule. Crown's case in chief has duly concluded. No prima facie case of the offense of affray has been submitted for consideration. Therefore, this case is dismissed, and the Defendant is free to leave. The jury is discharged."

With that, the gallery burst into excitement. Several spectators yelled their disappointment. Jurors looked to one another in confusion. Several in the gallery cheered loudly. Taliaferro stood and shook Desales's hand. "Congratulations, sir! Well played!"

The guard in the dock looked over to the confused Giroux and said, "You're free to go, mate." He opened the dock door to the courtroom. Giroux walked out, stunned. This had not gone as planned! Not at all! His avocat was engaged by IR to make several long speeches about the precarious environmental conditions on the earth, the criminality of Big Oil, the need for divestiture and the necessity of solar. Giroux would lose his case, of course. DeSalés was to be dragged away with Giroux and charged with contempt. The resulting media attention and protest would bring further credibility to the IR! But now, it was all gone!

He began walking angrily to the trial table. Desales didn't notice. He was handing the brief back to Taliaferro. He figured he'd better bail Roy out while he still had the robe and wig costume. *Might be easier.* Then they could pick up his backpack and award at the check-in room. He headed back toward the dock.

Giroux grabbed Taliaferro by the shoulder from behind. "Cochon! Fils de pute! Con!"

Taliaferro was shocked. "Sir! What's wrong? You just won your case? Do you understand that?"

The guard saw Desales approaching and opened the door. "Thanks! I just need to visit the holding cells for a minute. I have a real client down there."

"Yes, sir."

He found his way to the administrative officer in Security. "I'm here to bail out one Roy G. Biv?"

"Yes, my lord. He's cleared for 'own recog,' so he is all yours." Desales was escorted to the cell.

Desales saw Roy's eyes light up. "Sonny! Well look at you in that fancy wig! An you got a gradiatin' gown on, too! Go to war, Miss Agnes! Boy, the things they make a feller do here, just ta get someone outta the hoosegow! So, I learnt it ain't legal crabbin' here. Can ya b'lieve that?"

He and Desales hugged warmly. "Love ya, Roy!"

"Yep, love ya too, Sonny!"

"Guess what. I won a Forensics award! They had a mock trial!"

"Way to go, Sonny! That's muh boy!"

"Yes. Was a pretty easy one." He thought, *Just like Coach Crowder always said: "Never forget the actual elements of the crime."*

Desales quickly signed off on the paperwork. They picked up Roy's bags from the property clerk.

"I need to drop this outfit back upstairs and pick up my backpack and award. Let's take the elevator."

As they headed down the corridor to the lift, Roy noticed a strange man being brought into the lockup in handcuffs. He was struggling fiercely against two police officers, one on each side. He ranted loudly in French and broken English. Something about not being an imposter. And several harsh phrases in French.

"What's that feller complainin' 'bout Sonny? Sumpthin' 'bout avocados?"

They found their way over to the check-in room. The room was dark. The guy running the mock trial was gone. Desales found his backpack and phone. But he didn't see any awards. He and Roy then heard an alarm bell ringing in the distance. One of the Security officers entered the room.

"Oh, sorry, sirs. Time to lock this room up. And they are asking for members of the public and attorneys to head to the exits, so you'll need to leave."

"Wow? That's odd? May I leave this wig and robe here?"

"Yes, sir. I'm sure it will be attended to after order is restored."

He saw their quizzical looks.

"There's been a disturbance following a trial upstairs. A defendant attacking his own barrister and several jurors attacking the Prosecuting Attorney for some reason. Quite an affray, I'm afraid."

. . .

Mick the Flick had not visited the Savoy for several years. He thought back to his last visit. It terminated with an unplanned and entirely unwelcome departure, courtesy of an unfortunate disagreement with management regarding some business or another. But, clerical turnover being what it was, he was willing to let bygones be bygones. And these lads had scored quite the suite.

"May I assist you with the safe? It can be challenging to operate."

Robbie said, "Sure. The combination is 2019."

"Very good. Oh, here it is." He rummaged through the contents of the safe. He pulled out the passports and confirmed the lack of "folding money" within and tossed them back in. He brought forth the dark velvet ring box. He opened it before the boys.

"Decent. Passable, I'd say."

Robbie chimed in. "A whale made it. My cousin said it was from some whales."

"Ah. Fascinating. In that case, 'save the whales!' We may be able to just squeeze 100 quid out of it. Pounds sterling, that is."

"Okay. Do you know the place to take it?"

"Certainly!" He quickly searched his memory for the closest pawn shop that would not summarily eject him upon entry. *Yes. Perfect.*

"So, it's very simple. We shall taxi up to the Circus Pawn on Oxford Street. Lovely establishment and usually generous with their payments."

After a tedious twenty-minute taxi ride, they finally arrived. Mr. Mick paid the taxi driver and provided a remarkably frugal tip. The driver drove away, seeming displeased.

"Now, you lads are not adults and may not enter these premises, sadly, under threat of arrest. But, leave it to Mr. Mick to take care of this transaction and obtain the hundred pounds plus proper receipt. After you bail out your unfairly imprisoned uncle, he need simply bring you lads back here, where, armed with the receipt and the 100 quid, plus modest carrying charges made by the establishment, you will receive back the whale ring. Easy peasy."

"Okay, Mr. Mick."

Within a few minutes, Mick the Flick had successfully pawned the ring for four hundred pounds sterling. He organized the notes:

three hundred twenty in Mick's breast pocket; eighty in hand. He met the boys outside the building.

"Well, there was some minor difficulty, lads. After extended bargaining, Mr. Mick was only able to obtain eighty pounds." He held out the money for them to see. "This is unfortunate, as you would need twenty more quid. But let me think on this for just a moment."

He put the bills in his trousers pocket and began rubbing his chin. Several lengthy moments passed. "Yes! That would work."

Robbie looked up. "What's your idea, Mr. Mick?"

"Well, there is a mild risk involved. But look just over there." He pointed to Purefoy's Offtrack Shop.

"What's that?"

"Well, it's a place where one may place a wager on a particular horse that is racing. If the horse wins, you receive a good deal more back besides your wager. The amount depends on the wager and various things like 'odds.' Let's take a walk that way."

They stood in front of the betting parlor. Doyle spoke up. "You know, I don't think so, Mr. Mick. Our mom and dad are against gambling and stuff. They say it's a good way to lose money."

Mick adopted a serious demeanor. "Well, your mum 'n dad are quite correct. I would never make a blind wager on a horse that wasn't reasonably certain to win. Good advice, those two. Of course, I do have some knowledge of these things and believe your money will be reasonably secure. But, it's up to you if you want to bail your uncle out of a miserable jail cell. I'm just as happy to turn these funds over to you and send you back safely in a taxi."

Robbie looked over to Doyle. "I think we should let Mr. Mick take a chance since he thinks he can win the extra money?"

"Well, lads, that's 'reasonably certain.' But these things are never guaranteed. 'There's many a slip twixt cup and lip' says Mr. Mick."

Robbie and Doyle weren't sure about the cup and lip, but Doyle said, "Okay, Mr. Mick. Let's go in."

Mick sighed. "Well, boys, again, you are underage, so you'll need to wait outside for just a touch. But Mr. Mick will be right back."

Once inside, he checked to make sure Horatio was not on the floor. He breathed a sigh of relief. He walked over to the refreshment counter.

"Kathy gal! Looking lovely."

She looked on cautiously. "Well, well. 'Mick the Flick. Fastest fingers on Fleet.' What ya want, Flickers? Gotta be cash, though."

"Oh, I am quite flush, presently! Could you pour me one of your special coffees, neat? And, Kathy, pour one for yourself!"

"Ha. There's laughs. No thanks, Flickie. Wanna keep this job. But if ya want plain old hot coffee just ask."

"Ah, very well! I shall abstain." He went about the business of rearranging his bills in his coat pocket, placing seventy-five with the three hundred twenty in his coat pocket. He made sure that Kathy and everyone else around took note of his current "solvent" circumstances. Good for PR. He kept out a five-pound note for a taxi for the two sprogs. He figured he'd better get out quick before Horatio showed up.

"Kathy gal, I must bid my tatty byes. Toodles."

"Ta, Flickers."

Outside, Mick adopted a disgusted and forlorn look. "Lads. The worst imaginable has happened. Mr. Mick had been given concrete 'inside' information on a dazzling gelding. But it was a lie! They took us for everything but this five pounds. I am so sorry, lads! I have failed you. The gelding failed us both. We've just enough for the taxi back home!"

He held out the five-pound note for Doyle to see.

Doyle looked at the note. He knew they were in trouble. And Uncle Roy would be stuck in jail. Not good.

Robbie looked at Mick, puzzled. "We didn't get a hundred pounds?"

Mick shook his head forlornly. "Correct, young chum. Correct. Shall we fetch a taxi back?"

Robbie, like Doyle, was in a state of shock. "Okay."

Mick hailed a taxi. One came over immediately.

"Sir, here's a fiver. Take these lads back to the Savoy or as close as five quid will take them. He handed over the pawn receipt to Robbie. "Here's your ticket for when you spring the whale's ring. Now, sadly, I must say g'bye, lads. Must take my leave and head back to my office. Laters!" He slammed the door shut.

Robbie yelled out the window, "Aren't you coming with us?"

But Mr. Mick must not have heard him, because he just kept walking away.

Amir Khalifa looked at the five-pound note. It was not going to get them anywhere near the Savoy. He craned his neck back to get a better look at his fare. Two little boys. In matching blue suits. He wondered what was going on.

"So, boys. You want to go to the Savoy?"

Robbie spoke up. "Yes, sir."

"Who was that man?"

Doyle jumped in. "A businessman or something. His name was Mick. He was helping us get our uncle out of jail. But Mr. Mick made a bad bet and lost the bail money we had gotten for the wedding ring they need for tonight."

Amir's head was spinning. "Ah . . . okay."

The boys were very quiet. He hated to raise the issue because he could tell they were just two little kids. And they looked defeated. "Now guys, I'm happy to take you as far as I can, but the five pounds won't be enough to make it all the way to the Savoy. But I could take you all the way there, if you had additional money available to you, once you get to the hotel? You know, someone like your mom or dad?"

Robbie spoke, "Desales will! He has his dad's wallet!"

"Okay, okay." He felt bad for the little guys. Something odd was going on. He figured, even if he didn't get the full fare, he had done quite well for the day. Two trips back and forth to Heathrow and plenty of work around town. Traffic had been horrible all day due to the demonstrators, and frustrated bus riders had been hailing taxis, right and left. This would be his last fare, anyway.

They finally wiggled their way through Soho and Leister Square and over to the Savoy. "Okay, guys, we're here." He held the door for them. He handed the five-pound note back to Doyle. "Tell you what, guys, the fare's just a little under twelve pounds. Hang onto your five pounds. I will pull over, just down the drive, and wait for ten minutes. If you don't come back down in ten, I will just drive on, and it will be a free fare. How does that sound?"

Robbie looked up. "Really? Well thank you, sir!"

The two made their way through the lobby and over to the bank of elevators. They wanted to get back to the room and find Desales as quickly as they could. They didn't notice the ruckus occurring at the front desk. The Reservation Manager was trying to smooth over the waters.

"This is outrageous! We've been loyal customers of the Savoy for decades! We'd like our suite right now, thank you! We have a wedding to attend in a matter of hours and must get ourselves readied! We've suffered through an absolutely horrible day of travel—I doubt we'll ever come into London again! Traffic's bad enough in Sussex!"

"Ma'am, I do understand your displeasure. We will get this resolved ASAP. Most likely, there was some glitch in the system. Please, if you and your party could just have a seat in one of our very comfortable sofas, just back there." He pointed. "I will find you once this is straightened out. And our bellman, Romney, will take care of your luggage. Romney?"

He couldn't figure it out. Clearly, some party had been checked into suite 1245. Perhaps that first party was placed in the wrong suite? That would mean a different suite would be open under some other name. But whose name? Which suite? He'd have to phone up to 1245 and discretely ask for the names of that party. He could then determine the suite they should have been placed in and offer it to the Youngley-Houghs. Hopefully that suite will have been paid in advance, too. Worst case scenario, he'd have to refund a portion of the 12,000 pound booking on 1245 to make things even.

. . .

Desales and Roy had taxied back to the Savoy. The ride took forever, thanks to endless traffic jams. Desales looked at his watch: nearly three p.m. But still plenty of time to get everyone over to Uncle Roland's.

"Glad ya got us checked in awhile, Sonny. Ya know, they usually make ya wait."

"Yes, Royal. I think you'll be satisfied with the room."

Desales unlocked the door with the electronic key and held the door open for Roy.

"Well, go to war, Miss Agnes! Look at this big fancy place!"

"Yes! I thought you'd approve! Right up there with the Ho Jo, huh?"

"Cheese 'n crackers! This may be better!" Roy began exploring the massive suite. "Look at that, Sonny! If ya have ta go ta baffroom, there's three of 'em!"

"Yes, Roy!"

Roy checked out each bathroom. "Looks like all the shairs 'r broke, though. Ain't got no doors? Might havta go downa celler an look for a tarp or somethin' ta throw over 'em. But the terlets look okay."

"That's good, Roy."

Roy looked around some more. "So, where's the boys at, Sonny? Outside in the park?"

Desales looked around for Doyle and Robbie. *Uh oh.* He called their names. He called them again, louder.

"Ah . . . I'm not sure, Roy. I told them to stay in the room and to wait for me." He thought, *Of course, that was hours ago.* He didn't blame them for going out. "So, yeah, they probably went to the park. Once you get settled in, I'll run down to fetch them."

The lock clicked and the door opened. Desales saw it was the boys. *Thank God!*

"Hey, there's the fellers! I wuz just askin' Sonny 'bout ya!" Roy noticed that they both looked anxious. "Everthin' okay, boys?"

Doyle let Robbie explain, "So, the taxi is down there and waiting for like twelve pounds if we have it. Because we had to come back from the horse place near the place where the ring is now."

Desales tried to make sense of it. "Slow down! What did you say about a ring?"

"Ah . . . you know, the one the whales made that was in the safe."

Desales ran over and quickly entered the combination. He looked in. He jammed his hand in. It was gone! He turned around, shocked. "Guys, did you take the ring out? Where is it?"

Doyle spoke: "Ah, like Robbie said. The man, Mick, said he saw Uncle Roy being sent to jail. So he said we'd need a hundred pounds for bail money. But we didn't have it, so he thought the ring would be good enough, and he took us up to a pawn shop somewhere, but he only got eighty for the ring. So he said he could get the other twenty if he bet on a horse at a place, like, just a few doors away. But he lost seventy-five. But he gave us five so we could take the taxi back. But Amir said it wouldn't be enough, and he'd wait ten minutes. Then it would be free."

Desales shook his head. He felt the onset of panic. Something he had trained himself not to feel. Uncle Roy simply stood with his mouth open.

Desales caught his breath. "Okay. You said there's a taxi down there waiting to be paid. And he knows where the pawn shop is?"

"Yes."

"Did the guy give you a receipt?"

"Yes. Here it is."

Desales looked at it. Four hundred pounds plus interest and carrying charges! He felt his heart palpitate.

"Shit. Okay. Everybody, let's get down to that taxi and get the ring back!

Amir checked his phone. *Time to move out.* He began pulling out of his makeshift parking space. He checked the rearview mirror to find a sea of blue seersucker, waving and yelling. He stopped.

. . .

They were nearly back to Oxford Circus. Robbie had to sit on Desales's lap the whole time. He was not going to complain. Roy had been remarking about the sights and sounds of London. "Jeezy Christmas. This place is busier than a one-eyed dog in a meat house!"

Amir was on his mobile phone. "Yes, my love. I know. I know. It is kind of an emergency for these guys. Yes. As soon as I can. I promise. You and the boys should just go ahead and eat without me."

They heard a tinny yelling sound coming from Amir's phone. He held the phone away from his ear. "Yes, I know, my love, but I will get takeaway tomorrow instead, okay? Ah . . . I don't know. We have some tinned things, right? Tuna and ghormeh sabzi and . . . hello?" She had rung off.

Desales had been trying without success to phone Uncle Stef. They would need cash to get the ring out of hock. Somehow, the calls would not go through. Amir noticed. He handed back his phone.

"Here, try mine. Sometimes phones from other places don't work here."

"Thank you, sir! I really appreciate it!"

Stef's phone vibrated. He had left it on his dresser and didn't hear it. He was too busy looking at himself in the bathroom mirror, reciting his wedding vows. *Crap!* He kept getting nervous and messing it up. He'd keep trying.

Desales left a voice message. "Hey, Uncle Stef! Just wanted to say hi and uh, also, when you get this could you please, please call me? But use this guy's number. Super nice guy, Amir. My cell's not working. Okay. Bye." He handed the phone back.

Amir squeezed the taxi into an "almost" parking space a few doors from the pawn shop. He figured he'd better go in with them. They were a mess.

Desales showed the pawn ticket to the clerk. "Sir, so what happened was, my cousin, who is that little guy there, was tricked into handing over this ring to a crook who brought it in here and pawned it." He pointed to Robbie.

Robbie thought, *And Doyle skates again!*

The clerk responded in a heavy accent. "Yes. You pay this, you get ring." He grabbed his calculator and punched in numbers. He pointed it toward Desales. "See." The calculator read £482. Neither he nor Roy had that kind of money. Desales had a secured credit card with a whopping balance of $68.00. Roy had never owned a credit card. And Desales knew converting the pounds to dollars would be extremely painful. And Stef had not phoned back.

Amir came forward and began speaking Farsi. Loudly. He tapped on the glass counter. He pointed up to the security camera. The clerk responded back in Farsi, even louder. And then the clerk pointed over toward the wall, to the sign warning of carrying charges and interest in bold letters. Amir continued speaking even louder and smacked the palm of his hand down on the glass counter. He pointed to the boys and then back up to the security camera. The clerk argued back some more. But then he went over and brought back his laptop. He looked at the ticket and clicked on the digital recording of the security camera feed.

He saw the face of the pawn customer. He scowled. He turned the laptop toward Robbie. "Him?"

"Yes, that's the man."

Roy looked at the screen. "That feller's sneakier than a red-eyed weevil in a ketchup factory."

The clerk and Amir began discussing things more quietly. It went on for many minutes. Finally, they were done.

Roy whispered to Desales, "Cheese 'n crackers, feel like I'm in some fern country!"

Amir turned back to the group. "Okay. Here's the deal. He will give you the ring back in return for your agreeing to not bring the cops in and for fifty pounds. That is the best he is willing to do."

Desales thought quicky. He had about twenty pounds with him, and Roy had almost thirty. He reached for his wallet. "Okay. Okay. I think that would work." He was about to ask Roy for his wallet when the clerk handed Desales a fifty-pound note along with the ring box. Desales was stunned. He looked at the fifty and quickly put it in his breast pocket. He opened the box for inspection. He pulled the ring out of the box and held it up to the florescent lights. He saw the squiggly lines for the river on the inside surface of the band.

"Yes. Yes. This is it. Thank you, sir!"

The clerk did not respond and looked on stoically.

Amir nodded to the clerk and said, "Merci."

As they walked back to the taxi, Amir explained. "See, they all have a list of the criminals who sell stolen goods, and all the pawn shops ban them. But whoever was clerking at the shop earlier didn't do a good job. The video showed it was a known criminal. So, we promised to not file a theft report with the police if he would return the ring, plus pay fifty pounds. And, by the way, my fare is going to be around fifty pounds." He smiled and opened the passenger door to his taxi.

. . .

They were pushing up against the clock. The traffic back from Oxford Circus was nightmarish. Roy and Doyle had nodded off. Desales tried to make small talk. He had to speak a little louder than usual because Robbie, seated on his lap, was blocking the sound. "So, Amir, were you a policeman back home?"

He smiled. "This is my home! But I know what you mean. Yes, we are from Iran. But this great country took us in. We had to flee oppression. I was not a policeman. I was an attorney. And a professor, too, at a university. But here, I am a taxi driver."

"Wow! I want to be an attorney, too! I'm planning to go to law school. But I haven't started college yet."

"That's good! I'm sure you will be a good one." He thought back to the crazy story he'd seen on his phone while waiting back at the Savoy. "So, you will like this news story I read. Today at Old Bailey— that's the famous criminal courthouse— some imposter lawyer snuck his way in and handled a big trial of some sort. And he won the case for the defendant! Can you believe that? Beating the Crown is very hard to do even with the correct attorney! And then there was a fight in the courtroom! The defendant was beating up his own attorney, and the jurors were beating up the Crown's attorney! And on top of that, they arrested the actual attorney, thinking he was the imposter! And, crazier, the defendant was interviewed later and says he wants to be tried again, even though he won? Isn't that madness?"

"Wow. That's insane!" Desales thought, *Just my luck. I was right there at Old Bailey and missed it all . . .*

They were hitting more traffic snags. It was just about 4:30, but they still had another mile to go. Desales looked around at the group. He nudged Doyle and Roy awake. "Hey, hey guys. Do any of us even need to get back to the Savoy? We're all dressed in our clothes for the wedding? We don't really need anything, right?"

"Well, yeppers, Sonny. Ain't got no need on my count."

"Doyle?"

"All good."

"Marionette?"

Robbie had no idea what Desales was talking about. But he didn't need the hotel. "No."

"Okay, Amir. Let's change the destination just a bit. The Saveloy. Wellington Street, Covent Garden. It's not far from here."

"Okay, sure. I know it, I think."

Within minutes they had pulled up in front of the hotel.

Desales handed the fifty pound note over to Amir. "And we have more if you need it."

"No. The fifty is fine. And that includes the tip."

They saw Roland walk out the front door in his tux. "Oh, thank God you're here! But there's no sign of Stef. There's supposed to be a car to pick us all up?"

They heard a vibrating sound. Amir clicked on his mobile. "Yes. Yes. He is here."

He handed the phone to Desales. "Stef? Yes, good! Well . . . I was . . . just calling to see how you were." He figured Uncle Stef was somewhat high strung to begin with. Best to avoid unnecessary details. "So, where are you? What? Hang on, I'll put you on speaker."

"Hey, Roy and Rol and guys. So, traffic is completely screwed up. The guy assigned to cart us around is stuck somewhere a few miles away. Are you guys in the lobby?"

Roland yelled, "We're just outside the entrance."

"Okay good. You'll see me in a second or two. Look down the road. I see you guys."

They looked over to see Stef in his tux walking toward them. "Shit, Gremlin! You walked all the way over?"

"Yeah. But that doesn't solve the problem. I'll be there in a sec."

Desales handed the phone back to Amir. Within moments, Stef was standing with them. "We need a ride to St. Paul's. We could walk it, but it's a long-assed haul." He was thinking Roland and Roy would never make it. Flo had gotten to St. Paul's earlier before the traffic went completely tits up.

Amir looked to the sky. *Here we go again.*

Desales said, "Amir? Can you do us another solid? Stef, Robbie would have to sit on your lap."

Amir thought, *Well, having one passenger without a seatbelt was illegal, so may as well go for two.* "Okay, guys. Yep. Consider it my wedding present."

Desales gave him a high five. "Thank you, man! You rock!"

They piled back in. The sight of Roland squeezed next to Roy was worth it to Desales.

"So, Uncle Stef, did people look at you funny for walking around in a tux?"

"The tux? Nah. This is London. Hang around long enough, you'll see a lot crazier than that."

They finally made it to St. Paul's. A crowd of photographers had gathered, clicking away at the comic clown car dismount. Roland was cool with it. He was quite satisfied with his look, certainly the biggest and most successful combover of his entire life.

Stef's phone warbled. "Hey? No, no apologies required, man. All good! Yeah, we're here at St. Paul's. So, maybe try to pick up as many guests as you can who've called in stranded?" Then he had an idea. "Uh, wait a minute. I may need you, after all." He held his hand over his phone.

"Amir, I know it's late notice. But could you come to my wedding? And the reception will be awesome. It's right there at the Royale." He pointed just across and down the street. "Plenty of good food and a vegan option. And I have a guy that can pick up your spouse and family, if you have any."

Amir was shocked. He had to admit this had been the craziest taxi day of his life. Why end it now? "Well, you see I'm not dressed for it? Is that going to be okay?"

"Oh, hell yeah! We're not that formal."

"Three kids, too?"

"All good!"

"Okay. Hang on, and I'll call my wife!"

He walked away a few paces to make the call. A minute later, he came back.

"What kind of car will be picking them up?"

Stef spoke back into his phone, "Which one are you driving? Ah. Perfect—hang on."

"Well, it will be a black limousine driven by a member of the Queen's Protection Command. Nice guy. I've met him before. His name is Manfred. Former RAF."

Amir walked back a pace and spoke on his phone. He clicked off. "Yes. She said that will be acceptable."

. . .

It had been a batshit night. The limo was jammed full and loud with laughter. Roland was playing the videos he took, holding his phone up for each person to view. "Look!" The entire wedding party was performing the Chicken Dance.

Roy saw himself and his nephews dancing. "I look loonier than a one-legged dodo at a hillbilly hoedown!"

The limo dropped off the others and pulled up to the Savoy. The four dragged their way through the lobby and up to their suite. The hallway was dim, and they had appropriately quieted themselves down. Desales placed the electronic key into the lock. He did not hear a click. He tried a few more times. No click. Then he noticed the small envelope attached to the door with a tiny piece of cellophane tape. He opened the envelope. The note was typed. "Please see Reception Desk."

They made their way back down to the front desk. Desales kind of knew what was coming. Mr. Jon, the Reception Manager, saw the seersucker sea approaching.

"Ah! 1245? You've received our note. So, folks, very sorry to have locked you out. Another party had booked that suite and somehow, through our fault, no doubt, it was mistakenly provided to your group. If I may, under what name was your reservation made?"

Desales spoke up, "Biv. B-I-V."

Mr. Jon clacked away on the keyboard going through the motions of checking for a reservation. He knew there would be none. Every single room was now properly accounted for and occupied.

"How unfortunate. I do not see any reservations under that name. Perchance did you arrive here mistakenly? Perhaps you reserved at a different hotel?"

Desales admitted, "Ah, yes, that may be possible."

"Yes, that happens sometimes. Travel can be so confusing. Disorienting even. Now, shall we fetch your group a taxi or two to get you safely over to your destination?"

"Ah . . ." Desales looked over to Roy who was looking on dazedly. "Well, I think we could just walk there if we could get our luggage from the room?"

"Certainly! We've stowed your luggage and belongings for you." He clicked some more on his keyboard. "We are holding two small wicker attaché cases, one backpack, two . . . ah . . . green utility bags, one orange-colored hip pack featuring smiling bird, four US passports removed from safe, and four standard-sized bricks. I'll have the bellman bring the items over!"

. . .

Dawn arrived, bringing a fresh new London day to the Saveloy. Robbie and Doyle were in their bunkbed watching Uncle Roy sleep.

They tried not to giggle too loud. They didn't want to wake him. But his snoring was hilarious! His nose always made a funny shape just before he snored. His nostrils got extra large! The volume of nose hair was fascinating! And then his lips flapped as he exhaled! Desales had taken off for somewhere. His cot was empty.

And then they heard a key in the lock. Desales entered holding a cup of Starbucks. He looked over at Roy splayed about the tiny twin-sized bed. "Roy's still asleep? We have to wake him. We've got to get over to that breakfast."

Doyle reached over and nudged Roy's shoulder. He stretched a little and began waking up. "Holy moly, I ain't slept this good fer a long time! Nice accommodations. Feels like I'm back home!" He sat up in bed and then stood, shakily, barking his shin on Desales's cot. "Ouch, Sonny! Ding dang! That cot's made 'a cast iron! He looked over to see Robbie's face in the top bunk, nearly level with his. "Well, hello there, tadpole! Looks like you growed up big overnight!"

Robbie giggled loudly.

"Okay, boys, let's get warshed up and over ta that fancy breakfast party."

"Uncle Roy, do we have to wear those same suits again?"

Roy looked puzzled. "Well 'a course we do, Doyle. It's supposed to be fancy. But, tell ya what, oncet we're done, we can all come back here 'n change into our comfy clothes and go ta that big Ferris wheel we been seein.'"

Robbie yelled, "Yay!"

. . .

The entourage made it back to the Savoy and went straight to the bank of elevators. They were all feeling a little embarrassed about being tossed out the night before. And they had left the four bricks behind. They figured that they'd steer clear of the front desk.

They entered the foyer to the massive tea room. The sign said "Biv-Stour Breakfast." The hostess checked their name on the list and led them over toward a large table. Along the way, Roy noticed the shiny, black baby grand piano. "Well, jeepers! Look at that piany!" They were some of the first guests to arrive. They saw a few other well-dressed people scattered about other tables.

"Looks like we made it in plenty 'a time! Don't see Stef 'n Flo yet." Roy looked around. "Sonny, are those the buffet tables?" He pointed to the English Breakfast warming tables with chaffing dishes. "D'ya think they mean ta feed us a buffet?"

"Oh, yes, Roy. Definitely a buffet. Probably those toaster waffles you like or maybe Pop Tarts. I hear they have those little tiny donuts with the waxy chocolate. Maybe some scrambled eggs and scrapple? This is pretty fancy, after all." He was trying not to smirk.

"Well, at sounds good! Sometimes these places have crab balls, too. Ya think they'll put out Old Bay with the crab balls?"

"Certainly, Roy!"

Servers slowly came by, filling cups with hot coffee or hot water for those preferring tea. Roy was getting hungry, but figured he'd ask for tea at least. "So, hon, ya got Lipton's? Or if not, you know, Safeway brand is durn good, too?"

The server opened her selection box. "Well, we have English Breakfast, Earl Grey, Twinings Ceylon Orange Pekoe and several varieties of herbal teas. Feel free to choose any!"

Roy fingered his way through the box looking for Lipton's. "Hmm. Ain't seein' Lipton's?"

"Well, sir, if you like a black tea, the Earl Grey is a nice choice. A little citrussy. But the Orange Pekoe is less so."

Roy looked confused. "So, yer sayin' the Orange tea isn't citrus tastin', but the Earl's tea is?"

"Yes."

"Do ya have plain coffee?"

. . .

Guests began arriving and quiet, polite conversation ensued. Roy and his entourage were introduced to Lady Rolf Harris and her adult twin daughters, Penelope and Persephone. Roland stopped by the table to wish everyone a "good morning," before taking his place with the wedding party. Finally, the English Breakfast was announced, and Lady Flo stood to lead the group in a short prayer of thanksgiving. All who were able stood and bowed their heads. Stef provided an "Amen" at the end, echoed by the others. Roy clanged his spoon noisily against his water glass and added, loudly, "Here here!" The photographer began taking candid shots of the wedding party.

"Sonny, are they callin' us up to the buffet table by rows, or d'ya just get on yer horse and giddyup?"

"Sure. Go anytime, Roy!"

Stef and Flo were just approaching the serving tables. The photographer had set up for a nice shot of the couple. The morning sunlight played fancifully against the chaffing dishes. And then she saw the odd man in the seersucker suit. He was pulling off the chaffing dish lids, one at a time, and inspecting each. He was shaking his head. He yelled loudly, "Hey, Sonny. I don't see no crab balls? What the heck d'ya think this round black stuff is?"

Stef quickly walked over. "Hey, Roy!" He whispered, "That's blood sausage. It's like a mixture of fat and pig's blood and stuff."

"Go to war, Miss Agnes! Sorta like scrapple with blood in it?"

"Exactly."

"Yick! Why would they ruin good scrapple with the blood? No thanky, sir! Are those some kinda baked beans?"

"Yes. Exactly."

"Fer breakfast?"

"Yes, that's normal here."

"Geezy Christmas! That's bass ackerds. Beans are for supper."

"Well, they do things differently here."

"Looks like they got some ham slices at least. Funny they ain't got no bacon or sausages."

"Well, the meat that looks like ham is bacon."

"That's bacon? Now, c'mon, little bro, stop pullin' muh leg!"

Stef couldn't respond. Flo was nudging him. He looked over and rolled his eyes.

"Ain't they got waffles or pancakes? Most fancy buffets do? Or them little donuts? Powdered sugar ones 'r okay if they ain't got them good chocolate ones."

"Well, like I said, breakfast is a little different over here, Roy. But, look. Right there are toast slices and fresh jellies and marmalades?" He figured that Roy would not be interested in the vegan plate also available upon request.

"Okay. And I seen them fried eggs. They look purdy good. 'N that ham stuff. I'll grab a couple of 'em fast, 'cuz everbody else'll want 'em too once they get a load 'a that blood scrapple."

"Sure, Roy."

Roy completed his first visit to the buffet. The photographer quickly got back to work.

Once Roy got back to the table he warned the others, "Look out for that black lookin' round stuff cuz it's got pig's blood in it if you can blieve it! The eggs 'n funny ham look fine if ya can get to 'em quick. Imagine they're goin' fast!"

Penelope Harris said, "Did you say there was black pudding?"

"Pudding? No, ma'am. I didn't see any."

Roy realized he'd forgotten to grab a couple hot biscuits. And there should be some nice ham gravy. He got back to the buffet and looked around. A kitchen worker was replenishing the blood sausage.

"Hon, d'ya know if they're gonna put out biscuits?"

She looked at Roy puzzledly. "Well, I doubt it, sir. I've never seen that done for a breakfast." Looking at Roy she felt a tad concerned.

She was majoring in Health and Nutrition. "Sir, diabetes is a serious disease. You know, as we age, we have to be a lot more careful about our ingestion of sweets."

Roy looked over, puzzled. "Well, thanks, hon! I'll remember that for later."

"Yes, when you get to pudding, it's best to go easy."

Roy was puzzled as there did not seem to be any pudding out for dessert. "Yer the second person ta mention pudding." He thought it was way too early in the day to have dessert. He'd pass on it once they put it out. He went back to the table.

. . .

Mimosas were poured, and the breakfast was under full sail. The loudness of the conversations increased as everybody relaxed and enjoyed the food and beverage. Desales tapped Roy's shoulder. "Royal, you know, I think the piano player is a no-show. You know how some of these musicians are. Unreliable. Probably out partying the night before."

"Yeppers. Know'd a few of 'em in my day."

"Why don't you get a couple good tunes going over there?" He pointed to the baby grand. "The crowd seems ready for a little fun, right!"

"Well. Don't know if yer supposed to. What if that piany belongs ta somebody?"

"Oh. Don't worry. It's there for use by the public. Otherwise, they'd move it to storage. I think you'd be doing the newlyweds a favor? Especially since the other guy didn't post."

"Well, I have been kinda itchin' to rev things up a bit!"

Roy walked over and took his place at the piano, unnoticed. He stretched out his rough-hewn hands, cleared his throat, and began to play a reckless and boisterous version of "Roll Out the Barrel." And, as an added feature, Roy occasionally added an enthusiastic vocal accompaniment.

The breakfast host looked over in horror. Musical entertainment was not on the agenda! He looked over to Flo and Stef to get their attention, to signal that he would take care of it. But the newlyweds had already stood up from their places at the head table. They appeared to be leaving! Who the hell was that strange man ruining his breakfast?

The host followed quickly behind Flo and Stef, trying to catch up with them, hoping to convince them to stay once Security was called in to remove the man. And then he saw them dancing! They were performing some sort of Polka!

Roy saw them and nodded, happily. He yelled out loudly. "C'mon, everbody! Gather 'roun the piany!"

Soon most of the tables had emptied as various breakfast guests tried out whatever physical movements their bodies seemed capable of making. Roy moved the repertoire along to other favorites such as "Camptown Races" and "In Heaven There is No Beer." And only a few dancers toppled over. Desales, Robbie, and Doyle had been dragged onto the floor by the Harris twins, who thought they were absolutely adorable children!

Time passed, and Management had some concerns as the concert had exceeded the agreed-upon limits for the breakfast booking. Considerably. "What shall we do? We can't yell, 'Drink up and piss off'?"

"We'll do the next best thing." The Booking Manager began flicking the light switches. Several in the crowd groaned. They didn't want to stop.

Roy took the hint. "Okay, folks, here's the last tune!" He immediately broke into "We'll Meet Again." The crowd roared approval.

. . .

November 2050

"I'm happy to see and speak with you, Mr. Elders, but like our com. stated, your test falls into the 'inconclusive' category." Mr. Desai, customer service rep, was choosing his words carefully.

Robbie was glad the company representative was at least wearing a lab coat. "Understood, but can you tell me in lay person's terms exactly what that means?"

Desai sighed to himself. *Here comes the "fun" part.* "Well, we can only presume that the sample you sent and that we processed got corrupted somehow, at some point. This happens occasionally, through no fault of our company or our customer. That's why our policy is to deliver replacement kits at no charge to the customer. In the hopes of obtaining a successful sample, ultimately."

"Yes, I get that. But I don't understand why all of my attempts failed somehow. I followed the instructions in detail. To the letter. What could I be doing wrong?"

Desai worded his response as carefully as possible. "Well, it's also possible that you've done absolutely nothing wrong and that our testing procedures have failed. We are certainly willing to refund your money. We want all of our customers at 23 HistoryHouse to be completely satisfied."

"Okay, thanks. Sure. I'll take the refund. But, tell me, looking at the test results from the two failed tests, what are you actually seeing?"

There was a long pause. "Well, we see that there's definitely been some sort of corruption in the sample or glitch in our testing mechanisms, because the test indicates that some of the DNA is unlike that which we usually encounter. At the molecular level, several of the DNA samples appear to utilize a triple-helix configuration, not a double helix, which we know can't be correct. That's how we know there's been some corruption of the sample.

Some problem in collecting or processing. But again, we'll get that refund back to you ASAP." He was glad to get that over with.

"Well, that's bizarre. DNA has two strands, not three, right?"

"Correct. Something like a virus may have a single DNA strand, but all living things have DNA with two strands. DNA molecules with three strands do occur in nature, but not in stable, complex organisms, like humans, plants, animals, etc. That's why we know there's probably been a corruption of the sample, somehow. Or, our testing is just not reading your sample correctly. Impossible to know."

"Okay. Thanks."

"You're welcome. And it has been a pleasure to communicate with you today, Mr. Elders. Once we end the call, could you please stay on-port for a thirty-second customer service survey?"

"Sure."

"Thank you, and have a nice day."

It made no sense. He'd just tell his book circle friends that he'd decided to take a pass on a DNA test. Thinking about tim tim had unsettled him. The DNA stuff reminded him of the crazy things tim tim used to say about the Bible and their family tree. He had virtually forgotten all that. Excised it from his memory. He needed to stay on his regimen. It had kept him sane, and even for many, many years. He needed to forget tim tim and those few strange episodes.

. . .

Spring 2023

Will needed to create an intervention. Watching his little brother "dance" foolishly in public hurt his brain. He walked up toward the bandstand. As he walked, he put his fingers in his ears because the sound was so loud.

"Tim! Hey! What's up? How've you been?" he waved his arms.

Tim tim saw the man approaching. It was his brother! He slowed down his frenetic pace but kept dancing, moving in place.

"Bill bill! What's happening?" He wiped the sweat from his forehead with his crumpled Orioles hat. It was a wet dishrag. He put the hat back on his head.

"Well, the whole gang is here! Look over there. It's Megan and Robbie. See?"

Tim tim shielded his eyes and looked out onto the green space.

"I see them! Let's go. I can say 'hello!'"

Will gently placed his hand on Tim's shoulder and held him back. "Let's wait. We'll hang back here. Megan . . . has concerns about COVID . . . and distancing. You know . . ."

"Oh. Okay, bill bill. Could you bring rob rob over for a minute? I thought of something else I needed to tell him."

"Okay. Well. Just tell me, Tim, and I'll relay the message. It's better that way, right?"

"Oh. Okay! Yes. Tell him that his time is near and to stay on mission. Tell him I dance because I'm happy. And rob rob will be happy, too! He just needs to stay on mission. I know he can do it!"

"Thanks, Tim. You know, Robbie's pretty happy now as he is! He's going into sophomore year!"

Tim tim's demeanor changed. He stopped dancing in place and looked down to the ground, despondently. "That's going to suck. That was a bad year for me."

"Well. Don't worry, Tim! We've got it! Robbie is seeing some people that have been helping him. It's all by Zoom. You know. Counselors and similar . . . cool people. To bring him out of his shell. Help him meet his full potential."

Tim tim sighed heavily. "Yeah. That's good, but I flubbed up."

"Flub . . . what? No! You did not! No flubs! You hung out with him and bought him comics! You were the perfect uncle! All good, man!"

"Yeah. But probably not good enough. If I could just talk to him? He may have questions."

Will saw Megan waving her arms and pointing to their picnic blanket. That meant the conversation was over. "Well. I'm really sorry, Tim. This is not a good time. You know, with the pandemic and everything. Definitely later. Right?"

"Sure, bill bill." He watched Will wave to Megan and then head back to their blanket, fingers back in ears.

Tim tim moved away from the bandstand and found a spot by himself on the lawn. Rob rob was going to need help. He had failed him. He thought about his own tutelage. Baz baz had come through for him, just in time.

. . .

December 1998

Will didn't recognize the voice on the other end of the phone line.

"Could you repeat that?"

"I said it's me, Will, Tim."

"Tim! Are you crying? What's wrong?"

"Can you bring me back home?"

He couldn't believe what he was hearing. "Home? Back to Mom and Dad's?"

"Yes. I'm not feeling well. I need help."

"Well, you know, you never took their phone calls or answered their letters? They thought they might never see you again."

"I'm here."

"Yes. Yes! That's good. I'll come get you."

Will sighed to himself. He had been studying for his law school exams. He didn't want to lose precious prep time. And then he realized. "Well, there is one minor complication."

"What?"

"Grandma's been sick and had to move in with us. She had to take over your room."

"I can stay in the basement?"

Will thought of the current chaotic state of the basement. They had moved almost all of his grandmother's furnishings and clothes into the basement. It was hard to even navigate through the mess. There was no bed in the basement anymore.

"Crap. It's all jammed up with Grandma's stuff."

There was a long pause on the phone line. And then Will remembered.

"Wait a minute. It's a coincidence, but Uncle Basil was just asking about you. He actually called Mom and Dad to see if you were there. He said he wanted to see you. He told me that if you ever needed a place to crash, he would take you in. He said this, like, just last month."

"Really?"

"He's living in the 25th Street house. I can phone him and tell him I'm bringing you over. Would that be okay?"

There was another long pause.

"Okay."

. . .

January 1999

"It's in there. I'll show you." Basil turned away from the stove top and pointed to the thick, worn-out Bible on the Formica-topped kitchen table. The tea water had not yet boiled. He stooped down to look at the flame and edged the burner knob a bit higher, watching the flame dance against the blackened bottom of the kettle. He took a seat next to tim tim.

Tim tim picked up the Bible. "Well, I've read the Bible many times, baz baz, but I don't remember reading anything about our specific family being mentioned? How could that be? That seems a little crazy, right? Not that I don't believe you though."

Basil motioned for tim tim to hand him the Bible. "Here." He opened to the beginning part and placed it back on the table in front of tim tim. "See, it's right in Genesis. This spot. Right before the story of Noah and the Flood." He glanced down, moving his index finger over the pica text. "Let me find the exact spot. Here." He pointed to a passage and pushed the book over to tim tim, holding his finger on the section.

Tim tim read the part to himself. "Wow. That's us? We're related to those guys?"

"Yes. But, we've gotten a bad reputation over the generations because of confusion about the name. It got mistranslated in the Latin Vulgate centuries ago and now is mistakenly interpreted as 'fallen people,' as though we fell away from God or something. We didn't. It's just a word based on a combination of ancient words that mean 'nephew' and 'people.' Basically, the words 'nepos' and 'phyle.' You know, the Latin word nepos, where the word nepotism comes from. Meaning like favoritism shown to a nephew. And phyle meaning a group of people. So, the word is saying that we are the 'nephew people.' And it's always the second nephew. That's just how it is. Don't ask me why. It's in our blood. Our people were legendary for doing good deeds. We were men of renown. Heroes of old. Giants among men. But, not physically, but more like really well-known for doing good."

Tim tim thought back to his Bible study group. "Well, they told us that those guys were supposed to be bad guys and wiped out by the Flood along with everybody else? Because people had been so rotten that God said that all the people had to go. Except for Noah and his wife?"

They heard the whistle of the tea kettle. Basil held up his forefinger to indicate a pause. He poured each a cup of tea in mismatched cup and saucers. Basil's saucer was chipped and heavily tea stained. Tim tim watched his teabag float to the surface of the water in his cup. He pushed it back down with his spoon.

"Okay, about the Flood. Yes, God spared Noah and the ark, but he spared our people, too. We had always done good things. We were sons of the father—he loved us—and we married and blended in with the other people alive at the time so that our lineage could survive and continue to do good deeds. All of which was specifically approved by God." He moved the book closer and peered over. He found the passage. "See, it says we were 'on the earth in those days and also afterward.'" He tapped the passage with his finger. "'And also afterward.' And then it talks about the Flood. So it's saying we survived the Flood. And, of course, we did. We're still here. In part, of course. We're mostly regular people, but our ancestry is in our blood."

"Okay. Good!"

"Our mission is to do as much good as possible for people. To always help people. We look to see ourselves. To find and know ourselves. When you do see yourself, you'll know it's time for a good and remarkable deed."

"Okay?"

"We do these things for the Lord. He's always with us. Always surrounding us. Jesus said, 'Split a piece of wood and I am there. Lift up the stone and you will find me there.' You'll see. Jesus also said, 'The kingdom of the father is spread out upon the earth and men do not see it.'"

"Okay."

"He told us, 'The kingdom is inside of you and it is outside of you. When you come to know yourself, then you will become known, and you will realize that it is you who are a son of the living father.' And he told us, 'Be passersby.'"

"Passersby?"

"Yes. Not taking part in all the everyday nonsense of life. Letting all of that flow by. Rather, being an observer. A bystander. Because there will be times for action. And you'll know when it's time."

"Really? How?"

"When the time is ripe, look to see yourself. Look inside to feel and to know, and look outside for the bystander that you must make one. Jesus said, 'When you make the two one, you will become a son of man, and when you say, 'mountain, move away,' it will move away.'"

. . .

Late August 2019

"Look at our baby!" Megan moved the photo album over to Will. They could finally relax now. Dr. Brigand had the problem well under control. Their evenings were so much more normal now. Will had opened the bottle of Chianti. They were enjoying life again.

"Wow! Such an adorable little kid! I can't believe he's ours!"

"Stop it, tiny brain! Look at him, splashing around in the tub. I would always help him get his soapsuds beard! He would laugh and laugh!"

"Yes!"

"And he always did the cutest thing before his bath. Do you remember? He would always pull his clothes off to the ground and then stamp on them with his little tiny feet! Almost like a little dance on his clothes!"

"Tim? Yes, he did do that! I remember!" He thought back to the home on 25th Street.

"Tim? You mean Robbie? Are you having a brain melt, geezer?"

Will quickly pivoted. He had never actually seen Robbie do that. Megan usually drew Robbie's baths. He knew it was something Tim always did as a child. He breathed in. *Wow.*

"Oh, yeah. Sorry, Meg. We've been talking about Tim so much that I misspoke."

. . .

Tim tim heard the door buzzer and opened the door immediately.

"Hey! Robbie! What brings you here?"

"Tim tim, you should check to see who's outside before just opening your door to anyone. I could have been a bad guy."

Robbie walked back to the kitchen and took his usual seat at the tea-stained table. Puzzled, tim tim closed the door behind him and followed.

"And you should keep your door locked, tim tim."

Tim tim took a seat next to Robbie. "Okay, chief, understood!" There was silence.

"Do your folks know you're here, Robbie, because your dad said that you were grounded for some reason?"

"Oh that. No. It was more like they didn't want me getting onto the mission. But I do want the mission."

"Well, that's a good step, Robbie! But I'd feel more comfortable if they knew you were here. I can phone your dad?"

"No. Probably not a good idea. He's at work. He's busy, and the same with Mom. Doyle's in charge, and he's not around, so I figured being with an adult would be a good thing."

"Okay. Sure. How did you get all the way over here?"

"I took the bus, mostly, and walked the rest of the way."

"Okay, Robbie. Wow. That's a haul. Just as long as your folks are okay with it." He figured he'd call bill bill later, after dinner.

Robbie looked on, earnestly. "So, I was thinking. I like the idea of doing good things for people. I think that with God on our side, we can do a lot of good things. Those special things you were talking about, like when you helped that lady with the purse."

Tim tim sighed. "Well, yes, those are good ideas, Robbie! But there's one correction. God is not on our side."

Robbie felt shocked and deflated. He inhaled. "What do you mean? I thought you said we do these things for God?"

"Well, yes! That is absolutely true. But here's something I learned from baz baz—God doesn't take sides. He is a side."

"What?"

"What I mean is that we have to take His side. He is all good. His side is goodness. We have to constantly align with His side. But when we do, we will feel a connection with God as we perform good deeds. Do you see?"

Robbie sighed and nodded.

"Don't worry, Robbie. Your instincts are good. As you get older and more able in the mission, you will begin to understand and know yourself and eventually see yourself. God will help you feel those moments of oneness of self when action is warranted."

Robbie shook his head, confused. "Could we maybe have some ice cream?

. . .

September 2019

Will took him outside the house to tell him. He didn't want any chance of Megan or Doyle overhearing. He had learned of Robbie's bus travels to see Tim.

"Robbie, I have to tell you the truth about Tim. Some of this stuff even Mom doesn't know."

They each took a seat on the swing set in the backyard. Robbie hadn't used their swing set in years. The dirt patches beneath the two swings had mostly grown over. Robbie held a weathered chain in each hand. He rocked gently. He heard a low creak.

"Tim may seem like he has it together. He's got a home and a car and takes care of himself. But the home belongs to Mom and me. One of my uncles willed the house to Tim. But Tim lost it because he couldn't pay taxes. He had no money and no job."

Will waited to see a reaction. Robbie stopped rocking in the swing. He looked down at his running shoes in the dirt patch. He moved the swing just a little. He looked up and stared out to the fire pit at the end of the yard.

"Tim has never been able to hold a job. He was diagnosed by several doctors as having mental health issues. Psychological disorders. Some of them were worsened by the drugs he voluntarily took. So how does Tim survive without a job? Because I got him a financial settlement from the US Army, that's how. I had to take our own government to court over the drugs they had given him. They had convinced Tim that he was a soldier and that they'd take care of him. But Tim was never actually in the Army. Did you know that? He thought he was, but he was only a civilian volunteer. The Army tried to disavow any responsibility for Tim and his condition. But, finally, with pressure from the Court, they officially categorized him as a veteran and cut him a settlement check." Will didn't want to mention that right before the trial, the State Police found the unclothed corpse of one of the other volunteers in the woods near the base, which helped make the settlement happen.

Robbie had stopped his slow swinging and held himself in place. "I manage that money for Tim. If I didn't, he would spend it all. He would give it all away. Before the settlement came in, I found out that Tim had lost the house for non-payment of taxes. He had been receiving bills and notifications about the court action, but ignored it all. I had to quickly strike a deal with the City to get the house back. It cost us a lot of money. Do you remember the summer when we couldn't take a vacation? I fibbed to you about having a busy court schedule. You and Doyle were mad. But the truth was, we couldn't afford a vacation because of all that. And it took me throughout that summer to get the house back and taxes straightened out. If we hadn't, Tim would be homeless and out on the street. And, your Mom and I bought him that Toyota, years ago, just so he could get around and get food for himself and get around like a normal person. Otherwise, Tim would have to get his groceries by taking a bus or walking a half mile. So, you see, Tim needs a lot of help to get by. He obviously loves you like a son, but everything he told you has to be taken with a big grain of salt. I mean really big."

Robbie looked up. "What about the religious stuff? I kind of think there's something to it."

Will sighed. "Look, you know your mom and I are not religious people. We have strong views about religions. Religions are used to hurt people. To bully people. To force people to believe in things that simply are not true. To control people and take their money. Yes, some people need religion to make them feel accepted or to tell them what to think or how to act. These people are sheep. They follow along, sadly. Have you heard the saying, 'lambs to the slaughter'? A sheep doesn't think for itself. It just follows some other sheep to disaster. We don't want you to be a sheep. You're going to be a man. You're going to make your own life. Make your own choices. Doctor Brigand is helping you with that."

"He said that tim tim's religious talk was a big lie . . . that the mission is a lie. But I just don't believe that tim tim would ever lie to me." He shook his head gently.

"I know. I know. I'm sure Tim didn't mean to hurt you with all that. He actually believes it. But that doesn't make it real. I think you're now beginning to understand that what Tim told you was all fantasy. Silly stuff. He didn't mean any harm. He lives in his own dream world. That world is not for you, Robbie."

Robbie looked back down at his shoes. "You said drugs messed up tim tim, so why do I have to take that pill every day? Why won't that mess me up? I don't like it. It mellows me out too much. It upsets my stomach, too."

"Well, that's why you have to take it with a meal. You keep forgetting to take it, and then we have to remind you to take it after you've already eaten. Take it with your meal and your stomach will feel okay."

Robbie thought, *Or maybe I'll just stop taking it.*

. . .

October 2019

Robbie wasn't loving the ride with the top down. It was fall, and it was freezing back there. The drive south along Pulaski Highway was torture. He could tell Doyle was cold too. But he knew Doyle would be too cool to complain.

"There's one."

Desales spotted the "We Buy Houses" sign just outside the fence of a closed warehouse. The industrial area was bleakly deserted. It was the weekend.

He pulled the Mustang in along the sidewalk and hopped out. He unlocked and opened the trunk. He paid no particular attention to the dark SUV parked twenty yards away. He yanked the sign out of the ground and let out a war whoop. He flung the sign into the trunk with two others.

Robbie noticed the very big man exiting the SUV and walking their way. "Desales?"

Desales looked up. "Shit." He saw the muscular giant in a Gold's Gym tee shirt and gray jogging pants. He quickly closed the trunk lid and hustled over to the door.

"Hey, you! Hold it right there!"

Desales stopped in his tracks. He looked around to see if perhaps the man was hailing someone else. He really hoped so.

"Yeah, you, Sambo! I'm talking to you!"

Doyle noticed that another skinny man in dark jeans and black tee shirt was now making his way over from the SUV. He was holding a tire iron.

Desales shuddered. "Is there a problem?"

The big guy was now in his face. "Problem? Oh, fuck yeah, you little piece of shit! You just pulled up one of my fuckin' signs. So, yeah, there's a problem!"

The big guy grabbed Desales by his collar and led him back to the trunk. "Open it!"

Desales shakily placed the key in the lock and opened the trunk. The big guy peered in. His friend arrived.

Doyle continued to look straight ahead, hoping that ignoring them could make them go away somehow. Robbie's hands were beginning to quiver. He didn't dare look behind either.

"Well, take a look at this, Cyr." He picked his way through the signs. "That's two of ours."

Cyril nodded. "Fucked up."

"Yeah, truly fucked. Gimme that."

Cyril handed the tire iron over to the big guy.

"Okay, you other two assholes, get out of the car."

Doyle temporarily froze. But he steeled himself and opened the door unsteadily. He took a spot a few paces back from the passenger's side. Robbie squeezed his way out of the rear seat and took his place next to Doyle.

"Okay, you three. You owe me. You've been pulling up my fucking signs for months. And now I finally caught you in the act! So, it's time to pay. I'm a businessman, and fucking with my business has a cost. Each one of those signs cost me a hundred bucks to make. That's a lot, but I make it up from the houses I sell. But every time you pieces of shit pull your little stunt and pull up my signs, it costs me both the sign and a way to pay for the sign by selling a house. Get it?"

The big guy's face was an inch from Desales's. He felt the guy's spittle and smelled his very bad breath. Desales gulped and shook his head "yes."

"What? Nothin' to say, ass wipe? How the fuck you gonna pay me back?"

Desales tried to rally. "Uh, well, I have some money on me. About thirty dollars?"

The big guy looked over to Cyril. "You hear that, Cyr? The monkey's got thirty bucks."

Cyril nodded and smiled malevolently.

"Nice try, dickhead. So, here's what I'm going to do. I'm going to take my signs and your thirty bucks. And then I'm going to smash the fuck out of your cute little car. Just a little payback. Then you'll have to spend your money to fix it just like you cost me my money."

Desales blurted out. "No. Please. That's my dad's car! Please don't!"

The big guy looked over to Cyril and chuckled. "You hear that, Cyr? Daddy might get mad!"

Cyril laughed loudly.

"I would actually rather beat the fuck out of you with this, kid." He raised the tire iron. "I was trying to be nice and just fuck up your car. But if you'd rather me fuck you up, that's fine! Your choice."

Desales felt his eyes water in fear. "No. Please. No."

"Okay, stand aside, shithead." He walked over to the hood of the Mustang and raised the tire iron into the air, about to strike.

"Sir, I have an idea."

He stopped and looked over. It was the little kid. And the kid was slowly walking toward him.

"Idea, kid? What idea? Do you have thirty bucks too?"

He sneered and began to raise the tire iron again.

"Well, here's the idea. My brother and I can add in whatever money we have with us. So you'll get more money that way." The kid spoke so soothingly. He brought the tire iron back down.

"Okay? Like how much?"

"I've got about three dollars." Robbie looked over to Doyle. Doyle looked down to the ground. "Uh, I've got like six."

The man scowled and began to raise the iron. Robbie continued. "There's something else, sir. You have to be careful because there are a lot of security cameras around in an area like this. They might catch you hurting his car. And people are always taking videos with their cameras and uploading them. You don't want to get caught."

The big guy was barely listening to the actual words. He was beginning to feel calm. Something about the kid's voice was calming. Very calming. He didn't know why.

"And one more thing. If they find you and arrest you, you won't be able to have ice cream." Robbie nodded and breathed in. He was mentally tasting his favorite ice cream. A Pepsi float with a slowly melting slab of Neapolitan. The big guy realized that he was somehow tasting a malted milkshake. He loved that flavor. He hadn't had a malted milkshake in decades. It took him crashing back to his childhood. He was happy then. And then he smelled and could almost taste another favorite: vanilla ice cream with warm caramel topping. He loved it. The warm gooeyness of the caramel. The coolness of the vanilla. And then he sensed the texture and sweetness of whipped cream sprayed on top. He could taste it all somehow. He wanted to get some ice cream. He handed the tire iron over to Cyril.

"Okay, you three. Just don't do this shit anymore. Cyr, get our signs."

They walked away with two signs and the tire iron.

Desales steadied himself against the rear of the car and exhaled. He pulled himself back up and looked at Robbie in bewilderment. "Holy shit, man! You saved us. He actually listened to you. I think he was afraid of being caught on video and arrested." He pulled the remaining sign out of the trunk and placed it, gently, on the sidewalk. Lesson learned. He closed the trunk lid. "What made you think that he liked ice cream?"

Robbie looked on blankly. "Everyone likes ice cream." He thought to himself, *Just like tim tim said.*

Robbie and Doyle got back into the Mustang. Desales reached behind Robbie and stretched the vinyl rooftop back over the convertible's frame. He secured the two rooftop latches. The fun was over. Desales pointed the car back toward Catonsville. He drove on, quietly.

Doyle looked over his shoulder at Robbie. "Man, you have been very weird since we got back from Uncle Stef's wedding. Ever since that day at the beach."

Doyle turned back around and sat waiting for a response. There was none. He looked back over his shoulder again. "I mean, what's gotten into you, man?"

"Well, I think I've been fine. I'm okay." He was definitely not going to tell them about how he caught a glimpse of that guy out of the corner of his eye again today.

. . .

August 2020

The news was bad. Frightening. Will clicked off his cell. "That was the police. They found my number in Tim's wallet as an emergency contact." His hand began to quiver. His eyes teared.

Megan heard the fear in Will's voice. "What's happened? Something's happened to Tim?"

Will took a deep breath. "He's alive, thank God, but at Mercy Medical in intensive care. Someone beat him up with a baseball bat. Really badly. The officer said the doctors had to wire his jaw shut."

"Oh my God! That's bad!"

"A witness said Tim intervened in some sort of dispute. Some thugs were threatening some neighbor. He gave me the surgeon's name and cell number to phone. I'm calling right now."

. . .

"I don't think we should bring the boys, Will. Especially Robbie. We've worked so hard to wean him away from Tim. Seeing Tim in the hospital could trigger a reconnection, or it may make him incredibly sad. Brigand warned us about that. It's been hard enough getting him out of his funk these past few months."

"I hear you, but he knows Tim's in the hospital, and he's going to want to visit him. I don't know how we'd even stop him."

"I know. I know. It's a no-win situation. We could tell him 'no' because of COVID? My hospital is only allowing two visitors at a time. We could check into it?"

"Well, I already did. They told me two visitors in the room at a time would be okay. So, we can manage that. And I think letting Robbie visit is the right thing. The lesser of two evils. Firstly, he'll be with us, so we can control the visit. And, yeah, Tim's jaw is wired shut, so he's not going to be all that conversant."

. . .

"Now, guys, I want to prepare you. We told you that Uncle Tim had his jaw wired shut. And he's been beaten up very badly. He has two black eyes. He's very weak because they have him on meds and well . . . he's just very beat-up looking. But don't let it frighten you. Tim's getting better. But he's low energy right now and has to use a whiteboard and marker to communicate. So Mom and I don't want to stay too long and wear Tim out."

Robbie and Doyle both nodded. Robbie spoke through his mask. "Okay, Dad."

"Let your father and I go in there first, okay? Just hang out in the hallway. There's a bench there."

Will and Megan walked to the side of tim tim's bed. Tim tim was sitting up, but had nodded off. Will touched Tim's shoulder, gently. "Tim? Are you awake, buddy?"

They saw tim tim open his eyes and blink. He mumbled through his clenched jaw, "bill bill . . ."

They could barely hear him. He pointed to his whiteboard and marker on the side table. Will handed them over to Tim. They watched as he slowly wrote, "Boys here?"

Will nodded his head. "Yes, yes, Tim. They're just outside in the hall. We wanted to see how you were, first."

Tim tim nodded.

Will made small talk. "Have they been feeding you okay?"

Tim tim raised his hand from the bed and made a "so-so" motion.

"Understandable. Probably all fluids. No solids yet?"

Tim tim used the napkin from his tray table and erased the earlier sentence. He wrote: "fluids."

"Oh, okay."

Megan asked, "Has a doctor been in today? Did a doctor come by earlier?"

Tim tim made a shrugging motion. Megan interpreted. "Ah, you're probably not sure, because . . . of sleep and meds."

Tim tim nodded affirmatively.

Will had been staring at tim tim's face: a masked clump of white puff pastry dough imbued with splotches of deep blue and black. Will's eyes began to tear at the sight. He took a breath and quickly composed himself. He didn't want to frighten everyone even more.

Megan continued. "I spoke to your surgeon yesterday, and she said your maxillomandibular . . . I mean she said you won't have your jaw wired shut for more than a couple weeks, so that's good. And she said that the social worker was organizing occupational therapy to help you get around in your home in your weakened condition. And we've hired a nursing team to help you around your house for a few days, to make sure you can handle it!" She smiled encouragingly behind her mask. She and Will would be paying for it.

Tim tim raised a weak "thumbs up."

"Okay. Well, let me send the boys in to say hi."

Megan stepped back into the hallway.

"Boys, Uncle Tim is only supposed to have two visitors at a time, but go ahead in there with Dad. I think it will be all right as long as we keep it short and don't make it too obvious." They nodded.

Tim tim saw Robbie, and his eyes lit up.

Robbie slowly gazed at tim tim's outstretched frame. But he didn't want to look at his face right away. He was afraid. He gave a series of quick glances toward that direction, just to ease the shock. Finally, he looked at tim tim's face and began to cry quietly. He looked away.

Doyle said, "Uncle Tim. What happened?"

Tim went back to the whiteboard and held it before Doyle. "Butt kicked."

"Oh. Okay."

Tim tim pointed to Robbie and began erasing and writing again: "mission." He held the board up to Robbie. He waited for Robbie to look at the board. Then he began erasing and writing, "timing off." He pointed to his face with his other hand.

Will had seen enough. "Okay, guys, Uncle Tim needs his rest. Tim, we're going to head out now, buddy. Megan and I will be back tomorrow."

Tim tim held up his hand to signal for them to wait. He went back to board: "mission = you." He pointed the board over to Robbie and tapped at the board with the forefinger of his free hand. He tapped louder. Robbie looked on and continued weeping.

Megan stood at the doorway. "Okay, guys. Give Uncle Tim his space." She began to usher them out into the hallway. Tim tim began frantically erasing and marking, "See you." He had underlined "you." He began tapping at the board and mumbling "rob rob!" through his clenched jaw. But Robbie was walking away to the hallway.

Will placed his hand on Tim's shoulder. "Calm down, buddy! It's okay. I'll let Robbie know you said, 'See you! See you later.' I'll let him know. No worries!"

He gave tim tim a pat on his shoulder and left to catch up with the others. Tim tim didn't notice. He was frantically writing on the board. He held up the message: "Know you." but there was no one left in the room.

· · ·

Late August 2019

Tracey had given up on the idea of a tailgate party. Only a few of the group had ever attended one. Many had never even heard of one. And a lot were vegan or were gluten-free or had allergies or other dietary requirements incompatible with a standard tailgate. And only about a third of the crew even liked beer. And for those who did, their beer choices were all over the place, provided the place was not the US Anything but domestic. Cusquena Gold from Peru or Six Fields from India or Bintang from Indonesia. *So, forget it. No tailgate. Let 'em get their own food and beer.* They'd all just park in Lot E and assemble outside the Southeast Lobby entrance like they were told.

Roland arrived with two kids in tow and gave Tracey a man hug. "Hey, Trace!"

"Hey, big bear! How ya been?"

"Been well, bro! So, these are my nephews Doyle and Robbie!" He patted each on the shoulder. "Guys, this is Mr. Trace, who's in charge of this event."

Robbie spoke up, "Hi, Mr. Trace!" Doyle nodded.

"They love the Ravens too, so I figured 'what the heck,' they'll get a kick out of this!" Roland hated to admit it, but he had actually grown to like his two nephews. They were okay. Desales, not so much.

"Cool, Roland!" Trace held out his hand. "So, you're Doyle? Welcome aboard! And you're Robbie?" He shook hands heartily with both boys.

"So, Roland. I heard you went to London?"

Roland shook his head dramatically. "London. Don't ask me about London! Royal wedding, so the paparazzi were all over it. Absolutely insane!"

"Yeah, somebody said you were in a tabloid, dancing or something?"

"Really? Hmm. Possibly." Roland had already professionally framed the article. He had only six remaining copies of the dozen or so of the Sunday Mirror he had obtained to hand out to friends or to leave in discrete places. He was still living off of that particular thrill. And tonight would be easy. He didn't have to be too concerned about his hair because he was wearing his favorite Ravens cap. It would only be removed for a couple minutes. *What they don't know.*

Slowly the group of a dozen or so assembled. The Ravens' second preseason game was not going to be a barnburner, but the event itself could not be missed. To get the group assembled, Tracey held up and waved a folder-sized sign that read "Rainbow Ravens."

Karla yelled, "I thought we were the LGBThespians? When did we become the Rainbow Ravens?"

Trace yelled back, "Two separate groups, Karla. But pretty much the same people. Anyway, for this event we came up with Rainbow Ravens to be more inclusive. Not all of us are actors, and not all identify as LGBTQ."

"Okay. But no tailgate?"

They were soon greeted by Evelyn Barker, Public Relations Coordinator for the Ravens. "Hi, everyone! Thank you for participating in this event with the Ravens. The Ravens embrace art and culture, especially homegrown in Baltimore!"

Several members of the group cheered enthusiastically.

"So, Art and Culture Night is big for us. And, we've got a special treat planned. We're going to wait until the Ravens are out of their locker room and introduced on the field. That's our cue to take you through the locker room for a quick tour. Yes! Can you believe it?"

Several in the group cheered.

"Then we'll get y'all seated in the primo seats. Section 115. You'll be super close to the field. You may run into the family members of some of the Ravens. Maybe even a few ex-Ravens from what I understand. So, it's going to be a fun night at the Bank!"

Roland let out a loud "Woo hoo!"

Doyle and Robbie both yelled, "Yay!"

Evelyn continued. "Yes, don't be afraid to get loud!" She heard a few more whoops. "That all ya got? C'mon, let's hear it!" The group got into it and started whooping loudly. "That's more like it!"

Roland saw Waxley jogging over.

"Shit. I parked in the wrong lot!"

"All good, bro. We're just getting started."

Evelyn continued. "So, another treat—our superstar kicker, Justin Tucker will be singing the National Anthem tonight! Yeah! The guy can handle more than just opera and chicken!"

Several in the crowd laughed loudly.

"So, Justin's actually flying in from New York. Coach Harbs has him inactive tonight to work out another kicker. But Justin lives here in B'more, so he said he was glad to pop by and belt out the anthem!"

The group whooped some more.

Roland looked to Tracey. "Wow, Trace! This is awesome. I'd love to meet the guy!"

"You and me both! Maybe we will?"

Evelyn ushered the group inside to line up for the metal detector.

"So, Chris, these guys are my nephews—my favorite nephews—Doyle and Robbie. Guys, this is a fellow actor, and a good one, Mr. Chris."

They both shook hands with Waxley. "Hi, Mr. Chris!"

They had worked their way past the metal detector. Evelyn could hear the Ravens starters being announced and then finally the big Ravens cheer and sound effects for the rest of the team.

"Okay, gang, follow me."

They found themselves walking through the locker room. It was surreal. They saw the crazy decorations and bling on some of the lockers. Roland was thunderstruck. "Waxley, isn't this awesome! Guys, what do you think?"

Robbie let out a loud, "Amazing!"

Chris high-fived Roland. "Hell yeah! I've been looking forward to this all summer!"

The group had made their way through the tour and were being assembled at the other end of the locker room to get to the seats. Roland lingered a bit longer. He wanted to see if he could find where Ed Reed's locker used to be. He poked around a few rows, but wasn't sure. He poked around some more. He saw a man standing in the hallway, sticking his head into the locker room, looking for someone.

"You're with the Ravens, right?"

"Yes! Art and Culture Night! Go Rainbow Ravens!" he said proudly.

"Okay. Stan called down for me to tell you guys that they need a replacement for Justin Tucker. Do they have the backup ready?"

"Oh, Evelyn said that he was inactive for tonight, so I would think they have their guy ready."

"Okay. Great. Just let upstairs know who it is and tell them that the plane was delayed."

Roland figured "upstairs" meant the stands where he'd be going in a sec. But all those folks knew Tucker wasn't playing. Didn't quite make sense . . .

A moment later, another man in a Ravens cap and gear poked his head in. "Oh super. Greg said they had someone. Are you ready? Let's go."

"You bet." He figured the guy was there to help him catch up to his group. This was going to be exciting! And then it dawned on him what the other guy said about the plane being delayed. *Uh oh! Shit.* The man led him just to the edge of the Ravens entrance to the field!

Suddenly he heard the crowd growing silent. The announcer yelled, "And singing our National Anthem tonight is none other than our Ravens great, our three-time Pro Bowler, place kicker and opera singer, give it up for Mr. Justin Tucker!!" The crowd roared!

The man with the cap looked over to Roland. "Sorry, man, someone forgot to call it upstairs. You're Green, right—Harvey Green?" Roland's face had turned green. He couldn't speak. "Okay, showtime. Get on out there to the mic!" The man gave Roland a friendly push.

Roland felt faint and began jogging out onto the field. He nearly stumbled but kept going. The crowd saw the huge man jogging slowly onto the field. The stadium broke into laughter at the sight. And loud laughter.

Robbie yelled, "Look! There's Uncle Roland!"

The Rainbow Ravens could not believe what they were seeing! Trace looked to Waxley. "Is that Roland? What's he doing down there?"

Roland composed himself. He took a deep breath and walked the final few paces to the mic. He said, "Obviously, I'm not Justin Tucker."

The crowd roared again with laughter. Roland chuckled a little too. He tossed his Ravens cap onto the field. He didn't think about his hair.

Evelyn asked the group, "Is he in your party?"

Waxley yelled back. "Hell yeah! That's Roland! Roland G. Biv. B-I-V." She grabbed her cell and made a quick call upstairs to the box.

Roland spoke quietly into the mic. "Okay, so when we get to the 'O' part, don't do . . ."

Suddenly, the opening bars of the National Anthem blared through the stadium. Roland began singing. And he knew the words, thanks to many choral opportunities in the past. He wailed, hitting every note, enunciating every line, powerfully. He got slightly distracted when he got to the "O" part because the damn jackasses had to yell along as usual. But he regained his composure and finished it out with style and panache.

The stadium broke into a standing ovation. The applause lasted for minutes. It would not cease. Roland nodded proudly and then bowed several times.

The announcer yelled, "Let's give it up some more for our guest singer, Mr. Roland G. Biv of the Rainbow Ravens!"

The crowd again began applauding and cheering loudly. Roland picked up his Ravens cap from the ground and waved it to the crowd, heroically. He jogged back into the entrance. It was undeniably and absolutely the happiest moment of his life.

Waxley was in awe. He had begun a "Roland" chant with Robbie and Doyle. He had clapped his hands red. But he was just a tiny bit jealous, too. He couldn't help but think, *Maybe I could have sung it better?*

. . .

April 2033

"We're going to have to let Robbie know. He would hate us if we don't." Will had stopped off at the 25th Street home to pick up suitable clothes for the funeral. He was still holding two brown paper shopping bags.

"I know. I know. But we haven't told him Tim was even sick. He may not like that."

"Well, people get better. You're not expected to make an announcement every time a family member gets sick, right?"

Megan shook her head. "Yeah, I guess."

Will had made the funeral arrangements. They had phoned as many family members as possible. They weren't really sure if Tim had any friends, besides his acquaintances at the American Legion. He'd phone the post and see what they would suggest. He found a list of people Tim sent Christmas cards to. Looked like mostly neighbors. But there were no phone numbers for any of them. Tim didn't even seem to maintain a book or a list of phone numbers. Will just saw a few numbers on scraps of paper. Mostly his and Megan's.

He put the bags down and pulled out an envelope heavily sealed with cellophane tape. It was simply addressed "rob rob."

They sat on their living room sofa. Will handed the envelope to Megan. "God knows what this will be."

She stared at it. "Why did he call him rob rob sometimes? And he told a lot of people to call him tim tim." She shook her head, forlornly. "We can't just hand this over to Robbie. Not after all we've done, all we've spent to get him better. No way. It could start everything up all over again."

"Yeah, I know. I agree. I think we should just throw it out. Pretend we never saw it. Robbie won't ask about it because he won't know about it."

"What if Tim told him about it in the past?"

"Well, then we'll just say, 'too bad,' we didn't find anything."

"I hate to have to lie our boy, Will."

"I know. It sucks."

They sat a bit longer. Will said, "Okay, what if we at least read it to see what it says? If we think it's harmless, we just tape it back up and give it to him? With all that tape already on it, Robbie's not going to know we looked at it if we tape it some more?"

Megan sighed. "Okay, you do it."

Will retrieved his letter opener from his home office. He sat back down on the sofa and carefully sliced the envelope open. He unfolded and held the letter open for both of them. It was handwritten.

"rob rob

Pit stop and time to replace the old piston. Yes, you are ready! Don't forget, even though we may not have kids of our own, being an uncle is pretty cool! I wish I had done a better job. But I know you will get your chance and do a great job! I've enjoyed being your uncle but also your friend. Always remember that. I hope you see yourself happy and know yourself what a great life we have!

tim tim"

They each read it a few times more. Megan handed it back to Will. "No way. It suggests that Robbie will never have his own kids. We can't let him see that."

Will sighed. "Yeah. It kind of does suggest that. Crap. The rest is not too bad. At least there's no mention of the 'mission.'"

"Yes, but it's just weird. Too weird."

"Yes. It's weird. Any second thoughts?"

"No."

They took the letter and envelope out to the fire pit.

. . .

Will was glad to see Robbie looking so together. Acting so normally. Yeah, he had put on a few pounds and his hair was getting thinner, but he looked fine. Nice business suit and tie. He watched Robbie kneel in front of the casket. They had done a nice job on Tim. He had an intelligent, professorial expression on his face. Robbie rejoined Will, Doyle, and Doyle's toddler, D.J.

"So, Robbie, man, we haven't seen you in like forever? How's work?"

"Oh, it's been great, Doyle! I got a promotion last month. I'm now a delinquent accounts supervisor, which is a notch or two higher than just a manager like I had been before."

"Cool, man. Are you still based in Wilmington?"

"Yes. I have a condo now! Nice place, but the fees are high. Oh well. Condo life. Are you guys still in Syracuse?"

"No. We moved to Rochester for my work. For some reason they think that Rochester is a hotter lacrosse market. Ridiculous, but they pay, and I go!"

"Yep. I hear you!"

Peg joined the group holding their youngest, Mack. He was a little less than a year old.

"Hey, Grandad. You want to hold this one?"

"Sure!"

Peg handed Mack over to Will. Will rocked him a little. "He's getting heavy!"

"I know. I know. We keep feeding him for some reason!" They all chuckled.

Doyle noticed that Will's arms were beginning to tire. "Dad, I'll take him. Hey, Robbie, want to hold Mack?"

He chuckled. "Oh no, no. I'm not good with that stuff! I don't want to screw up and drop him."

"Okay, man!" Doyle chuckled too and grabbed him back.

Peg watched Doyle holding and rocking Mack. D.J. was now hanging onto Peg, restlessly.

"Hey, Uncle Robbie. What do you think of these two?"

Robbie laughed. "I can't believe how big they both are! Reminds me of Doyle and me!"

Doyle chuckled. "Yes, we have a lot of childhood stories we could tell on each other!"

"Yes! That's why I'm getting out of here tonight!" Robbie laughed some more.

Will said, "Aw . . . you're not coming to the funeral tomorrow? You'll miss Mom?"

"I know, I know. I'm sorry, Dad. I've got some deadlines I have to meet. So, I've got to drive back tonight. Tell Mom I love her and will see you guys soon!"

"Oh, that's okay! I'm just glad you had a chance to, you know, pay your respects and see us and all. We all know Tim was a little 'out there,' but he was a good guy and loved hanging out with you back in the day." Will wished he hadn't added that part, but he would have felt bad if he hadn't. He was half glad that Megan was on duty at the hospital. She would not have wanted him to even mention Tim even though it would be a little hard not to, under the circumstances.

"Yeah! I know! I now understand that Uncle Tim was a good guy and actually meant well. I have a much better understanding now of his problems. I look back fondly on our friendship!"

Will was happily surprised at how well Robbie appeared to be handling it. The therapy had definitely paid off.

They saw Desales enter and waved him over.

"Hey, guys!" He shook hands and gave everyone a warm embrace. He looked over toward the casket. "Beth and I are both so sorry to hear of Tim's passing."

Will looked on solemnly. "Thanks, Desales. We're going to miss him."

"So, Beth's with the baby and Roy. Roy said he'd give Beth a hand with babysitting, which means Beth is babysitting both of them."

The group chuckled politely.

"But we'll all be at the funeral tomorrow." He looked around the room. "Has anyone seen Roland?"

Will responded, "Megan told me he's stuck in New York and can't make it down. He's in that musical that his friend wrote. Remember, the guy who got shot during a holdup at a store or something like ten or fifteen years ago? Made all the talk show rounds? That's the friend. Won a Tony, I think. His show is Off Broadway, but it keeps getting held over. Like maybe ten years, now. Megan said it got nominated for an Obie."

"Oh, yeah. Beth and I actually caught that a few months ago. I think it's called 'Black Friday' or 'Good Friday.' I forget, but it was cool." Desales recalled that Beth enjoyed it more than he, because of her science background. He just wasn't sure what some of the scientific terms meant. But the singing was at least not horrible.

"So, another thing to report to you guys. We're moving back to Baltimore. I'm taking a position with a local nonprofit."

"Whoa, Desales! Way to go! So you decided against that partnership offer?"

"Yeah, Uncle Will. Working for a big DC firm was cool and great training. But that's not for me. My heart isn't in it. I mean, how many corporate tax cases do you have to defend before you literally become a zombie?"

The group chuckled some more.

"I made some decent money, and we have a baby now. I'm getting back to what I love—consumer law, consumer rights, etc. I hate seeing the little guy getting screwed by financial predators and similar . . . types." He was watching his language. "There's a huge need in Baltimore. It won't pay much, but we're both working, and we think we can make it."

"That's great, Desales! We're all excited for you!"

The rest joined in with their approvals.

Robbie spoke up. "That's really great, Desales! Hey, I was just telling everyone that I've actually got to get out of here now and drive back to Wilmington. I've got a bunch of deadlines to make for tomorrow. It sucks, but I'm going to miss the funeral tomorrow."

"Oh, that's a shame, man. Well, I'll let you say your goodbyes, and I'll pay my respects." He nodded over to the casket. "But let me walk you out."

. . .

The April air was chilly. But they could look up and see the stars.

"So, Robbie. I know that Tim meant a lot to you and that this has probably been tough. I just want you to know that if you ever need anyone to talk to or anything, I'm here. Yeah, I was a dickhead when we were young. I still am! But, hanging out with you and Doyle was always great. You guys are a big part of my childhood memories. My best memories! Let's not let that go."

"Thanks, Desales! Yeah, I think back on those days very fondly. You and your Mustang! We were like the Three Musketeers."

"Yes. Man, I wish I still had that Mustang!"

They arrived at Robbie's Toyota. "Look! Here's my Mustang!"

Desales laughed and gave Robbie a warm hug. "Okay, man! Be well, and keep on rockin' it up in Delaware! And don't forget. I'm here if you need me!"

"Thanks, Desales! And congratulations on moving back down here!"

Robbie sat and looked in his rearview mirror. He watched Desales head back into the funeral home. He wept quietly as he turned the key in the ignition.

. . .

September 2019

"We shouldn't be here. We're going to get in trouble with Mom and Dad." Robbie had to yell to be heard over the noise of the surf.

"Shut up, wuss. Whoever heard of closing down a beach?"

Doyle intervened. "Man, it's too cold here, anyway. The wind is a bitch!" He could barely hear himself over the rushing sound of the wind in his ears. He shivered and folded his arms against his windbreaker. He yelled, "Let's go back to the condo."

The three stood together as the waves thundered against the beach. Although it was nearly ten a.m., the sky was twilight dark. Desales pointed. "Holy shit, look at that one!"

They watched, spellbound: the swelling movement of the surf; the undertow sucking up water, exposing a nearly dry beach in creation of a monstrous wave. The wave rose and rose as it prepared to strike the beach. It grew impossibly tall. Suddenly, it flung itself against the beach with a deafening fury, the noise of the crash crushing the ears of the three watchers. Each boy flinched. Robbie ran back two paces in retreat.

"Oh my God! That was awesome!" Desales looked to high-five Doyle who was still staring out into the surf, open-mouthed.

Robbie rejoined the two and yelled, "Man, we should get back. It's cold, Desales!"

"No, puss! This is a chance of a lifetime. When are you ever going to see something like this again?"

Then they heard the buzzing sound of an engine. They looked toward the source, a compact, four-wheel drive rescue vehicle just behind them, driving parallel to the surf. They saw the driver stick his bullhorn out the window.

"You three! Get off the beach, now! This beach is closed! There's a hurricane warning! Get off, immediately, or you'll be arrested!!"

Desales waved to the driver and yelled, "Sorry, man. We're leaving."

The lifeguard closed his window and continued his patrol, southward.

"Okay, we've got to go for sure, now!"

"Robbie, don't be a pussy! He's gone now. He's not going to arrest anybody. He's a dipshit lifeguard, not a cop."

Doyle was still staring out into the churning surf. "Hey. What's that?"

All three looked out. "I don't see anything, dickhead. What do you think you're seeing?"

Doyle pointed out and to his right. "Look! Look just out there! See! Is that somebody swimming?"

The three followed his direction and looked into the surf. They began moving closer toward the surf to get a slightly better look.

Desales began pointing too. "Fuck! That's some asshole swimming! I can't believe it!" He shielded his eyes with his left hand and continued pointing, tracking the movement.

Doyle yelled, "It's a kid! I think it's a kid. I think they're in trouble!

Desales yelled. "Shit! You're right! They're trying to swim but they can't get anywhere! Let's get that lifeguard!"

They looked and saw the rear of the four-wheel moving farther and farther away.

Desales yelled, "Shit. He's gone! Should we try to get somebody? Like your mom and dad?"

Robbie had moved closer to the surf. Another enormous wave crashed in, surprising him and driving him back. Doyle looked up to the condos. "We wouldn't make it back there in time, Desales! Use your phone!"

"I don't fucking have it! Shit!" He pointed to the condos. "I wonder if anyone up there sees this? Maybe they're calling for help?"

Robbie said, "I think one of us has to go in and help them!"

Doyle looked at Desales. "Man, we don't know how to swim! You live on the water. You know how to swim, right?"

Desales looked down. "No, man. I don't know either. Roy didn't want me to get my head in the water because of all the disease and shit. And, even if we did, we couldn't go out in this shit! This is nuts!"

Robbie was watching the figure struggling more and more. They were losing energy. And then he couldn't see the person's head anymore.

Another thunderous wave struck the beach just a few paces before them, driving them instinctively back to safety.

"Shit, man! What can we do?"

Robbie spoke up, quietly. "I think I can do it."

Doyle went white. "What? No! No, you can't, Robbie! You're too little! You can't even swim!"

"No. It's okay. I've seen them do it on TV. You know, like the Olympics." He took off his sweatshirt and windbreaker. "Hold these." Doyle took the clothes and looked on blankly, too shocked to speak.

"Fuck no, man!" Desales waved his arms in the air in front of Robbie. "No, man! You can't go in there! That's crazy!"

Robbie waited for the last wave in the set to crash to shore. He ran forward, splashing into the receding water. He knew it felt cold, but it didn't really bother him. He dove in and began to move his arms, stroke by stroke against the swirling surf. Another wave pulled him upward and threatened to toss him against the shore, but he continued stroking as hard as he could and pushed himself over the crest. He continued swimming along the water's surface, but the choppiness of the surf worked against his arm motions.

He pushed himself below the surface where there would be less resistance. He thought of how the great Olympians seemingly attacked the water with their arms and hands. He tried to do the same, grabbing and thrusting at the dark green water before him, kicking his legs like scissors. He was getting closer and closer to the child. He saw it was a little girl. She was flailing in the surf, occasionally bobbing above the surface where she'd gasp for air and then sink below, where the cycle would repeat. But now she was weakening. He saw her drop below the surface and barely make it back for a breath. Her arms and legs were giving out.

He remembered that he needed to breathe. He could push himself to the surface, but his progress would be slowed. He thought back to tim tim's advice: always breathe, no matter what. So, he breathed in and kept stroking forward. He felt an icy punch at his lungs, like a thousand icicles, but he breathed in again and felt warm. It was okay. He continued breathing and attacking the water. He was getting closer to the child.

He saw that her head was barely breaking the surface. She was breathing in a mixture of air and saltwater through her nose. She dropped down again below the surf. He saw her nearly still body suspended below the surface. She was drowning.

With a final pull he met the child and grabbed her by the waist. He pushed her upward to the surface with all of his might. Her head broke the surface of the water and she gasped for breath. He continued treading water in the choppy surf, pushing her upward, making sure her head was above the water, making sure she could breathe.

He pushed himself above the surface and flattened himself on his back against the waves, holding her to his chest and stomach. "Just breathe. I've got you."

She coughed and said, "Okay!"

He grasped her with his right arm and used the left to stroke and navigate in sync with the rip current. They floated parallel with the coastline. He carefully preserved his energy. He had read about riptides, and he let the current do its work. He felt the force of the child's body coughing and shivering. He could feel her whimpering, trying to stifle a full cry. "Hang in there! We got it!"

Finally, he felt the current becoming weaker. He began slowly stroking toward shore. He watched the swirling dark sky. Tiny cracks of sunlight leaked through from time to time. He felt the roughness of the surface and knew they were close to shore. "Okay, now don't worry. Take a few breaths because we're going to be hit with a few big waves on the way in." The child coughed out an "Okay."

He rearranged his grasp and began to dogpaddle them forward, closer and closer to shore. The rip current had taken them blocks and blocks away. Finally, he could feel sand just touch beneath his feet. He got his footing and began walking them in, suddenly feeling the weight of both of their bodies as they emerged from the surf.

He avoided another enormous breaker and stumbled them both onto the beach at the shore's edge. They both fell to their knees. A man and woman ran forward with a beach blanket and helped the shivering girl to her feet, wrapping her in the blanket.

"Are you two okay? We saw you from our balcony! Should we call someone? Your folks?" They were yelling against the swirling wind.

Robbie watched them as he coughed out a mixture of seawater and air from his lungs. Robbie slowly rose to his feet, shivering. "Not for me. I'm okay, but the girl needs help. She's freezing and almost drowned."

"Okay, we'll get her inside. We called 911." They each took a side of the girl and began walking her up toward the building. The man looked back. "Do you need help?"

Robbie stood shakily, hands on hips. He bent back over to cough out more water from his lungs. He looked back up. "I'm okay! I'm okay! My brother is going to be looking for me, so I'll stay here. I'm okay."

"Okay! Look, we're at the White Swan. Unit 517." The man pointed toward the buildings. "Come up and get us if you need help! And nice job! You saved her life!"

"Okay." Robbie looked toward the buildings and saw the flashing lights of emergency vehicles in the distance. He saw several uniforms running toward the three as they approached the buildings. He looked to his right and saw two tiny figures running along the beach toward him.

He stood shivering. They finally caught up, exhausted. Desales bent over to catch his breath. "What the fuck, Robbie! Who are you, Aquaman?"

Doyle had collapsed onto the sand, first on hands and knees and now sitting. He handed Robbie his sweatshirt and jacket. He yelled, "Is the kid okay?"

Robbie quickly put the shirt and jacket on. He continued to shiver. "Yeah, she's okay. A little girl, like a second grader. Some people are taking her up there." He pointed to the flashing lights and activities at the building area.

"Man, way to go!" Doyle stood and gave Robbie a high five.

"Yeah. And now he's got a date for his sixth grade dance!" Desales laughed.

"Yeah right. Thanks, man."

"Give 'em a break, man!" Doyle scowled.

Desales continued. "Okay. Sorry, man. But, how the hell did you do that? You said you didn't know how to swim?"

Robbie took in a breath. "I didn't. I just imitated what I've seen on TV. Swimming isn't that hard, actually."

They were both staring at Robbie. "Okay, look, dickhead, I know you're going to want a parade in your honor and all that shit, but we can't tell your parents, or they will flip out that we went on the beach when we said we wouldn't. We'll all be grounded. And it's bad enough that we get this shit weather. Think if we're stuck in your parents' condo for the rest of the week."

"Yeah, that's okay." Robbie didn't want to get grounded either. Last time, they took away *Peppa Pig* for a week, although he did sneak a little in thanks to the YouTube app on his mom's phone.

. . .
December 2050

Mack glanced around his dorm room. Five p.m., and it was already dark outside. And gray. His roommate, Oswald, was dining and hanging out with friends. Mack hadn't been invited. He was alone and very lonely as usual. He felt a deep ache in the pit of his stomach.

He walked over and looked out the massive glass window. He couldn't see much outside, save the bird droppings flung against the window. The lighting in the dorm room was clinically bright. He cupped his hands around his eyes and pressed them to the window. Only a few cars were parked in the lot below. Many of the students had finished their exams and had headed home. He was stuck taking a make-up exam for Bio I. He had suffered a "health incident" just before the exam. The professor had cut him some slack and allowed him to take the make-up. He had simply freaked out over the stress.

He walked over to the bathroom and looked at himself in the mirror. Balding and fat at eighteen. He had no girlfriend and no prospects for a girlfriend. And he didn't particularly care. And why did he feel this way? So uncertain about everything. So empty?

He walked back to the window. He gently slapped his palms against the glass, just as he had done many times before. The distance to the ground would be sufficient, but he would never be able to break through the high impact glass. But he thumped at the glass a few more times.

He had thought it all through before. Even if he could break through the glass, he couldn't do it because he could seriously hurt or even kill someone below who might happen to be exiting the building at the wrong time. Just like he had checked out the grade-level railroad crossing a quarter mile away. He could muster up the nerve to jump in front of the engine, but there was always that risk of derailing the train and injuring the conductor and passengers. He couldn't do that.

Something was missing, and it was killing him. His dad didn't understand him. Or maybe it was the other way around? He loved his dad. And he knew his dad loved him. But being here was not working for him.

What was he feeling—what was he looking for? He needed to find whatever it was, but he knew it was not here. And maybe not in anyplace he'd find in this lifetime. That's what made it unbearable. Thinking made his stomach hurt even worse.

He had been researching poisons. But, post reunification, there was no way to access a poison freely online. He'd be web-blocked by the censor walls if he even tried to research it. His mind turned to poison plants. He could grow his own. Something like hemlock. Maybe researching a less obvious plant would not be web-blocked? There had to be a few.

He heard his port warble. Bizarre. An incoming, for him? No one ever contacted him these days.

He nodded the port open. He saw the username, but the face was blurry. He wasn't sure who it was. "Yes?"

"Mack, is that you?"

The voice sounded familiar. He thought for a split second that it was Dad or possibly big brother, D.J. They sounded a lot alike. But it wasn't.

"It's your uncle, rob rob. Do you remember me?"

He felt shocked. He hadn't seen or even thought about his uncle in years.

"Uncle Robbie? Is that you?"

"Yes! So, let me ask you, have you been thinking about leaving school recently? For good?"

He inhaled. His heart pounded. "Well, yes, actually. But my dad would never allow it. I'm stuck here."

"Okay. Does your window look over the parking lot?"

"What? Yes?"

"Good. Look out your window. Do you see a car parked next to the light pillar?"

He cupped his hands to his face and saw a car. Then he saw the headlights being flashed.

"Yes?"

"Okay. That's me. I screwed up. I should have hung out with you more when you were growing up. But it's not too late. I know how you've been feeling, and I can explain everything. There's a lot to do. A lot to learn. I'm getting you out of there. Are you willing to pack a quick bag and leave all that behind? My house is not much. I just moved back on 25th Street in Baltimore. Are you ready? Do you feel it's time?"

Mack looked around his depressing dorm. He felt something almost like adrenaline. Almost like hope. It was even better. Way, way better. He was becoming happy.

His eyes began to water. He breathed in. "Yeah! . . . Heck yeah! Don't go anywhere! I'll be right down!"

About the Publisher

Pearls Before Press is a book publisher of unusual and trend-setting fiction and outstanding non-fiction.

Advance Reviews for *The Big Comb Over*

"A wonderfully comic novel packed full of eccentric, fun to get to know characters. Highly recommended!"

The Wishing Shelf - 5 Stars - Award Finalist

_____

"In *The Big Comb Over*, the author takes the reader on a hilariously absurd journey into the heart of a Royal Wedding, where family dynamics and satirical wit collide in a riotous tale. This cleverly crafted novel explores the lives of three nephews and their uncles as they navigate the chaos and eccentricities surrounding this grand event."

The International Review of Books - Gold Badge rating

_____

"Spanning multiple timelines and incorporating multiple perspectives, the book takes readers on a hilarious journey through the lives of one extended family. ... If you are in the mood for a laugh-out-loud comedy that defies reason and revels in ridiculousness, this book is for you!"

Readers' Choice Book Awards - 5 Stars

_____

"*The Big Comb Over* is a lighthearted and thought-provoking exploration of family, identity, and the unexpected twists that come with discovering one's roots. ... I recommend this riveting tale of self-exploration and the surprises which come with it."

Pacific Book Review

Read more at https://www.pearlsbeforepress.net/.